Dublin, Written In Our Hearts

Previous One Dublin One Book Titles

2006　*At Swim Two Birds* by Flann O'Brien
2007　*A Long Long Way* by Sebastian Barry
2008　*Gulliver's Travels* by Jonathan Swift
2009　*Dracula* by Bram Stoker
2010　*The Picture of Dorian Gray* by Oscar Wilde
2011　*Ghost Light* by Joseph O'Connor
2012　*Dubliners* by James Joyce
2013　*Strumpet City* by James Plunkett
2014　*If Ever You Go* edited by Pat Boran and Gerard Smyth
2015　*The Barrytown Trilogy* by Roddy Doyle
2016　*Fallen* by Lia Mills
2017　*Echoland* by Joe Joyce
2018　*The Long Gaze Back* edited by Sinéad Gleeson
2019　*The Country Girls Trilogy* by Edna O'Brien
2020　*Tatty* by Christine Dwyer Hickey
2021　*Leonard and Hungry Paul* by Rónán Hession
2022　*NORA* by Nuala O'Connor
2023　*The Coroner's Daughter* by Andrew Hughes
2024　*Snowflake* by Louise Nealon

Dublin, Written In Our Hearts

Edited by Declan Meade

*An anthology celebrating 20 years of
Dublin City Council's One Dublin One Book*

The Stinging Fly

A Stinging Fly Press Book

Dublin, Written In Our Hearts is first published in March 2025.

2 4 6 8 9 7 5 3

ISBN 978-1-916914-00-1 (paperback)

The Stinging Fly Press
PO Box 6016
Dublin 1
www.stingingfly.org

Dublin, Written In Our Hearts. Copyright 2025 by *The Stinging Fly*.

All rights reserved.

See also pages 257-259 for individual copyright information.

Epigraph by Eugene Sheehy, *The Joyce We Knew* (1967) edited by Ulick O'Connor (Brandon). Reproduced by kind permission of The O'Brien Press.

Page 7: 'J.P. Donleavy's Dublin' by Derek Mahon from *The Poems: 1961-2020* (2021) is reproduced by kind permission of the Author's Estate and The Gallery Press.

Set in Palatino

Printed in Ireland by Walsh Colour Print, County Kerry.

ONE DUBLIN ONE BOOK

One Dublin One Book is a Dublin City Council initiative co-ordinated by Dublin UNESCO City of Literature and Dublin City Libraries.

arts council schomhairle ealaíon | funding literature

The Stinging Fly Press gratefully acknowledges the financial support of The Arts Council/An Chomhairle Ealaíon.

Contents

Foreword		ix
Introduction		xi
Anne Enright	*Dublin Made Me*	3
Caitriona Lally	*Eggshells*	11
Paula Meehan	*In Solidarity*	23
Deirdre Madden	*Authenticity*	27
Keith Ridgway	*Undublining*	39
Karl Whitney	*The Hidden Rivers of the Liberties*	47
FELISPEAKS	*Dublin: A Poet's View*	63
Kevin Curran	*Adventure Stories for Boys*	67
Estelle Birdy	*Ravelling*	79
Kevin Barry	*There Are Little Kingdoms*	97
Niamh Mulvey	*Stringing Up The Brides*	111
Sean O'Reilly	*Levitation*	123
Belinda McKeon	*For Keeps*	131
Sarah Gilmartin	*Service*	143
Niamh Campbell	*We Were Young*	159
Thomas Morris	*all the boys*	171
Róisín Kiberd	*The Night Gym*	191
Peter Sirr	*Noises Off: Dublin's Contested Monuments*	201
Nuala O'Connor	*Jesus of Dublin*	215
Stephen James Smith	*Dublin You Are*	217
Réré Ukponu	*Famine Days*	225
Roddy Doyle	*The Buggy*	239
Contributors		251
Permissions		257

My sister, Mrs Sheehy Skeffington, told me that at a later date she had another such interview with Joyce. Half dazed with his cascade of queries, she at last said to him:

'Mr Joyce, you pretend to be a cosmopolitan, but how is it that all your thoughts are about Dublin, and almost everything that you have written deals with it and its inhabitants?'

'Mrs Skeffington,' he replied, with a rather whimsical smile, 'there was an English queen who said that when she died the word "Calais" would be written on her heart. "Dublin" will be found on mine.'

—Eugene Sheehy, *The Joyce We Knew* (1967) edited by Ulick O'Connor

Foreword

Every April for the past twenty years, people across Dublin were to be seen on buses and trains, in cafés and in libraries, reading the same book. At first glance this might appear to be an incredible coincidence, but these readers have been participating in Dublin City Council's One Dublin One Book initiative, the annual programme managed by Dublin City Libraries and Dublin UNESCO city of Literature.

City-wide reading campaigns began in Seattle in 1998 when librarian Nancy Pearl thought it would be interesting to expand the notion of a local book club to a city-wide initiative with everyone reading and discussing the same book. Other cities, including London and Berlin, followed suit; Dublin came on board in 2006, choosing Flann O'Brien's comic masterpiece *At Swim-Two-Birds* as its first title. Eighteen other books have been selected in the years since then, written by icons such as James Joyce, Jonathan Swift and Oscar Wilde to contemporary authors such as Christine Dwyer Hickey, Roddy Doyle, Andrew Hughes and Louise Nealon.

Some of the One Dublin One Book titles were linked to the recent Decade of Centenaries programme. James Plunkett's *Strumpet City*, Lia Mills' *Fallen* and Nuala O'Connor's *Nora* were selected to commemorate the Dublin Lockout in 1913, the 1916 Rising and the publication of Joyce's *Ulysses* respectively. Scorned by Ireland in the 1960s, the late, great, trailblazing writer Edna O'Brien appreciated the city selecting *The Country Girls Trilogy* in 2019, bringing the books to whole new generations of readers.

During the COVID pandemic, Rónán Hession's quietly powerful debut novel, *Leonard and Hungry Paul*, chosen in 2021, resonated deeply with readers. Publisher, Bluemoose Books, credits the campaign for bringing greater attention to Hession's novel, helping to fuel its international success.

This year's book is the third anthology to feature as the One Dublin One Book choice. In 2014, *If Ever You Go*, an anthology of poetry edited by Pat Boran and Gerard Smyth, was commissioned by Dublin City Council. This unique volume continues to be widely used as a resource. *The Long Gaze Back*, Sinéad Gleeson's ground-breaking anthology of short stories by Irish women writers, was selected for the campaign in 2018.

Dublin, Written In Our Hearts was commissioned to showcase the work of some of the many writers who have been writing about the city during the first quarter of the 21st century. It offers a unique snapshot in time, a celebration of the various different styles and approaches adopted by writers whose work continues to be inspired and animated by the city.

Dublin City Council is grateful to the twenty-two writers and poets who have kindly contributed their work to this collection. A special word of gratitude to Declan Meade and his team at The Stinging Fly for editing and publishing the book. Sincere thanks must also go to all those in the Dublin UNESCO City of Literature office and Dublin City Libraries who work with great flair and imagination on the One Dublin One Book campaign each year.

The main objectives of any reading campaign are to put a good book into a reader's hand and to encourage others to pick up the book and to stretch their imaginations. Without the loyal following of the city's readers, One Dublin One Book could never have been such a wonderful success. We applaud all our readers and book lovers across the city. We hope you'll enjoy this special anniversary collection.

Mairéad Owens
Dublin City Librarian

Introduction

I grew up about forty miles from Dublin city centre, but it may as well have been forty thousand miles or four million. I grew up in rural county Louth in the 1970s and 80s and I had no great sense of the city and very little curiosity about it through my childhood and teenage years. Any interest I might have shown would not exactly have been encouraged in any case. 'It's Dublin you're in,' someone marvelled on one of my recent trips home. 'It wouldn't be for everyone.' (We had only just met, but he had no trouble sharing this conviction.)

It's Dublin I've been in for the past thirty years, having moved here in the summer of 1995. That was a beautiful long hot summer, the weather helping to convince me that Dublin was the right place for me. The city may well not be for everyone, and although I might be slow to say this out loud in Louth—or Laois or Longford—it has been good and right for me.

Back in that long hot summer, I got a job on a community employment scheme doing the bookkeeping for the James Joyce Centre, eventually and briefly becoming the Centre's administrator before taking on the editorship of the annual *Bloomsday* magazine, a job I did for several years while also editing and publishing early issues of *The Stinging Fly* magazine. This all served as an education in what it was to be a writer writing about the city. James Joyce had seized his opportunity to put Dublin on the literary map of the world. He knew that by doing so, by focusing his enormous talent on capturing the city in all its everyday glory, he could immortalise both the city and himself. We can only salute him—and be grateful for his legacy.

One hundred years after Joyce walked and mapped the city's alleyways and streets, this book brings together some of the writers who have been writing about Dublin during the first twenty-five years of our new century. It does not lay claim to be in any way definitive or complete. It offers my selection of writing—fiction, non-fiction and poetry—about Dublin; a selection made over the course of a few months with the aim of producing a book of roughly this size. There are, of course, plenty more writers writing in and about the city than the twenty-two you will get to read here. There are more anthologies to be published. We have an abundance of great writers, not a shortage.

Working on this book and connecting in with Dublin City Council's One Dublin One Book initiative has been an honour and a privilege. Whatever else, it is a wonderful thing to play a part in the city taking such an active role in celebrating its contemporary writers and their writing. Joyce, I imagine, would be bemused, perhaps even pleased.

Declan Meade
Editor

Dublin, Written In Our Hearts

Anne Enright
Dublin Made Me {essay}

Whenever I pass along Earlsfort Terrace I remember the fact that I was born on this street, in number 17, which was once the Stella Maris nursing home. As a child, I used to sit on the top deck of the 15A bus on my way home from town and look at the bay window on the first floor. Behind that white curtain, I decided, was the room I first drew breath. I could never see inside.

When I asked my mother what time I was born, she said she could not remember. This felt like indifference to me until I had children of my own and realised a labouring woman might have other things on her mind than the position of the big and little hands on her abandoned wristwatch in the locker by the bed. It was not a difficult labour, she told me, but she seemed a little vague about that too. There was chloroform, I was her fifth. Back at home, her husband was making porridge three times a day for four young children, and burnt rashers, because such was the extent of his culinary expertise. He was a willing and useful father but there were limits. In those days, you couldn't expect a man to know how to cook—he would just be useless at it.

I think my mother would consider it wrong to tell a child

how much it hurt to bring them into the world, and when I had my own children I understood that too. No, she said, it was an easy labour. Later, she talked about a nurse, probably a nun, who glanced at her mid-contraction and said, 'Now you are paying for your moment's pleasure,' but I don't think that happened at my birth. The story from the Stella Maris was about a woman who shared her recovery room, whose husband came in to view the baby and 'pulled across the screen', after which there were 'noises'. It took me many years to understand what was going on in this story. Certainly, in the days I passed on the 15A, I knew very little about such things. I was a student in Trinity, having the time of my life.

On the other side of Earlsfort Terrace was The National University building where the UCD departments of medicine and architecture were housed. Now partly occupied by The National Concert Hall, it was from this neo-classical behemoth that architecture students protested the destruction of the Georgian buildings in the surrounding streets. Years after they were all gone, I walked its abandoned, yellowing halls. One long corridor gave way to the next, fallen plaster squeaked underfoot, doors hung open and light fittings dangled askew. In the distance: the clink of ghostly forceps, the unheard sound of saw through bone. My mother's brother was a pathologist who studied here in the 1940s and, like every medical student, he teased his sisters about the body parts of the dead. I remembered this when I walked into a narrow, high-ceilinged dissecting room and saw a steel table bolted to the wall. There was a drain at one end of the table for blood and formaldehyde, another drain below it, set into a corner of the tiled floor.

Behind this building was the secret garden, now returned to its proper name, The Iveagh Gardens. In the 1980s, there was only one entrance to this urban wilderness, through an ordinary doorway in the back wall. The place was always deserted and ghostly in a different way; abundantly overgrown, its dappled paths rustled with a sense of possibility. It was the most romantic place in Dublin town.

This is what I see, even now when I drive down Earlsfort Terrace in my modern electric car. I see my mother labouring across the road from generations of medical students, including my sister in the 1980s, when she ate her sandwiches in the secret garden from folded waxed-paper parcels, on the outside of which were the words 'Brennan's Bread'. I see myself as a student, coming home on the last bus. But also, these days, I sense the restored gardens running to the back of MoLI at St Stephens Green, with the tree where James Joyce was once photographed. I see my grandmother at the same tree, and also my mother, who went to UCD for a term before leaving to take up a job in the civil service. I think she missed student life. She talked about a dance in Newman House; how she was walked home to Phibsboro by a poet who did not click with her.

'You were well out of that one,' I told her, when she finally divulged the name. And she said, 'Do you think?'

This is a street I experience in many dimensions; the map gives way to previous maps as the decades swop and speak to each other. A tree grows and is not chopped down. Some of the stones endure.

And now, for the life of me, I can't tell you what way the

15A goes. When they change the flow of traffic, when the roads switch from one way to the other damn way and they alter the routes of my childhood buses, it really messes with my head. How am I supposed to get home?

The poet Paul Durcan was also delivered in the Stella Maris, eighteen years before I emerged in the same spot. He wrote a poem about the event, telling how his obstetrician, nicknamed 'Wee Wee', was a drunk whose trembling hands botched the birth with a slip of the forceps, leaving the poet with a scarred eye. I asked my mother about Wee Wee but the name meant nothing to her. She never had need of an obstetrician, she said, though they always put their head round the door when the birth was done, 'So they could collect the fee.'

All this, and we have not yet turned the corner! We have not lurched, on the growling Bombardier, past the tiny opticians, like a last tooth, alone and un-demolished, where Mendel Stein held out against the office block developers. I have not made it up over the hump of canal bridge and down, past Observatory Lane into Rathmines. There on the right is my primary school, with its terrazzo steps and the parquet corridor that we polished by skating along wearing old socks. I have not put my father in there, smoking in front of a fawning nun, my mother in a hat made of wrap-around feathers, dyed a jaunty orange. I have not yet recalled or discussed my First Communion breakfast of pancakes in the school hall, the railings we used to tumble around, behind what is now the public swimming pool.

I could have gone Northside with my mother as she walks

home from that dance in Newman House, now MoLI, in 1943. Past the Abbey Theatre and the Gate Theatre where she saw Micheál MacLiammóir and Siobhán McKenna, where I saw Olwen Fouéré and Gabriel Byrne perform. Past the Black Church, which you could hop around on your left foot counterclockwise three times and meet the devil. Past the entrance of Blessington Street where Iris Murdoch was born (I set a novel over that wall) and St Peter's Church where my granny used to see Walter Macken, a censored writer, at early Mass, on his knees. Although she does not recognise it, a few yards from the church, my mother passes the house where May Joyce died while her son James stood in the room and refused to pray for her soul—he would later steal, for a silly old book, the white china bowl by her deathbed, as recalled by Stephen Dedalus looking over Dublin Bay with his waggish friend, the medical student Buck Mulligan.

Derek Mahon, the late, great poet, knew how the city yielded without warning to every past version of itself. In his poem 'J.P. Donleavy's Dublin' he wrote:

> For the days are long—
> From the first milk van
> To the last shout in the night,
> An eternity. But the weeks go by
> Like birds; and the years, the years
> Fly past anti-clockwise
> Like clock hands in a bar mirror

'Your first day in Dublin is always the worst,' John Berryman said of his visit in 1966, but I am not sure it ever gets better.

I met an American once who said—and I had no reason to disbelieve her—that on her first day in the city, while crossing Trinity's Front Square, she met a one-legged nun who'd had an affair with Ezra Pound.

Of course I can't give my entire heritage, my home town and my family in it, to Irish literature. I am capable of walking down Nassau Street without looking up at the sign for Finns Hotel. I can pass the corner of Merrion Square and ignore the first floor conservatory where Oscar Wilde's father, another doctor, examined his patient's eyes in full natural light.

I can resist! I can get on the bus and go home, past the room where I was born, up over the canal (where I do not consider the work of Patrick Kavanagh). Down past my first school, and the library with its floors of green linoleum. Beyond the intersection, my second school where we learned another poem about Dublin, this time by Donagh MacDonagh which has the rousing opening lines:

> 'Dublin made me and no little town
> With the country closing in on its streets
> The cattle walking proudly on its pavements
> The jobbers, the gombeenmen and the cheats'

On Rathgar Road, I can forget which window belonged to Siobhán McKenna whose last performance, in *Bailegangaire* by Tom Murphy, I saw in 1985. When I passed her house as a schoolgirl, you could see gilt wooden chair-backs in the drawing room window—very delicate and theatrical, as she herself was. I can ignore the road where Tom Murphy was waked thirty years later and a hundred or so yards away. In Terenure, I do not have to acknowledge the house where he lived, when I met him first. I do not even know which gateway on Whitehall Road belonged to the Irish poet, Mairtín O Direáin whose work, like Murphy's and Macken's, pulled the Irish reader's heart west.

I am a Dubliner, born and reared. I spurn these lyrical types with their yearning for the rural; what MacDonagh called, 'The lean road flung over profitless bog/ Where only a snipe could nest.' For me as for him, it is the 'arrogant city' that 'stirs proudly and secretly in my blood.'

Past the house of the poet, which ever one it was, and the seminary filled, in my childhood, by African priests, is the place I was taught, at six, to reach the string that rang the bell. The day I was brought back from the Stella Maris my siblings waited by this bus stop because how else would I get home? They did not consider the idea my father would drive the distance in his black Volkswagen Beetle. My mother probably sat in the back seat. No safety belt. Me in a wicker basket, or maybe in her arms. This was my first journey; bearing left, turning right, stopping and starting along this same route. My father drove it slowly, with a crack in the window to let out the smoke from his fag. One last corner. The other children running down the footpath to see the new baby. A neighbour standing by her open door to say all was well. Home.

Caitriona Lally
Eggshells {novel extract}

I wake up in a frown. Things don't seem right already, and I have barely opened my eyes. It was a struggle of a night, one of those nights when I felt itchy all over: itchy arms, itchy scalp, even itchy breath. I coughed up a tickle all night. I can hear the wind whistling through the gaps where the walls join: the sound that a comb makes when I put a tissue over it and blow. I can't stay in my pyjamas today—they're marshmallow-coloured and would get mucky on the streets—so I peel them off and pull on some clothes from the floor and go downstairs.

'Morning, Lemonfish,' I say.

He's looking more ragged by the day, and a dark thread of waste hangs from his underside. Maybe he needs more roughage. I cut up an apple and throw in small pieces, which he ignores. I tap on the bowl and shout: 'Drink more water!' at him, but that would be like trying to cure human constipation with gulps of air. I put a pouch of chocolate buttons in my bag, a big pouch to share, along with a Greek drachma coin from my coin collection in the hoardroom, and leave the house. People seem to be crossing my path, and I have to swerve to avoid them. I press the thumb of each hand onto the side of its first finger and whisper 'safe safe safe' to get me through the streets. I turn off Berkeley Road onto Eccles Street, because I need to walk on a street that's also a cake. At the junction with Dorset Street, I wait for the lights to turn red. The Eccles Street sign has been entirely blue-ed out, but, higher up on the same wall, the letters of an old green street sign haven't been greened out—either the leprechauns are seriously unmotivated, or their union doesn't allow them to climb ladders.

I need to go to the toilet so I head for Clerys on O'Connell Street. A scrawny grey-faced man is splayed against the home furnishings window, being searched by two guards. The man looks unsurprised, as if this is as normal as window shopping. I walk up the carpeted middle staircase—I might be an elegant rich lady going to a ball or a passenger on the Titanic staircase, and I struggle with the urge to wave daintily to my subjects. I join the queue for the toilet, trying to ignore the big mirror to my right. An elderly lady with a fresh hairstyle smiles shyly at herself in the mirror, and cups the bottom of her hair as if she's catching drips of water. When I'm finished, I walk back to North Earl Street and look at the carved stone face of a woman above the café on the corner. I call her Naomi because she looks like she deals mostly in vowels. Today she is calm, which is a good sign. I follow North Earl Street until it turns into Talbot Street, then I cross at Connolly Station and walk up Seville Place. On Seville Place I think of orange marmalade, and on Dawson Street I think of damson jam; maybe the streets should be twinned in a cross-river fruit-preserve initiative.

When I reach the church, I turn left onto Ferryman's Crossing. The houses have pale tops like pebbledash shirts and orange bottoms like brick skirts. I need to find Charon, the ferryman in the Greek myth, who brought dead people across the River Styx to Hades, the Otherworld. I'm not dead, but if I stay very still, I could pass for a corpse. The Liffey is not the Styx, but I don't want to travel to ancient Greece—crossing so many time zones would make for unbearable travel sickness. I walk to the end of the street, looking into the porches of the houses for oars, but the street ends in a wall topped by a railing, the river on the other side. I put the drachma in my mouth: it tastes thinly metallic, like blood when I bite my tongue. I look out over the railings at the tall grey office buildings and wonder if they are in Hades. A man walks by with a dog.

'Are you looking for something, love?'

'I'm looking for Charon.'

My words come out thick and spitty with the coin in my mouth.

'Sharon Larkin or Sharon Eliot?'

'A different Charon,' I say.

The dog is sticking its nose between my legs quite strenuously, and I push it back.

'He likes you,' the man says.

'I'd prefer if he didn't like me so much,' I say.

I cover my legs with my hands and the dog starts licking them. I say goodbye to the man, and walk back down Ferrymans Crossing. A taxi is parked outside one of the houses, and a man comes out and walks over to it. Maybe this is a motorised, land-based version of Charon.

'Are you a taxi driver?'

The coin clogs my palate and my tongue stumbles over the 'X.'

'Yeah, why?'

'Could you drive me over the river?'

'Alright, where to?'

'Just over to the other side. Or maybe over and back a few times.'

'Okay,' he says. 'Different bridges?'

'Yes, there's more chance of it happening then.'

The coin clacks against my teeth. I have to clench my jaw to form words, but they come out tight and distorted.

'Of what happening?'

'Of me finding my way back.'

'Are you Dorothy or what?'

'Not today,' I say. 'I tried looking for the Yellow Brick Road, and also Emerald Street and the Emerald Palace, but I had no luck.'

The man looks at me as if I'm an interesting disease and shakes his head slowly.

'Right,' he says, 'hop in.'

He sticks his fingers into his belt loops, yanks up his jeans, walks around to the driver's side and opens the door. I stand on one leg and hop the few steps to the car because, if this is Charon, it's important that I follow his instructions exactly.

'Is your leg hurt?'

'No, you said to hop in.'

'Jaysus,' he says, 'I've a right genius here.'

I look at the name on his identity card on the dashboard: it's Charlie Larkin. I'm glad he's Charlie and not Charles, because a middle 'I' is more friendly than a final 'S.'

'Do you know Charon?' I ask.

'The missus is called Sharon,' he says. 'Why?'

He starts the car.

'Wait!' I say. 'Does Sharon want to come too?'

Spit wells up in my mouth every time I say Sharon. Charlie turns around in his seat.

'Are you for real?'

'Yes, Sharon can sit with you in the passenger seat and I'll sit back here, and we can all drive over the bridges together.'

He looks at me like there's something behind my eyes that I don't know about.

'I'll pay you double fare, for two drivers.'

He turns back to the steering wheel and stops the engine.

'Wait here.'

He gets out of the car and walks back into the house. I'm so excited I could burst out of my face. A woman is standing by the window looking out at me. I wave, but she looks cross and doesn't wave back. I know from watching television with the sound turned down that they're arguing, because her mouth is opening wide and her lips are moving quickly and her face is jutting forward. She disappears from the window, Charlie comes out of the house, and she follows, slamming the front door behind her. Charlie walks around to the driver's seat and she gets in the passenger side. I lean forward between the seats.

'Hello, Sharon, thank you for coming on the journey.'

My jaw is not moving as fast as I need it to and the coin goes *clack clack clack* against my teeth. Sharon stares at me with an expression that contains a menace of question marks, and lets out a sigh the length of a caterpillar. Charlie starts the car.

'Alright to start with the Eastlink?'

'Yes, thanks.'

Sharon stares out the side window even though the view

is better from the front. She's wasting the front seat but I don't want to make her angrier by asking to swap. I take out the pouch of chocolate buttons, open it, and hold it through the gap in the seats.

'But-tons?'

The coin shifts in my mouth and it comes out like two separate words.

'No, thanks,' says Charlie.

Sharon just stares out the window. We turn onto Seville Place and head for the river. I sit back content because I'm going for a spin with two adults in charge and I have chocolate in my hand. I take out the drachma and stuff some buttons into my mouth and chew them quickly before we hit a bridge. Sharon hasn't talked yet but I know how to get her to talk, I've read the covers of women's magazines in the shops.

'What's your favourite hair colour, Sharon?' I ask.

She keeps staring out the window and shakes her head and mutters something short that ends in 'Christ.'

'I like clothes,' I say. 'I like jumpers best because they are warmest and cover the most area but cardigans come second.'

'Sharon, you like clothes too, don't you,' Charlie says, and there's a quiet tightness in his voice. She turns her head slowly to me.

'Yeah, I like clothes.'

Her sentence changes the situation to an almost friendship, even though her voice sounds like jagged rocks.

'It's the gaps between the buttons that let in the cold,' I say. 'That's why cardigans come second to jumpers.'

'Got it,' she says.

Charlie starts talking about the bridges he can drive over and the ones he can't and the ones he can drive south over but not north and the ones he can drive north over but not south: the Eastlink Toll bridge, Samuel Beckett Bridge, Talbot Memorial Bridge, Butt Bridge, O'Connell Bridge, Grattan Bridge, O'Donovan Rossa Bridge, Father Mathew Bridge, James Joyce Bridge, Rory O'More Bridge, Frank Sherwin Bridge, Islandbridge.

His list spans the city, and I realise I don't know many of the people the bridges are named for. A bridge is currently being built for the tram, and I have half a hope it will be named after me if I do something noble and grand, but I must do it quickly.

When I've swallowed all the chocolate, I put the coin back in my mouth. It's not so bad when it tastes of chocolate.

'Sharon,' I say (because she likes clothes), 'if I swallowed a whole bag of chocolate buttons, would it be like swallowing one-fifth of a chocolate cardigan?'

Charlie snorts. Sharon turns fully around in her seat to look at me, and this time she is an inch from a smile.

'Are you taking the piss?' she asks, but her voice is not like rocks any more, it's like pebbles, pebbles that have been washed smooth on a lakeshore.

'I don't think so,' I say, and now the two of them laugh. We cross the first bridge and I close my eyes, because this is what you do when you make a wish.

'Charlie?'

'Yeah?'

He looks at me in the mirror.

'Which side of the river would you say is earth and which would you say is Hades?'

'Hades?'

'Yeah, Hades, the Underworld.'

'Oh, well there's dodgy goings-on both sides of the river, I'd say there's parts of the criminal underworld everywhere.'

'Oh, okay.'

I look out the window. We're on the south quays about to cross another bridge back to the Northside. It would help if I knew in which direction I should be wishing the hardest. I close my eyes, but when we turn left onto the north quays, I open my eyes and look at my arms and my legs— they haven't changed. We continue over and back across the Liffey, making a shape like a wide-toothed comb. I squeeze my eyes shut for each crossing, but there is no change. When we cross Islandbridge, the final bridge, I feel sad that we haven't found the portal to the Underworld, but happy that we've had a nice trip. I direct Charlie back to my road off the North Circular.

'Ah, the Norrier,' he says.

'The what?'

'The North Circular, it's known as The Norrier.'

'Oh, does that make me a Norrierer? Maybe an honorary Norrierer if I wasn't born here. 'Honorary Norrierer honorary Norrierer honorary Norrierer," I say, until my tongue twists on the coin and there is too much spit to continue. Sharon shakes her head. When he pulls up outside my house, Charlie names the price of the trip. I reach into my bag and pull out my purse but (oh no), there are only small coins. I empty them out onto my hand, take the coin out of my mouth, add it to the pile on my palm and push my hand between the seats.

'Would you take this much euro and a wet drachma?'

Charlie and Sharon look at each other. Before they can respond with some words that would ruin our nice afternoon, I say, 'Only joking,' because that would be a funny joke, then I say, 'Please come in and I'll get you the money.'

They look at each other again. Sharon bursts open her car door.

'Come on, Charlie.'

I get out of the car and they follow me into the front garden and I feel so proud that I have visitors, that I'm leading people instead of following so I say very loudly for Mary's and Bernie's ears,

'Please follow me. I hope you enjoy your visit.'

I open the door and stand back to let them in. They come in slow and hesitant, like they're being pulled from behind by strings.

'Come into the living room.'

I sweep my arm forwards but now my arm is sticking straight out from my body and I don't know how to lower it casually, so I keep it stuck out in front of me.

'Do sit down,' I say, because I've heard this on *Fawlty Towers* and it sounds welcoming. Charlie and Sharon don't look welcomed, though—they look like they've just found out their child has a disease.

'Do you have any diseased children?' I ask.

People always enquire about the health of other people's children. Charlie makes a noise like a bark and says,

'Three children, two grandchildren, no diseases. Now love, have you got the fare?'

'Yes, yes, would you like a cup of tea first?'

'No, thanks, I've got to get back to work. So that's—'

He repeats the amount I owe him. The neighbours won't

think it's a proper visit unless I keep them for at least a quarter of an hour, so I say: 'You can choose your favourite chair and sit in it, but you might have to squeeze through or climb over other chairs to get to the ones at the back.'

Charlie clears his throat and yanks up his jeans again. He looks like he's about to make a funeral speech, so I clear my throat too.

'Could you both turn around and close your eyes?'

'What?'

'I need to go to my secret hiding place and I don't want you to see where it is.'

Sharon growls. They have both turned into dogs with their noises.

'For fuck's sake, are you going to get the fuckin money or what?'

They stare at me as if they want to peel off my skin and put it in a scrapbook.

'Alright,' Charlie says, with a sigh as long as November. 'Come on, Sharon, let's turn around.'

'And close your eyes?'

'And close our eyes.'

They both turn and, when I'm sure that they're not peeking, I tiptoe to the bookshelf and take down *Grimm's Fairytales*. I open it at the Hansel and Gretel story, on the page where the woodcutter and his wife leave the children in the forest because they can't afford to feed them. I keep money between those pages so that the woodcutter can buy food for his family and Hansel and Gretel will be safe from the witch's oven.

'Okay, you can say *'ready or not'* now!'

'What?'

'We're playing hide-and-seek and you're both on,' I say. 'I'm ready to be caught now.'

'How about you just give me the fare and we'll head on.'

I hand Charlie the money, and they both walk quickly into the hall. I am considering the best way to say goodbye—whether handshakes would be more appropriate than a wave, whether I should take both of their phone numbers so as not to offend one of them—but Sharon has the door opened and they're wedged together in the doorway in their rush to get out. Once he's outside, Charlie waves and says, 'Cheerio, love.' I wave and close the door behind them slowly. If they have to leave so quickly, I'm glad it's while calling the name of a cereal. Next time I say goodbye to someone, I will end with a shout of 'Cornflakes' or 'Rice Krispies'—or 'All-Bran'—to a sturdy aunt. I sit down on the dark green patterned armchair and take off my shoes and socks and rub my bare feet against each other; this feels like a ritual performed at the end of a journey. The tops of my feet are butter-soft, but the soles are leathery, like one of those bath sponges with a soft yellow body and a green scouring base. I peel open the map of Dublin and plot today's route, just the part where I walked to Ferryman's Crossing, because Charlie might want to plot the drive on his own map, and it's really not mine to draw. Today I walked the ECG of a patient who flat-lined briefly, before rallying into a healthy peak.

Paula Meehan
In Solidarity {poem}

In solidarity
with the clouds which took the bare look off the sky the
day you died, you'll never die! Morning cargo on the wind
that smelled of the sea; with the gulls that flocked inland
upriver, stravaging past Liberty Hall, raucous, raucous,
raucous,
in solidarity.

In solidarity
with the moon, the wolf moon of January, a lamp in the
early dark your last night on this earth, Venus, a diamond,
studded the night, Pluto in Capricorn, Death drew down
the fatal night; with all the planets and stars that lined up
to light your path
in solidarity.

DUBLIN, WRITTEN IN OUR HEARTS

In solidarity
with the weather — who will forget the mildness of it, the
last days bathed in all that radiant light, midwinter sun hung
in the southern skies, as if stopped still, the solstice burning
like a flame for you; with our own lovely star of morning,
our seven stars on a field of blue, ploughing a sea of blue, our
scarlet banners high-streaked upriver, tattered flags of sunset
in solidarity.

In solidarity
with the people bereft by your passing, bearing the ordinary
weathers along with their grief, with the passage of time
your name will shine like a star in our private and our public
firmaments, banishing darkness; with time itself which brings
us to our senses, brings us to our knees, which teaches us
humility and our own true natures
in solidarity.

In solidarity
with the foggy dew, the waxy's dargle, the dicey reillys, the
heart of the rowls, the twangman, and the rocky road that led
you down through the songlines of Dublin to the river itself,
the seagull raucous Liffey; its smell, its swell, its angelus bells
ringing o'er it, its crescent moon above and the whole world
in a state of chassis
in solidarity.

In solidarity
with those who couldn't organize a piss-up in a brewery,
with the one who roared 'up the knocked down flats'; with

those who were elected chair and sat there through tedium
and tension of meeting after meeting where the soul of the city
was fought for and even sometimes won and done on behalf of
those who couldn't organize the proverbial
in solidarity.

In solidarity
with the children we have lost and who have yet to be born,
Janus who names the month of your death, looking both ways
at once; walking backwards into the future, remembering the
future, staring clear-eyed at the past, intuiting the ancient
lineaments of the ancestors in the month of the wolf moon
in solidarity.

In solidarity
with your dreams now that we inherit them, wearing the year
of your death like a union badge, wreathed in your dreams of
dignity and justice, like a mantle your dreams for the city, for
the people; with the people, always with the people
in solidarity.

In solidarity
with the hare. You were there for it. Elect it now your totem
creature, loping through the sky meadows over Dublin, away
off into eternity; leaving the beloved streets, the beloved faces,
the beloved songs
in solidarity.

i.m. Tony Gregory

Deirdre Madden
Authenticity {novel extract}

He spent all morning in his studio but achieved nothing; nothing that pleased him in any case. When William had last painted, many years earlier, the works he produced had been strong and assertive, making up in verve for what they lacked in technical accomplishment. On taking his canvases out of storage to look at them again he was surprised at how good he'd once been. His studies in oils of trees and rivers, his still lifes, had somehow got at the essence of the things represented, although for the life of him now he couldn't think how he had done it. This notwithstanding, his past accomplishments gave him confidence as he embarked upon his new phase of work. In the intervening years his interests and tastes had changed and what he wished to paint now were abstract works in watercolour. 'Good luck,' Julia had said to him when he told her this. 'Believe me, you're going to need it.'

To begin with his initial enthusiasm had carried him along, together with the excitement of having his own studio space and the time in which to work in it, but in the past week or so he had become bogged down and could make no progress. He found he couldn't control the colours, couldn't make them conform to the idea he had in mind and wished to express. Was that the problem—was he taking too rigid a stance, trying to impose a form upon the work rather than taking a freer and more instinctive approach? In the painting he was engaged upon this morning, executed in reddish brown tones of ochre and rust, the effect he wanted was of transparency and light, the colours seeping into each other in a feathered and delicate way. He was failing utterly in this: the more he struggled for a translucent clarity the more murky and opaque the whole thing became.

He gave up for the morning and after a short lunch alone—Liz was at work, the children off at day camp as they were on summer holidays from school—he returned to the studio. The painting looked even worse than he had thought, a heavy muddy daub, brown dominating red, the whole thing clumsy and ham fisted. There was nothing to be done but set it aside and start afresh. This time he tried to have no preconceptions but quickly found this meant he had no idea whatsoever of how or where to begin. William's mind was racing now so that he couldn't concentrate. It was precisely the worry of not being able to paint that was getting in the way and preventing him from even making a start. He stared at the blank sheet of paper, willing himself to pick up a brush as a deep sense of anxiety unfolded within him, immobilising him and putting paid to whatever last few shreds of his self-belief remained.

In mid afternoon he gave up and decided to go into the city, leaving a note for Liz to say he would probably not be back in time for dinner. As he propped it against the teapot on the kitchen table he reflected that she would be annoyed by this, but didn't consider changing his plans. Before leaving the house he went into the drawing-room to find a book to read on the train into town, and while he was there he caught sight of Roderic's painting, which depressed him even further. He saw in it exactly that combination of freedom and control that he had sought so ardently all day and that had eluded him so completely. The fields of green and blue paint complemented each other like voices singing in harmony, each depending on the other for its full resonance and power, the formal restraint serving only to accentuate a wild beauty that it barely contained. Compared to this, his own laboured efforts seemed ludicrous.

There were few people travelling into the city on this August afternoon and so he had no difficulty getting a seat on the train, but the book he had brought with him remained in his pocket. He looked out across Dublin Bay to Howth, the distant houses vague in the heat-haze. He had hoped that leaving the house would clear his head and permit him to think clearly, perhaps even to know what he might do when next he went to the studio, to break through the impasse in which he had found himself. The sea view, however, brought no enlightenment and still his mind was unfocused, was like a pack of scattered cards. The stations slipped past: Sydney Parade already, and he had given no thought to what he would do when he reached town where he often went now to wander aimlessly, to look in galleries and bookshops, to sit in pubs, wishing his life away.

William left the train at Westland Row, crossed the road and went through the back gate into Trinity College. He was aware as he emerged onto College Green that he was tracing out now a skewed version of his past life. Empty-handed and casually dressed he dawdled along the exact same route where, not so long ago, he had strode among the early morning crowds with business suit and briefcase, purposeful and directed and desperate. What had changed in his life? But *really* changed? His mind shrank from the thought. Julia. He would go to see Julia, he decided, as he proceeded up Dame Street. He knew enough now about the pattern of her day to know that there was a good chance of finding her at home at this time; and then just at that moment, he saw her on the other side of the road.

She was walking in the same direction as William; evidently she was on her way back to her house. He would have crossed over, called her name and joined her had she not been with Roderic. He trailed in their wake, hoping that her companion would leave her at some stage but that too, he knew, was unlikely. Logic said that he was also going home or, worse from William's point of view, was on his way to Julia's place. The sleeves of the blouse Julia was wearing hung down well past her knuckles, completely concealing her hands. From the depths of the left sleeve dangled a bag made of such thin white plastic that William could see through it and identify the modest haul of groceries it contained: a carton of milk, a loaf, some oranges, a tin of soup and a tin of cat food. Abruptly Roderic and Julia stopped walking and William stopped too, thereby causing a collision between himself and a woman walking immediately behind him, much to her irritation. Julia handed the plastic bag to Roderic and held on to his left forearm for balance while she stood on one leg and removed her shoe, a scuffed brown moccasin, then shook it to remove a pebble. As she did so, Roderic said something that made them both laugh, Julia so much that she wobbled and almost overbalanced. Dropping the shoe on to the pavement she shoved her foot back into it and playfully thumped him on the shoulder in response to whatever his teasing remark had been, herself said something and again they both laughed. Roderic was still holding her shopping, and by his gesture William understood that he was offering to carry it for her but Julia shook her head. He handed it back and they continued on their way. It never occurred to William how disconcerted they both would have been had they known he was observing their inconsequential but, as they thought, private stroll through the city.

Perched on a stool in a diner one lunch time not long before he had had to take leave from his job he had noticed, on glancing through the plate-glass window, a woman pass in the street. She was pretty in a rather conventional way, with blue eyes, carefully tinted blonde hair, and she wore a quilted rust-coloured jacket with gilt buttons. A silk scarf printed with Montgolfier balloons was folded around her throat. He noticed all of this, and also noticed that there was something spirited about her: the way her lips were pursed as though she were laughing at something she knew she ought not to find amusing but couldn't resist. She looked as though she was fully aware of how little her own monied elegance amounted to; conscious of how, underneath it all, she was wholly her own woman. In a fraction of a second William noticed all of this, and it was only then that he recognised his own wife.

As he walked up Dame Street now until it became Lord Edward Street, past offices and shops, past Dublin Castle, he consciously attempted to do the same thing in reverse with Roderic and Julia: to see them as though they were not people he had met, and, in Julia's case, someone he liked to consider a friend, but total strangers. How unprepossessing they looked! Ambling home in the late afternoon with their shopping and their shabby clothes—her floppy skirt, his faded cord jacket—there was nothing, but *nothing* about them, to William's mind, that suggested any kind of gift or accomplishment. No one could have guessed at their real selves, but then, wasn't that always the case? Wasn't that what was always said about murderers too, how unremarkable they seemed, and the more heinous their crime the more people insisted, marvelling upon their ordinariness? What did strike him today forcibly and surprisingly about Roderic and Julia was that they were a couple. As a complete stranger that was the only thing he could have intuited about them with any certainty. This was strange, for they weren't holding hands and apart from the moment when she had balanced on his arm there was no physical contact at all between them. And yet in their easy confidence and the relaxed way in which they talked and laughed together their intimacy could be read as easily as on the day when he had seen them in the shop, speculating on the names of the semiprecious stones. It was as though walking along the street together they were encompassed in a field of radiant light that was theirs and theirs alone.

For a moment William was overcome with jealousy, so powerful and acute it was like physical pain; it winded him and literally stopped him in his tracks. He resented Roderic so deeply that briefly he hated him. For all that he looked inconsequential he had what William wanted and yet would never, could never, have. Looking at the other man today he knew that. He was too alien, too unlike him; he would never be able to unmake himself to become what Roderic was. William had lost ground to the couple, they were still walking on and he followed them again, but half-heartedly now. Roderic threw back his head and roared with laughter at something Julia had said. It was worse than William had thought: it simply wasn't in him to be what he wanted to be. His confidence was all gone and he had no real work to set against it, nothing to prove that he had achieved something exceptional in the past and therefore might reasonably expect to produce good work again in the future. It pained him more than ever now to remember the muddy paper over which he had laboured that morning to so little purpose. Against that he set Roderic's painting and he recalled the beauty and energy of it, the tension there was between the rich pigment and the decisive intelligence of the form; and this was, moreover, far from being his finest work. There was a playful, even foolish side to him; the side that teased Julia and sported with Max, but this silliness did not negate, indeed had no impact whatsoever upon the detached genius that made the paintings. There was no denying the reality of the other man's gift: the magnitude of it.

They had come to the top of Lord Edward Street. Christchurch was before them and as Roderic and Julia waited to cross the road William hung back. There was no point in going any further. He couldn't face either of them now and he turned away, wishing that he had never followed them in the first place.

He rang Julia a few days later to arrange a meeting. She was cheerful as ever and asked him how his work was going.

'Better not to ask.'

'Do you know what the secret is?'

'Tell me.'

'The secret is that there's no secret. You just get on with it. You just do the work.' She could hear him snort at the other end of the phone. 'You think I'm joking? This is as serious as I get.' She suggested that he call by on Wednesday.

As he walked up the street to her house he smelt the smoke of a turf fire, even though it was August. He commented on it when they were on their way up to her flat and she stopped on the stairs, turned to him. 'Will you do something for me? Will you do me a favour?'

In the sitting-room, she gave him a pen and a notepad. 'I want you to write down what the turf smoke makes you think of, in as much detail as you wish to give me. Do you mind doing that?' It wasn't at all what he had expected, but he took up the pen and after a moment's thought started to write.

Turf smoke reminds me of the west of Ireland. We used to spend our family holidays there when I was a child. My mother was from Westport and we used to go there with her, my brother and I, for the whole summer. My father who was a lawyer came for occasional weekends and then for two weeks' holiday. I liked being there because my parents, especially my father, had more time for us children than was usually the case. I found him less stern, less forbidding than when we were in Dublin, to a singular degree, almost as if he were another person. We used to go to Achill. We used to go to Keem, to the sunken cove in under the headland. We were there one day, I remember, in late summer. The holidays were almost over, which I regretted, for soon we would be going back to the city and the old, rigid regimen would take over again. My mother had settled down with us children in the middle of the strand, we were paddling, playing, digging in the sand. My father had gone down to the end of the beach some little way off, was sitting in the shadow of some rocks reading. I strayed into his territory without meaning to and I thought he might tell me to go away, but he smiled when he saw me and asked me to sit beside him. We looked out to sea, to Clare Island with its mountains, where the pirate queen had lived. The atmosphere was strange that afternoon, bright and full of heat, the light before rain, the light before a big storm. My father was staring out to sea. The sea was the colour of pewter. To me he seemed very serious, very old, although I realise that he can have been no older than I am now, if that. I thought for the hundredth time of how I would never measure up to him, neither what he was, nor his expectations of me. I was I think about ten years old. The light was strong, weird, making all the colours too vivid, almost painfully intense: the green of the slopes behind us, the sand, the rocks; all the colours drenched, saturated, like in a cheap postcard. Soon the weather would break, and all would soften into greyness, as the water, although riddled with light, was already grey. I could hear the cries of my brother, my mother's voice calling to him. My father was still looking out to sea. 'Look,' he said, 'out there, a school of porpoises. Can you see them?' I looked to where he was pointing out in the bay, and I saw their dark fins shimmering in the water. It was a remarkable sight. As I write this, I can see them again. 'Shall I tell the others?' I asked my father, but he said no. He said that there would be other things for all the family but this moment was for just the two of us. We kept looking out to sea, at how the black backs dappled in the water, shiny as black glass, the water soft metal, now dark as lead, and it was as if my father and I were the only two people in the world, so that there was only this moment, this ocean, these porpoises, my father, me. It made me feel so close to my father of whom, generally, I was afraid.

And then the light reached breaking point. The sky darkened, and a bright fork of lightening tore down, there was thunder and my mother called to us. It began to rain, a few heavy drops, then more, then a torrent. I heard my brother shriek. My father and I stood up and together we ran along the beach, seeking a place of safety, a place of refuge.

He put the pen down.

'May I see?'

William nodded, and sat with his hands over his face, as Julia silently read through the text he had written. She read it slowly twice so as to give him time to compose himself. 'I had forgotten that,' he said at last when he could speak again. 'Forgotten it for all these years.' He looked up at her. Julia smiled at him and he struggled to smile back, looked away. Forlorn, he was the image of his own small son.

The task she had set him had created a strange atmosphere between them; an intimacy she did not want and was keen to dispel. 'I'm sure you're wondering why I asked you to do that,' she said, but oddly it hadn't crossed his mind. He had unthinkingly complied with her request. Julia explained the nature of the project upon which she was engaged. 'I have a list,' she said, taking it from a folder and passing it to him. 'I'm exposing people to particular scents and then asking what it evokes for them. When I have enough material, I'm going to create a work around it. These are the scents and odours I'm using.'

William looked down at the paper in his hands:

Hot chocolate
Clean linen
The ocean
Hay
Coconut
Rotting apples
Mint
Bleach
Tea
Cut grass
Turf smoke
Fresh bread
Roses

'It's turning out to be a more potent idea than I had expected. People are often surprised or even shocked by what they themselves come up with,' she said as though to console him. William sat nodding at this strange young woman in her dim room whom he really didn't know, and who had unwittingly forced open a closed chamber of his heart, where his own past was hidden from himself. She took a sheaf of papers from the folder and glanced through them, told him that what had struck her so far was the discrepancy between the thing offered and the thing remembered. So far no one had simply evoked the thing itself, and strange circular links had been created. For William smoke suggested the ocean, for someone else the ocean evoked roses, and for someone else again roses were redolent of smoke. 'For they told me of being in a public garden at the end of a day when the gardeners had been cutting the heads off roses and they were burning them on a great fire, as though it were an offering, a sacrifice. From then on, the person concerned could never disassociate the smell of roses from smoke.' She took another page from the folder. She had offered someone clean linen, a sheet laundered, pressed, fresh from the line. The woman said it reminded her of betrayal.

'How will you use them? Will you transcribe them?'

'I don't think so.' She didn't like to add that that would diminish their impact by removing, say, the contrast between William's precise handwriting and the emotional force of what he expressed.

She asked then for his permission to keep the text, to use it anonymously in any project she might subsequently develop.

'Has anyone refused you yet?'

'Just one man.'

'Was it your friend?' he asked as though she had only one.

'Roderic?' she said, deliberately naming him. 'No, it wasn't Roderic. It was someone else.'

He tore the page from the notebook and looked at it as though considering whether or not to destroy it, then leaned over and handed it to her, although in doing so he had the strange feeling that he was handing over to her too much of himself, that he was giving her some kind of power over him. 'I feel,' he said deliberately, 'that I'm giving you something private. Something precious.'

'Yes, you are. You're doing just that,' Julia said. 'That's why I asked your permission.'

'Is this,' he asked, 'what art has become?'

'This,' she said, 'is what art has always been.'

Keith Ridgway
Undublining {essay}

> The distance was full of sound as if many things were happening there.
>
> *The Informer*—Liam O'Flaherty

Dublin, of course—we all know this—does not exist. A synecdoche of an ever-changing collection of streets and neighbourhoods, histories and legends, literature and politics, hilarity and gossip, gathered by the sulking river Liffey as it stumbles to the gentle bay. That cannot be abstracted. There is no more a *Dublin* than there is a colour blue.

In this, Dublin is just the same as any other place on earth—unique. And it has, of course, a particular and very lovely shade of blue on its flags and emblems.

Nevertheless. The point stands. A name is an idea. A place is a place. The idea is constantly trying to make sense of itself—seeking balance, or clarity, or comprehensiveness, or accuracy, or truth. The place carries on regardless, not caring a jot. Well, of course.

*

My first novel was written on the North Circular Road, in a mousey little flat overlooking the much maligned O'Devaney Gardens estate, now demolished. The last time I went by my old building it was abandoned, boarded up, waiting presumably for some exotic financial instrument to activate, allowing someone somewhere to make a killing. I have very little memory of that time. Scenes and moments. There are some vague physical remnants (the flat could be very cold, I remember that, and the dust, there was something about the dust) that I still seem able somehow to sense. And there are emotional artefacts (a difficult and ending relationship, vivid encounters nearby) which form a small, intricate tangle of regret and sentiment. I suppose—given that I can name them—that I carry these sensations, regrets, feelings, all these years later. But not as a burden. Less like baggage, more like lint in the pocket. I do not feel in any real way connected to the young man who wrote that young book. He is not me. I am not him. I feel that I am entirely different. This is not something he should take personally, so to speak. I feel this way about all previous versions of myself. With regard to my sense of self I am what Galen Strawson calls a *transient*. I don't experience my life as a narrative (though of course I can relate it as such if required—with some discomfort). And I don't feel that I am the same person that I was—on an ongoing basis. I am perpetually startled and new. I feel I am an entirely different person to the one I was last month, say, or last week, or this morning.

Perhaps it is this always restarting sense of self—not very unusual, but probably not the experience of the majority of people—that has led me into my uneasy relationship with almost all of the writing I did before… well, before this very piece, which seems to me to be the only writing I've ever done that can properly be ascribed to me—the me that I currently am. You see the problem? That first novel *is not mine*.

Maybe if I could disavow it things would be simpler. But of course I understand and accept that I wrote it. I cannot and do not deny responsibility. I accept the pennies that sometimes arrive as royalties. My name is on the cover. But I do not feel any sense of connection, or particular insight, or even understanding. I no longer feel qualified to say very much about it. No more qualified certainly than anyone else who read it several years ago and has an imperfect memory of what it's about or how or whether it works. Sometimes a reader will tell me about a particular passage or scene they like and it comes as a complete surprise to me. Even when the reader is complimentary, I feel this chiefly as an embarrassment. Here is someone to whom a piece of writing has meant something, and they are kind enough to tell the author about it, and all they get is a blank look, and stuttering, and I fear sometimes that they worry that they're thinking of a different book, that they've made a terrible mistake, but no, it's far more likely that I have simply lost track, as it were, of myself.

It is—that first novel—the only novel I have written while living in Dublin. All the others have been written, more or less, in London. It was set in Dublin as well—that novel—for the most part. I haven't read it in years. The second novel—written in London—was also set in Dublin. I haven't read that in years either. Each of them contains a slightly different sense of the idea *Dublin*. In each of them a reader will now find an abstracted Dublin created by reference to a historical

Dublin (part abstracted, part real—though the notion of *real* comes with a large retinue of caveats) which in many physical, cultural, psychic, and emotional ways no longer exists, filtered through the creative imagination of a mind (mine) long since consumed and replaced by a countless number of subsequent minds.

So many Dublin, so many mind, so many me.

*

These days, on the rare (and always flattering) occasions when I am asked whether parts of these early novels (or indeed pretty much any writing previously published) can be anthologised, I say—as politely as I can and with not an insignificant amount of (again) embarrassment—no. Sometimes, due to contractual intricacies which I never really understand, I can't say no. Thankfully, after all these years, the rights to my first few books have reverted to me, and that's the end of that. Which is why you are reading this —essay?—by me, and not an excerpt from *The Long Falling*, or *The Parts*—books written by previous Ridgways now no longer with us.

Henry James described thinking of his early novels as "the work of quite another person than myself… a rich relation, say". That's very James, isn't it? My own sense is different. I'm not going to call the police, but it feels to me like I've been visited by a thief. Someone has been through my desk, or my brain, and has made off with some of the patterns and tics of my thinking, with some of my observations and memories, but has missed the really good stuff, which thankfully only the current me has access to. This thief has then travelled somehow back through time, and framed me.

The writing feels counterfeit.

It's not at all an enjoyable experience, this reading of counterfeit work. And I think I mean—currently—any writing more than about a year old. It's not that I don't think the work is any good, though I'm a better writer now than I was then. But the sensation is uncanny. *Well*, I find myself feeling, *I wouldn't write this… and yet it's familiar somehow… as if this writer knows things about me… how unpleasant… and my name is on the cover… that can't be right.* What is most discomforting is the feeling that *people will think this is me.* And of course, it's not.

*

So much for me. What, I wonder, might Dublin's sense of self be? How could we find out? We could ask its people. How? Ask them what? And is Dublin merely its people? If Dublin is an idea, how constant is it? How coherent? How communicable? Most importantly of course—whose idea is it? And if it was possible to embody, or at least personify Dublin, and give it a single sense of self, consider how uncanny it would find all the millions of words written about it. Dublin, wrapped in a dirty overcoat, sitting on a park bench, reading, shivering, her teeth rattling, her stomach slightly off, wanting to stop reading, but unable to. *People will think this is me.*

All nonsense of course. The simple truth of it is that Dublin, like anywhere else, is a subjective experience. Each one of us has a different idea of it. Each one of us is wrong, in our own particular way, and that's fine. Anything you read about Dublin is not about Dublin at all. It's about the writer. It's their attempt to align their idea of themselves with their idea of Dublin. Even when they are completely successful on their own terms, they require a great generosity on the part of the reader. They require the reader to say to themselves—*yes I suppose it could be experienced like this. I suppose so. I suppose.*

When I read other writers' depictions of Dublin (and here I'm including those depictions written by earlier versions of myself) I very often feel a great and shameful irritation. *This doesn't get at it at all*, tends to be the tenor of it. It's instinctual, and it's possible to reason myself out of it, but it's there. It's most pronounced with writers closest to me in experience (so, my earlier versions especially) and less so with writers long dead, writing about earlier versions of Dublin now definitively vanished. I love the Dublin of James Plunkett's *Strumpet City* for example. A terrible, grim, painful place, populated by exemplary Dubliners. I particularly love the Dublin to be found in Liam O'Flaherty's *The Informer*. It's not a Dublin I know. Though it has some curious coincidences of street geography with the Dublins I have been to. And he evokes familiar nighttime hours and their light—their vivid encounters—and I can hear the voices very clearly. As if his Dublin haunts mine. Or, perhaps more likely, as if the Dublins I have been in have read *The Informer* with me. The reader reads the writer and the city reads the city. We are—all of us in this arrangement—in an un-Dublined Dublin, several metres off any solid ground, a very long way from Clery's clock, or Thom McGinty, or the hats and the bridges of Jack Yeats's *Liffey Swim*.

Dublin is not a narrative. It has no sense of self. It is what it is now, unknowable, and altered slightly from what it was an hour ago, also unknowable.

I have recently finished a new novel. I wrote it here in London. After three novels set here, this new one is something of a surprise to me—it is set in Dublin. Well, I should be more precise. I have learned my lesson. It is set in *Dublins*. All of which are themselves set entirely in my mind—or some of my recent minds anyway. All now vanished. If they were ever there at all.

Karl Whitney
The Hidden Rivers of the Liberties
{essay extract}

I was born in the Liberties, in the then new Coombe hospital on Cork Street; and during my childhood in Tallaght we passed through the area when taking the number 77 bus into the city centre. I remember the tightly packed red-brick streets as a vivid contrast to the wind-swept housing estate where my family lived. I was always intrigued by the sharp turns the bus took at the junction of Cork Street and Ardee Street, and then again from Ardee Street into the Coombe—I didn't know, then, that every street in this part of the Liberties follows a river. During the medieval period, this S-shaped arrangement of streets was known as the Crooked Staff. Cork Street runs west to east alongside the Commons Water, while Ardee Street runs north to south above the course of the Abbey Stream, and the Coombe follows the course of the Commons Water towards where it joins the Poddle.

Today 'the Liberties' is a single district of the city, but the Liberties of Dublin are plural for a reason: there were four of them, originally created in the twelfth century. A liberty was an administrative division of the Lordship of Ireland, and until the nineteenth century each liberty was independent of the authority of Dublin Corporation. All of the Dublin liberties—Thomas Court and Donore; St Sepulchre; Christ Church; and St Patrick's—had their origins in charters granted to religious orders. Thomas Court consisted of the lands surrounding a large Augustinian monastery. After the Reformation and Henry VIII's dissolution of the monasteries, the liberty was granted to the Brabazons, Earls of Meath. The liberty of Donore was also added to their estate—thus Kenneth Milne, in *The Dublin Liberties, 1600–1850*, refers to 'Thomas Court and Donore' as a single liberty. In the Liberties, even a single liberty could be plural.

In my twenties, I lived for about four years in the Liberties, first in a new apartment block not far from Meath Street, and then in a red-brick nineteenth-century terraced house off Blackpitts. I didn't realize it, but when I thought of 'the Liberties', I was mostly thinking of Thomas Court and Donore. The apartment I lived in had been outside the liberty of Thomas Court, looking in; the red-brick house had been inside the liberty of Donore, looking out. The house would have had a good view of the Poddle from its front windows, were that river not channelled below the tarmacked surface of Blackpitts.

It was a bright, breezy morning in mid-September when I met Franc Myles at a café on the South Circular Road. We planned to walk around the boundaries of the liberty of Thomas Court and Donore and, at the same time, trace the paths of the underground rivers. Franc explained the logic of the excursion: 'What fascinates me as an archaeologist is the sense of difference and the sense of place. How different was your life ten metres inside the liberty or ten metres outside the liberty, or was there a difference at all?'

Franc is six foot five and in his late forties, with greying hair gelled straight up in spikes. On the day in question, he was wearing a bright-yellow high-visibility vest with the word 'Archaeologist' printed on it in black letters and a pair of streamlined Ray-Ban sunglasses; he wore both the vest and sunglasses throughout our walk, and pushed a bike alongside him.

He described his main area of research as the 'archaeology of the contemporary past'. He has personal connections to the locality: his aunt lived in Weavers' Square, close to the path of the Abbey Stream; his father worked in the Guinness factory at St James's Gate, through which the Liberties' ancient boundaries run. Franc himself grew up in Kilmainham, not too far from the outer boundary of the Liberties, and lived for a while just off Blackpitts. The pace of urban redevelopment in the Liberties, coupled with the historical interest of the district, has ensured that a large amount of archaeological work has been carried out in recent years, much of it by Franc. Things had grown much quieter by the time we met; in the aftermath of Ireland's economic crash, construction had all but ceased in the area. New apartment blocks were interspersed with sites that had been cleared in the expectation of further building. If the recent past was visible in the unevenness of development in the area, the more distant past was accessible through a subtle reading of the urban landscape.

The arrangement of streets in the Liberties preserves the geographical features of earlier eras in the most unexpected of ways. Leaving the café and turning a corner, Franc gestured east down Greenville Avenue—a quiet street lined on one side by pairs of semi-detached, pebble-dashed houses—towards where it took a severe hairpin bend. On a map, you can see that sharp corners and an unusually jagged layout characterize a series of streets that run from the south end of Blackpitts in an east–west direction: Greenville Avenue, Merton Park, the west end of Merton Avenue and finally Donore Avenue. This irregular arrangement of streets, Franc told me, reflects a line of fortification that dates back to the Renaissance era. The curve he pointed towards would have been a vantage point extending from the fortification wall 'to give a field of fire in every direction'. On the 1837 first edition Ordnance Survey map, he told me, you could see 'a zigzag laneway from the bottom of Blackpitts to Roper's Rest'. Roper's Rest was a house or tavern near the South Circular Road end of what's now Donore Avenue.

On reaching Blackpitts, Franc explained that we were approaching the edge of the liberty of Donore; across the invisible Poddle was the archbishop's liberty of St Sepulchre. Blackpitts follows the original course of the Poddle and sits in a just-perceptible depression running from south to north through the landscape. Maps from the sixteenth and seventeenth centuries show the river flowing along the east side of the road, but it was subsequently covered over—by the mid-seventeenth century, Franc thinks. There was slight incline towards Clanbrassil Street to the right, while, to our left, on noticeably raised ground, stood a terrace of five red-brick houses. I pointed out my old house, and Franc told me that before these houses were built in the late nineteenth century there had been an orchard on the site. Further north along Blackpitts the fortifications we were tracing had crossed over the Poddle and continued eastwards.

As we walked, Franc referred to his recollections of various old maps of Dublin, particularly the 25-inch Ordnance Survey map of 1912, which had been central to structuring his understanding of the evolution of the area. Continuing along Blackpitts, he drew attention to a ruined chimney stack that adjoined another building, telling me that it was a remnant of a gable-fronted house in the 'Dutch Billy' style once prevalent in Dublin, and especially in the Liberties, but now virtually obliterated from the city's streets.

'The 25-inch map was surveyed around here in 1912,' he said. 'If you can imagine what the chimney stack would look like on a map, it'd look like a building with a sort of a V-shaped protrusion. So what you're effectively looking at here is a blank space where they've knocked down the house but they've had to keep the chimney stack, which is integral to the structure of the other building. So this is a good way of looking, when you look at the 25-inch map: see how many blank spaces there are with these sort of Vs sticking out, and that can give you a good idea of how many Dutch Billy houses there were.'

We strolled towards Newmarket, pausing to look at the redeveloped site of an old distillery that had once drawn water from the Poddle. There had been a facility in the basement for taking water from the river; Franc had once got a look at it—'I just climbed in, really'—but hadn't had a camera to document what he found.

The terrain of the Liberties is mostly flat, but Newmarket sits on a plateau-like expanse at a slight elevation above the surrounding streets. To the north-east of Newmarket, surrounded by waste ground and, on its northern side, a tall fence, is St Luke's, a Protestant church built between 1715 and

1716 and now severely derelict. In 1975, it closed to public worship, and the building was damaged by a fire in 1986. It now stands roofless, its bell-cote empty—its bell having been moved to St Patrick's Cathedral for safe keeping—while its windows are filled in with concrete blocks and its grounds overgrown and inaccessible to the public.

In 1674, a royal patent was granted for a twice-weekly agricultural market at Newmarket, and construction began the following year. The marketplace was modelled on that of Smithfield, across the Liffey, and a plan for the site stipulated wide approach streets; sheep pens were to line Ward's Hill, at the eastern end of the market site. Water from the Abbey Stream supplied individual properties around the market—including tanneries and breweries—for which property owners paid twice-yearly rates to the Earl of Meath.

During the nineteenth and twentieth centuries, Newmarket underwent a decline in fortunes. The silk trade, which had been fostered in the Liberties since the seventeenth century by Huguenot migrants, disappeared from the area in the nineteenth, while the breweries that had grown up around the rivers didn't last much longer: mass consumption of beer meant that larger brewers such as Guinness thrived while the smaller breweries along the Poddle closed. Watkins' brewery at Newmarket dated from the early eighteenth century; in 1904, it merged with Jameson, Pim & Co., and by 1937 went into voluntary liquidation. This decline was reflected in the fate of Newmarket's architecture. In 1954, the architectural historian and conservationist Maurice Craig wrote that Newmarket was 'no longer of any architectural character'. More recently, the architectural historian Christine Casey noted that 'extensive rebuilding in the mid-1990s has if anything worsened matters'. Nevertheless, perhaps because of its location and vastness—and in spite of its relative disuse—Newmarket is a striking urban space. Franc listed some of the uses buildings around Newmarket were now put to: an evangelical church, a food co-op and flea market, a taxi company, a business manufacturing Indian sauces. Most obvious were the large sheds on the south side of the square with CCTV cameras at each doorway: warehouses used by a multinational data-storage company.

We stood beside a pub, long closed, at the corner of Brabazon Row and Newmarket. There was a murder here a number of years ago; subsequently the pub had closed, and remained shut. Dull pebble-dash covered the upper level of the two-storey building. 'This thing was a gabled structure originally, and when I got inside it, there were very thick walls, old brick. You can actually see behind the render—see the windows? And when you look at it over here, there is an element of a gable there. Believe it or not, there's a seventeenth-century building here. You'll have to use your imagination.' I narrowed my eyes and looked up, and a series of large square indentations, the former windows, were visible on what would have been a third storey. I pictured a three-storey, gable-fronted building, in brick or plaster, instead of a squat public house. A sign advertised 'beers and good food'. I imagined a damp, musty smell and a long-muffled act of violence. We moved on.

Just around the corner from Newmarket, we stood in a yard that belongs to Dublin City Council. Franc had said that if we walked up a concrete ramp towards a low wall at the rear of the yard we would glimpse the Abbey Stream below us, but the water had been channelled through pipes and covered over so that all you could see was a rectangular stretch of waste ground surrounded by high walls. A council worker told us that the owner of a neighbouring property had taken it into his hands to bury the stream, and that 'a case was being taken' by the council. As we stood in silence, a black and white cat gingerly picked its way along the top of the wall across from us.

We walked down Chamber Street, where a row of elaborate Dutch Billy houses had once stood, then took a brief detour: along Weavers' Square and down a narrow laneway to a little street called Cow Parlour, now surrounded by recent housing developments. (According to Clair Sweeney's *The Rivers of Dublin*, the name comes from the monastery of Conelan, which was corrupted to 'Cowbelan', then 'Cowparlour'.) In the laneway, stone cobbles poke from under a ragged carpet of eroding tarmacadam. Once you notice this, it isn't so difficult to imagine how the laneway and surrounding area might once have looked.

We doubled back northwards and began to track the Commons Water, along the north side of Cork Street. The river marks the boundary between the liberty of Donore to the south and that of Thomas Court to the north. One way of judging its path is to follow a line of likely-looking manholes down a narrow side street, but for us the trail ended where the river ran under a building. Picking up the river's path again on Ardee Street, Franc drew my attention to an old stone wall that was visible through the front and rear windows of the empty ground-floor retail units of an apartment building.

'See the wall in behind? That is a fucking amazing wall.

It's one of the few we've actually found a reference for—off the top of my head, it's either 1682 or 1692. We found a reference to its construction in one of the Brabazon leases. And it was basically constructed to separate land known as the Artillery Field—which was one of these places that during the disturbances in the 1640s [when the Irish Catholic gentry rose up against the English administration in Ireland] they used as an artillery park—and the brewery of William Cheney. Now William Cheney, it turns out, is an ancestor of the former American vice-president, Dick Cheney. So we wrote to him and said, "Any chance of getting a few quid for a publication?" We didn't receive a response. But William Cheney was the first person we know of to take a lease on this plot. Pretty soon afterwards he had developed a tannery, and just where that building stops, that's where the Commons Water comes through. So the site is divided by the Commons Water as such. So you're now in Thomas Court. Once you cross the far end of that building, you're in Donore.'

On reaching the Coombe, Franc and I began to trace the boundary of the liberty of Thomas Court. This was also the course of the Commons Water, but we broke away from that river at a small lane that leads uphill on to Ash Street. The Thomas Court boundary runs parallel to this street. On reaching Carman's Hall—a lane that connects Francis Street with Meath Street—we could look back down along the boundary line and see that it now cuts through the back gardens of the buildings on Meath Street, before continuing along a narrow lane in the direction of Thomas Street.

The lane was made narrower by the car wedged in the

centre of the alleyway. Two men, the car's owners, stood to one side and showed no sign of moving. For a brief moment, the situation felt a little threatening. Franc held his bike above his head and squeezed between the car and the wall. I looked to the left and, unexpectedly, my gaze was met by a horse's quizzical stare: along the lane stood a row of stables. A viscid yellow liquid trickled from below the stable doors, along a drainage trench carved in the centre of the alley, and dripped through an iron grating.

These horses pulled tourist carriages around Dublin's city centre, and, although it was a surprise to encounter them here, this was by no means the most unlikely place one could stumble across equine accommodation in the area: I knew of a tumbledown shack where a horse was kept on a corner near Francis Street. Across from it, I once saw a horse being led down the hallway of an otherwise unremarkable two-storey terraced house. I also knew of a large red-brick house off Clanbrassil Street where the residents kept horses and carts in the rear garden. Once, I walked past it expecting to catch a glimpse of the horses and instead saw a team of armed police pin down a handcuffed man in the centre of the street; all guns were pointed towards him.

On Thomas Street, Franc pointed out what he called a 'dog-leg'—a zigzag inconsistency in the frontages of the buildings that indicates construction on irregularly shaped medieval plots. Here, the dog-leg was visible between the Tesco and the Centra.

We cut down Hanbury Lane, parallel to Thomas Street, heading west. Here, we were tracing the old boundaries of the abbey of Thomas Court. Franc drew my attention to a gap in a row of nineteenth-century red-brick houses that led to some small industrial buildings which he thought suggested the persistence of a right of way: 'Every time I'm in the Registry of Deeds I go looking for the original deed to see how that's actually articulated, that little gap.'

'It wasn't a continuation of the street?' I asked.

'No, no—you're very much within the bounds of the abbey now.'

We turned left along the street named Thomas Court, and left again on to Earl Street South, where railings cordoned off a gate-like entrance to an empty yard that had been overgrown by weeds. A rusting street sign behind the railings indicated that this was the old Meath Market. After the monastery's dissolution, its buildings had been cleared by the Earl of Meath and replaced by a cattle market, a rectangular expanse surrounded by houses and abattoirs where butchers sold meat from their stalls to the public. A visit to the market by a sub-committee of the municipal council in the summer of 1876 was recorded by the *Irish Times*, which declared the 'loathsome' Meath Market to be 'the worst locality visited on the South side of the city' and alleged that not one of its twenty-two dwellings was 'fit for human habitation', partly as a result of overcrowding, but also because of their proximity to 'four or five slaughterhouses'. The newspaper report concluded by suggesting that 'the speedy clearance of this area would effect an improvement than which nothing could be more desirable'. Although much of the stone from the abbey had been taken away by the Brabazons, an archaeological excavation carried out by Claire Walsh in 1997 dug through the modern layers of red brick and limestone to discover medieval and post-medieval remnants—roof slates, window glass, sculpted stone, floor tiles. These finds suggest that a good portion of the Abbey of St Thomas Court is still buried beneath Meath Market. At the time of the excavation, the site was owned by a developer, who subsequently failed to get planning permission; now, as the result of a land swap, it belongs to Dublin City Council.

Franc drew my attention to the building to the left of the railings, a dull, single-storey, pebble-dashed construction: 'The funny thing about this is that it has a concrete floor, and as you walk in, the floor comes up. So . . .'

'There's something there?'

'There's something there. In my line of work you look for little hints and little clues—there's some reason why, when you walk into that building, the floor level rises. So I would imagine they're avoiding pretty heavy-duty masonry walls, which is screaming at me: gatehouse.'

The building was probably going to be cleared and a new building erected. Planning permission had already been granted. Before the demolition, Franc wanted to dig there, to see if he was correct in his hunch about what lay below the site.

Rainsford Street isn't the street it used to be. Approximately two thirds of it is now hidden behind the walls of the Guinness factory at St James's Gate. The abbreviated street begins as a continuation of Hanbury Lane but appears to stop short at an eastern gate of the factory on Crane Street. In fact, Rainsford Street continues beyond the factory gate and emerges, through another gate, at the western edge of the Guinness site, at Grand Canal Place. Through a security fence beside the entrance to the Guinness Storehouse, you can see an old green sign on the wall of a factory building still telling you the name of the road: 'Rainsford Street'. Before the Guinness factory divided it, Rainsford Street used to be a fashionable promenade which led in the direction of the City Basin, a substantial reservoir filled by the City Watercourse. Once, Dubliners strolled around the perimeter of the basin on sunny days; now, it had been filled in and built on: a park to the north, a school to the south, with the red-brick Basin Lane council flats in the middle. At the back of the schoolyard you could see a low stone wall with a squat cement staircase leading down into what had once been the basin.

The City Watercourse, which begins by branching off from the Poddle at the Stone Boat in Kimmage, travelled through the Liberties along a series of raised earthen ramparts known colloquially as 'the back of the pipes'. It had its origins in a command from the Lord Judiciary of Ireland, who on 29 April 1244 told the Dublin Sheriff to improve the city's water supply. In 1931, the City Watercourse was channelled into the Grand Canal, and in 1984 it was again diverted, to drain into a large sewer that ran along the canal. Channels were also built from the other rivers—the Poddle, the Abbey Stream and the Commons Water—to handle floodwater overflow.

Franc had told me that, even though they're now disused, the City Watercourse's ramparts were still partially visible, and we walked into a 1930s housing estate in hope of seeing them. At a break in the line of houses, beyond the end of a back garden, there was what looked like an overgrown laneway, hemmed in by the boundary walls of the gardens. The houses to the far side of the rampart were sited noticeably higher than were those beside which we were standing, indicating a fairly steep incline. At the end of the street, some waste ground was untidily fenced off. Grass grew between concrete slabs: below this, the old watercourse had run.

We cut down a lane past the Botany Weaving Mill—which used to be the Bethany mill. We reached some old stone bollards, on the other side of which was Cork Street. The path of the Commons Water cut across the lane: this was the edge of the liberty of Thomas Court, and the end of our trip around the rivers and boundaries of the Liberties.

The Liberties are sharply delineated—or were. In the nineteenth century, they were dissolved as administrative units, and now they persist more as a notion than anything else. But it's still possible to walk the edges of each liberty and to imagine the buildings that once stood where you're standing, and the people who've lived and died only a few footsteps away. Sometimes, on a still and silent evening, you can even hear the water rush beneath your feet as you cross one of the Liberties' long-buried rivers.

Our walk finished at Meath Street, a bustling shopping street lined with butchers' shops, bakeries, pubs and discount stores. Earlier, Franc had told me that, in a church on this street, 'they have the representations of all the saints in Ireland—they're along on either side of you, around halfway up on the left—and there's one suspiciously fresh-faced-looking saint. It's actually the death-mask of Kevin Barry. They couldn't find a representation of St Kevin, so they used Kevin Barry instead.' Kevin Barry was an Irish republican martyr who had been executed, aged eighteen, in 1920. Now, as Franc cycled up the street, he turned in his saddle to remind me to visit the church and see the statue he had described: 'He's the only saint without a beard!'

I went into the church and examined the statues of the saints, but they were all painted white and I couldn't distinguish one from another. Even though I had only recently had the statue and its exact location described to me, I was unable to find it. I could have done with a map.

FELISPEAKS
Dublin: A Poet's View {essay}

When my feet were still forming and my wits were just beginning, I heard of Dublin and I would gasp. When childhood teeth were still milky and my eyes were heavy with school books, fingers following lines to be read, schoolgirl charms still developing, when pen was still approaching paper, timid and unsure, I heard of Dublin. When train rides were still adventures and train tracks carried you to more than a destination, when metal bullet tanks took people at the speed of whatever was less than light, I heard of Dublin. When permissions were something sought from every adult with wisdom wicks lined around their eyes, when life was something vertically leaning, looking up to light greys fluffing heads I followed and obeyed, when dreams were something I took from sleep and wonder was anything found on the internet, I heard of Dublin. When Dublin was the home of every grand decision my mother had to comply with, when her hands shook with letters she interpreted in friendship groups, they arrived from Dublin. When the hallways hushed with contemplation amongst family members, the answers were always in Dublin. When my rewards were sweetest, they took me to Dublin, shopping centres, buildings tall and fat and thick and old and fun engulfed bambi feet, everything towered in Dublin, everything spun in Dublin, everything mystified and demystified in Dublin. The spire called all of us, every friend and I to claim it as our centre, our starting point, our remembrance spot, our forget-me-not, our find-me-here, our saving grace, our on-your-mark, get-set, our go!

*

I met Dublin properly, wide-eyed, the big city the country girl couldn't capture in a stare. I spent time with Dublin like a guest, I hid in its outskirts and took to it when I sought answers, when letters were complex, when poetry asked me to stretch, when job interviews were up next, I took to Dublin with much respect and it tossed me sometimes, it humoured me sometimes. It allowed me to swallow street names with time, it charmed me into recognising the best place to get the best this, the best that happened here, the only place to get this belonged here. I finger-pointed 'actuallys' to guests who hadn't met Dublin at all. I knew Dublin like the family friend you end up calling cousin. Close enough. Just about. Dublin and I could be merry when we met, and I didn't have to watch my bags around Dublin. I didn't have to watch myself in Dublin. I didn't have to use my inside voice around Dublin. I didn't even always have to have enough coins and wherewithal for Dublin to take me as I am. And Dublin would happily take, but me too, I was happy for Dublin to take. Phone or otherwise. I knew Dublin well enough at this stage. We bumped shoulders and then we would wink at each other, it was harmless.

*

For a long time, Dublin's sharp teeth never sharpened in my direction.

    The Lion only tears away at the bastard child in his Pride. My milk teeth had spat here, my bambi feet had run here, my awe had gasped outside Connolly station. My adult hands had toiled here. I even lived here. Tramlined through neighbourhoods on tracks I watched be built. I knew Dublin, I knew Dublin so well, till I didn't. I saw Dublin till it blurred my vision. I could say her name and not have to whisper, now I am hoarse. Dublin has become my bogeyman. I stare at Dublin and want to cradle her, Dublin slaps my hands away, Dublin slaps many hands away. Covid took her beauty and textured her skin with men in need of alms, the ones Dublin couldn't feed, couldn't save. Dublin is heaving with the unremembered determined to be seen. Dublin is shaking with the memory of safety now out of reach. Dublin is throwing out its own children and sending them away. Dublin keeps telling all of us, I have no more space. Dublin cannot hold any of her own softly anymore. Dublin is making us hard. Dublin is making us scared. Dublin is closing doors that took art in, it is spitting coffee beans at us, faxing us hotel receipts, HQs and HQs without so much as a fada in their names. Dublin has been through worse before we came, Dublin will go through better when we leave.

Kevin Curran

Adventure Stories for Boys {short story}

I pulled the yellow curtain behind me and never even noticed the lack of a swish.

'Alright, Da,' I whispered, soft, cause I was kinda afraid to disturb things. For one, I was on the bounce and didn't want to alert anyone to my presence, and two, the place felt like a library.

'Yer looking good, Da, yeah,' I said, easing my schoolbag to the ground and lifting the plastic grey chair around to face the side of the bed. I scraped myself in, knees up against the mattress and took a breath. Got myself together, like.

I found my da's hand—the one not bruised and hooked up to tubes—down by his side and rested my wrist on the cold metal rail. I lifted his fingers, just held them while I rested my thumb on his palm. I was always surprised by the warmth and feel of my da's hand. There was a roughness there like the hard texture of a stray dog's paw.

I had no memory of ever holding my da's hand before. I was what, fifteen. I'd no memory of holding anyone's hand. Other than Holly's when I had to bring her to school. But that didn't count. She had to or I'd bate her.

I quit inspecting his fingers and looked at his face.

'Sorry I'm late,' I said, 'it's not my... I had to go to class.'

It seemed with every visit I was discovering something new. Today it was his stubble. Normally he was freshly shaved. I remembered his line from a few weeks before the accident, mumbled while he was checking his foamy face above the bathroom sink, the razor about to draw down on his cheek, his eyes all bloodshot and dark, staring hard at his reflection, 'If you're feeling rough as fuck, son, never let them bastards know.'

A distant trumpet of daytime television played over the ward. A slight breeze from somewhere swayed the curtains, but couldn't budge the heat.

'Ma says she's been getting calls and shit.' I paused. I was trying to stay all upbeat like they said I should. Keep things positive. But it wasn't easy. 'She's telling me I haveta go in or the courts will be on and, like, then there'll be more trouble.'

A trolley and its rinky contents stopped outside our yellow enclosure. A voice—the nurse's muffled instructions—filled the gap in a big thick country accent.

The hair on me da's face was growing high on the cheekbones. Like something out of *Dawn of the Planet of the Apes*. He wouldn't have been impressed.

'So, yeah, Da, I went to a class.'

I gave his fingers a gentle squeeze and withdrew my hand and leaned down for my bag. I took out my only book and some cold toast I'd fleeced from Breakfast Club leftovers nearly two hours before. I settled the book on my lap and said, 'Where were we, Da?'

But I couldn't concentrate. I was drained. Absolutely bollixed. So instead, I said, 'I met a girl off the train yesterday, Da.'

And so, to fill the silence, I went on and told him about how the earphones were in and I was lost dealing with the awful bang of hunger when I heard Taylor call after me. I just strolled on, head down, trying to adjust my walk to stop the instep on my converse from wearing through to the socks.

'Hey Rory, Rory!' she shouted and suddenly she was there with her big giddy face beaming beside me, her cheeks pinched pink like one of Holly's old dolls we'd left abandoned in her bedroom.

'Hiya,' she mouthed.

I took out the earphones. She smelled fresh and clean, like Hubba Bubba.

'Hi,' I said, returning my eyes to the path, trying hard not to pull a redner.

She stood too close, but. My school shirt smelled like shit after Ma hand-washed it in the sink and dried it on the radiator in the bathroom in one of her manic fits.

'Ye need to turn yer music down,' Taylor gushed. 'I was calling ye for ages. I saw ye get off the train and followed ye over the wall. I had no ticket either so ye saved me. Were you on the mitch too?'

She was almost skipping with the excitement of it all. We were surrounded by suits and hands pocketing weekly tickets and cars reversing out of spaces. The train sounded so loud and sluggish pulling away from the platform.

'Yeah.'

She giggled and nudged me.

'Where'd ye go?'

'Eh, I, the usual place.'

'Usual place? Oh yeah, you do this a lot, don't you.'

'Suppose.'

She stopped walking. The crowd had thinned out.

'I used to think you were, like, a nerd.'

I shrugged it off, but still felt the sting.

'You going home?' she said, a glint in her eyes, the final word a little too rushed. The earphones clicked softly in the palm of my hand and I looked to the blue sky for an answer. She was exhausting.

'Suppose.'

'I'll walk with you then.'

And she waited for me to lead the way.

'I nearly missed the train,' she went on, her face lit by the horror of such a possibility. 'My ma would've been ringing the school if I wasn't back by five.'

I just nodded, watching our shadows ripple like ghosts before us over the path.

'She's mad like that. Stupid bitch. Though me da wouldn't give a shit if he found out. He's grand. What's yours like?'

I looked up to read her face. There was nothing only her wide eyes and stupid smile. 'Me ma's strict but me da is...'

I trailed off and Taylor giggled nervously and blurted, 'They're all the same. Do you know Shauna Boylan's da? She lives a few doors up from you. Like, directly behind my house. I can see into her back garden from my bedroom and everything, like. Her da does be out there naked. The state of him. Freak.'

And so it went for the next five minutes of walking, me nodding along to Taylor's shite talk until we reached the estate. It was still bright and sunny and there were kids out on their bikes pulling wheelies and circling lazily in the middle of the road. Taylor stopped at the corner beside the 'Drive Slowly Children Playing' sign and stretched up on her tippy-toes and peered down the row of houses.

'Looks like you're in the clear. Your da's van isn't there.'

She was nibbling at her bottom lip eager for something. I gave her nothing. So she said, 'See ye around then, and maybe the next time ye go on the mitch ye can give us a shout, yeah? What's your Snapchat?'

I went, 'Eh, I'm...'

'Mine's Taylorbyrne56. Add me.'

And she giggled and hunched over her phone and started typing while she walked away.

I watched her go and then craned to look where she'd just looked. See what she had seen. I lingered on the empty driveway a while. Thinking about the fading patch of oil near the porch from his work van. When I was sure she was gone I put my earphones in and felt myself disappear. I turned away from the road, the driveway, the kids' laughter, and started back towards town, to the empty hours ahead.

'Member we used go the cinema, Da?' The memory pushed forward a giggle cause right under it a sob was waiting to burst through. My da's chins were doubled up like Jabba the Hutt's, his eyes closed, his face frozen like Han Solo's in *The Empire Strikes Back*.

The nurses had said it was good for him to hear our voices. And since I was in no mood to read, I just kept talking shite.

I told my da the film had been cat and right at the end, when the lights had come on and I'd looked up from fixing my runners, the cleaner lad with the brush and pan was sweeping behind me.

'Excuse me, our...' the lad called. The dull soundproofing of the theatre, mixed with the earphones, dampened the young lad's voice and I didn't turn round.

I'd a good head start and so got into the lobby before the pan and brush appeared from behind the screen door down the hall. A girl in a red shirt was at the counter sifting through a thin set of twenty-euro notes for Wednesday night's takings.

'How many for Screen 3?' the young lad called, slightly out of breath.

I scarpered through the neon colours and echoing movie trailers on the HD screens, feeling an awful bang of hunger from the warm smell of popcorn. The girl looked up from her count, confused, and strained into the computer screen, 'Eh, three.' She tapped the screen. 'No, four. Four. Why?'

I didn't hang around for his answer.

I laughed when I told my da. I'm sure he would've laughed too. After he gave me a bollicking about not paying for the ticket.

Still the book lay heavy on my lap, and still my da lay there, the rhythm of his breathing the only constant in my life. And still I couldn't bring myself to read to him so I said, 'It was one of those days yesterday. Non. Stop. All I wanted to do was keep my earphones in and my head down.'

I looked around for a sup of water. My mouth was so dry.

'So I have yer one wrecking my head, and then your man from the cinema running me outta the place, and then, guess what, Da? I had me first pint.'

Once I'd got around the corner from the cinema I slowed down to pull my jumper over my head. The earphones managed to stay in and I kept my head straight, my stride consistent as if walking to a steady beat. My shadow stretched out and disappeared when I moved away from the streetlight, only to be replaced by two more mumbling and cursing silhouettes from behind.

I kept walking up Main Street, head down, until I got to the heavy oak door just up from The Front Bar. I shifted my bag on my shoulder and waited for the shadows to pass. The polished lustre on the gold handle had faded since morning. Once I thought the voices were gone, I went to open the door but my feeble attempt at a pull saw an arm stretch over my shoulder. I followed the arm and saw Martin Maughan smiling down on me. His cracked lips and freckly nose were nearly touching my face. The earphones were taken out and the hiss of Main Street and the whoosh of passing traffic filled the silence and I said, 'Thanks,' and Martin nodded for me to go ahead.

And so we stepped into the claustrophobic hush of reception—the plush red carpets and polished oak cases, trophies and black-and-white pictures of Gaelic and hurling and football teams from the town. No one was at the desk— thank fuck—and Martin leaned down to whisper in my ear.

'They serve you in here too?'

It was only then I saw what must've been Martin's da standing behind him, concern digging at his brow.

'I've never tried before,' I said.

'Are ye meeting someone then, lad?' Martin's da asked, stepping forward, tucking his shirt into his jeans, the question thinning his lips.

'No.'

Martin and the da exchanged a look, as if I'd just confirmed something, and the da's face immediately opened up and he threw his head back and blew out a small, surprised laugh. 'Well, you're here now, lad, so ye may as well go for a pint.'

I said nothing, did nothing.

'Come on inside,' the da said, clapping his hands together. 'I'll get ye a pint.'

The stairs past the front desk to the first floor were lit in a low yellow. I had no money on me. I never had any money.

We sat in a corner, hidden from the bar by a stained-glass harp with honey strings and a red shamrock on its body. Martin scrolled through his phone.

'You on Facebook?' he said.

I just shook my head as the da arrived back with a Guinness and two golden pints held tight in the triangle of his hands.

And so I took a timid sup, testing the weight of the beer on my tongue. It was rank, but I managed not to gag.

'Do you drink here much?' I said, just to say something.

Martin nodded, 'Now and then. They do know me from the boxing up in the function room.'

'This lad brings in the crowds so he does,' the da announced, licking the froth off his top lip. Martin nodded proudly.

'Wait'll I tell ye about this lad here, Da,' Martin said, 'real quiet lad, but always on the bounce.'

Up until that day I'd been convinced no one had noticed.

'It's the quiet ones ye haveta watch,' the da said.

'What class are we in together?'

'Can't remember,' I whispered and we chuckled.

'French,' Martin responded, smiling at his recall.

'Par-ley-voo fuck off,' I said.

The heads of the pints rippled with laughter. I felt satisfied with their approval. Cheap too, but, like I had to perform for my drink.

Their glasses were raised again. I wasn't sure how much

to swallow at each lift, and how quickly, so I followed Martin's lead. Only a few gulps in and my stomach was feeling hollow and my head a bit dizzy.

'Don't suppose you'll be here again tomorrow morning?' Martin said.

It was like I'd been sucker punched. They had me cornered. I didn't know where to look. 'Tomorrow morning?'

Their beermats stuck to the bottom of their glasses. They both took a long, long gulp of their pints. I didn't follow.

'The school awards, Rory. They're on upstairs in the function room.'

The da held out his Guinness. 'This lad here'll be getting sportsman of the year. Won't ye son?'

They clinked glasses.

'Oh,' I said, trying to keep my head steady. 'No. No award for me.' And I took a quick sup to catch up with Martin and hide the relief.

The harp darkened and the woman from reception appeared over our table.

'Out,' she snapped and to make things as painless as possible, I just ducked for my bag and mumbled, 'See ye,' and legged it.

'The lad deserves a break,' was the last I heard from Martin before I went through the door into reception.

'What ye make of that, Da? Me first pint,' I whispered.

The memory embarrassed me and after a while of just sitting there in silence I ducked out and found a small plastic glass and filled it with lukewarm water from a jug at the bottom of the ward. Got myself together, like.

I went back in after a while and moved the chair close to the bed again and took my da's hand. The book was resting on my lap. I'd nothing more to say. I certainly didn't want to talk about that morning. He certainly didn't need to hear it.

Ma and Holly were gone and I'd slept in again and even though I was rushing to get to school for period two, I'd stalled it at our front door with its silver 201 until I'd felt the earphones in my bag. But it was only after the door had clunked shut that I realised I'd left my keycard and coke bottle filled with water beside the bed. The light above the handle clicked from green to red and I knew I'd be parched for the day.

The lift was in use so I went down the hall towards the stairs to reception and there, like something from a nightmare, at the function room double doors, was one of the new teachers and a row of maybe twenty students all lined up in twos against the wall, going from the function room back to the stairs. All the conversations stopped and the faces went blank. If I'd had time to think I probably would've taken an almighty redner, but I just put my earphones in and forced myself to keep walking.

The teacher started tapping the toe of her high heel when she saw me approach.

'And where do you think you're going?' she said

I powered on past her.

'Excuse me,' she said, 'are you helping with the awards? The function room is here.'

I gave her a glance—that's all she deserved—but didn't stop.

Her voice went up a notch. 'I'm talking to you. Where do you think you're coming from?'

All the eyes looked to their crests, their school shoes,

intimidated and awed. I walked by and made the stairs before anyone had a chance to say anything.

The worn hardback trembled on my lap. The corners of the glossy cover were dented and curled, the cheap cardboard lurking under the golden title marked by my da's work stained hands.

The book was all I took with me. Ma had put everything, absolutely everything we had of worth up on Gumtree to cover the rent. And when that month was up and we got no deposit back, anything unsold that we couldn't fit in suitcases was left behind. Left behind like we'd evacuated our lives without warning—posters still on walls, jackets still on hooks, soggy tissues still under pillows, dolls still on beds, books still on shelves.

The ward was unusually quiet. I'd been silent for too long, so I pulled on the silk strip of cloth just like my da used to, and opened the book at the end of our last story. I took a breath and got ready to read.

Her voice shocked me with, 'I'm sorry, love, no phones or electronic appliances so close to the equipment,' and I slammed the book shut, freaked. I copped where the nurse was looking and put my hand to my ear and realised I hadn't taken the earphones out.

'Oh, sorry,' I said, like a little kid, and since I'd been caught off guard, I pulled the empty jack out of my pocket and held it up and said, 'I don't have anything to plug them into.'

There, the truth was out and I was exposed. All she did was press her lips together and nod as if to say, 'Isn't that nice?' and finished what she had to finish and left me there feeling the familiar burn on my cheeks.

The earphones clicked around in my hand like painkillers.

The new noises of the ward started to press in. The curtains looked real flimsy all of a sudden.

'Who'm I kidding, Da?' I said, a defeated laugh escaping into the high ceiling. The earphones had helped me ignore them, but as much as I tried to convince myself otherwise, people's words were getting through. The reality of it all was getting through. It was constant. Day after day after day. Ignoring them had me shattered. Taylor didn't need words, she was obvious. The girl in the cinema had asked the lad with the brush and pan who I was and he'd told her what I'd become. Martin and his da had talked about me before I got to the hotel entrance, and a girl's voice that morning at the function room—just as I ran down the stairs—had explained to the teacher they'd had a special assembly about me.

My da's stubble was dark, his face was pale. I thought of his eyes looking at me through the mirror while he'd shaved before work. They had been exhausted. He had been exhausted.

I opened the book and said, 'Where were we, Da?' wishing, really, really, really wishing today would be the day he'd answer back.

Estelle Birdy

Ravelling {novel extract}

On the Luas, Karl shifts out of the way of the woman with the buggy. Small and dark, linen dress, loafers. Brown Thomas, for sure. Balancing her iPhone and one of them bamboo coffee cups over her kid's head, she looks Karl up and down and thinks better of saying thanks.

His mam's voice's in his head, banging on about having to leave his job in Penneys now that he's in Leaving Cert, drowning out Kanye on the headphones. Would he have these AirPods if he wasn't working? No. Would he have these VaporMaxes? No. Would he have been able to buy her the birthday nails voucher for that swank gaff in Donnybrook? No. There's no chance, *no chance*, he's giving up this job. And it's not like he's going to do amazing in his Leaving in anyway.

He shoots Deano a message.

>Story. U going out after?

If he's hurling, Deano won't get back to him till lunchtime, but. At the earliest. Since the funeral and maybe Wino talking to him, Deano's started this kinda snakey shite that Karl can't quite work out. Wouldn't even come out to help last night when Karl was giving the brothers a dig-out, collecting for the flats bonfire. Karl and Deano are a bit old to be at it for themselves anymore, but Deano'd never normally pass up the chance to help the flats out—even not his own flats—with a bit of collecting, carrying tyres over his shoulders, steering shopping trolleys full of crates. And Karl could've done with Deano's long legs when he was trying to get back out over the warehouse wall with the pallets for Frankie and Jackie. Something's not right with Deano but he's telling Karl nothing.

*

He gets into the shop, dumps his bag in his locker and heads to the kitchen. It's good when it's quiet like this. The world is just beginning to wake up and you're the only one there to see it.

The lads keep on at him that he needs to lay off the fries and get back to the hurling but seriously, who can say no to the full Irish before work? And he hasn't actually played since primary school. Apart from the egg, he's taken to grilling everything. Healthier. Doesn't taste right but. This used to be his and Hamza's thing, the brekkie in the morning. Then Hamo got the Brown Thomas job over the Christmas and that was it. Says it's closer to home than trekking out to Dundrum but everyone knows it's because he wants to hang out with the yuppies, studying them, as he says. Not that it's all bad being out here without the boys. Sometimes, some things are kinda better without them.

Suddenly, his eyes are covered by hands that smell of strawberries. Tanya.

—Guess who? she says.

—Some Clonskeagh skank? he says, trying to sound bored.

—How's my favourite chipmunk? I swear you'll be the youngest heart-attack victim in the world with those breakfasts.

Tanya's tanned. Like real tan, from the sun, in Spain. Not Salou, but. The family has a villa near Barcelona. So, she'll be going for a little top-up at the mid-term, and the family pops over sometimes just for the weekend. Yeh know yerself. Then it'll be into winter and skiing. She comes back with a tan from that too. It's usually really sunny on the slopes, she says. The snow reflects the light. Karl never got a tan in Dublin during the big snow last year. That's all Karl knows about tans and snow.

She called him on the second day of that big snow and brought over her snowboard and gave all the lads a shot of it in the Phoenix Park. Best day ever. The boys think he spends all his money on clothes. Not all. Some goes to the Credit Union—into the secret holiday fund. Karl's going snowboarding for real. Maybe even skiing.

Tanya's last working weekend next week. She fought with her parents to stay at it, but she has grinds starting on Saturdays and it isn't like she needs the money in anyway. She wanted to get into Harvey Nicks, of course, or even House of Fraser but they were full up. She's happy enough now though. Penneys is pretty cool. All modern behind the scenes, it is.

She slides into the seat beside him. He grins at her, chewing hard on a gristly rasher.

—Gonna miss me?

—Get over yourself, chipmunk, she says, swiping a sausage and taking a bite.

Karl grimaces. She knows full well that messing with the brekkie proper pisses him off.

—I'd better eat the rest of that, hadn't I? Unhygienic for you otherwise, she says smiling, reaching for the sausage again.

He blocks her hand.

—Touch my sausage and I swear, I'll bleedin batter yeh, he says, his mouth still full of rasher.

She pulls her hand back, wipes her shellacked fingers slowly on a paper napkin and arches one perfectly shaped eyebrow.

—I wouldn't dare touch *your* sausage, Karl.

—Ah yeah? I wouldn't give yeh the chance, yeh minger.

She rolls her eyes.

—Aww, I love it when you do your skanger talk, Karlo. Do it again.

He cranks it up, enjoying himself now.

—You callin me common?

She laughs and sticks her feet up on the side of his chair, then puts a serious head on.

—Know the way I'm leaving here next week?

—Yup.

—Well…

Damien bursts through the door. Damo, the type of fella who wouldn't go north of Lansdowne Road without a Garda escort. Except for that one time when he was a kid and his *old mon* brought him to a corporate box in Croker for the England–Ireland rugby match. The atmo was electric mon. The Bollinger was flewing. Damien couldn't have been more than six or something—Karl looked it up—2007.

—Hello, hello. Ready for another day, are we? Damien chirps like a thick-necked canary.

Damien has the entourage in tow. All the new ones, following him around everywhere he goes. Karl overheard him telling his groupies that his job title was 'Customer Service Moving into Management'. Bit weird for a spa who only works Saturdays, but this lot are lapping it up. He'd have got a slap long ago if he'd started his crap round Karl's way, straight up. That's the problem with the likes of Damien, but. They've never got a slap, nor even the threat of a slap, and they never will get a slap, and that's the end of it.

Damien's told everyone his da is some big shot law fella or government fella or some shite like that. His da made him get a summer job, told him it'd be good for him, and now he's still here at weekends. Damien's kind'd normally be out playing rugby or whatever it is they do, but poor little Damien here has to hang out, tidying up the men's sportswear. The supervisors keep finding him sloping around the bras, but. Been thrown out of lingerie at least three times, Karl's heard.

—Hey, Ton! Looking gorge, Damien says.

—Hi Damien, she sighs.

—Doing anything I wouldn't do this weekend? he says, resting his hands on her shoulders.

He's fucking seventeen like. Acting like a fifty-year-old paedo. Karl pretends he can't see Damien, finishes up the breakfast, staring straight ahead, crunching down on the crackly bit of egg, thinking of his ma. She makes the eggs soft and smooth. Karl can never manage it. Like feckin rubber, they are.

*

The morning passes quickly, busy from the start. Which is good. The day'll fly and he wants to get out with the boys. Deano mostly. A woman crashes his daydream—asks him for the khaki capris in size ten. Ambitious, with those hips. Tells her that whatever they have is already out on the floor but then, looking at her disappointed face, says:

—Ah, no, maybe. I'll go check in the stockroom for you.

He bounces along the hallway, checking his phone, opening IRQaeda group chat.

Deano:
Later P4F smoke, round Hamzas gaff, his ma in Pakiland

Hamza:
No way. Going mosque.

Deano:
Fuck off ya snake. Saturday no mosque. U smashing candy?

Hamza:
Nah, going mosque. No Candy.

Benit:
Ye right know u hittin dat she got jungle fever.

Hamza:
Am brown. Not black, nigga.

Benit:
Black enuf for candys jungle fever

Deano:
Some snake, leaving the boys for randy candy

Hamza:
Not with Candy. Leave her alone.

Deano:
Yup u hittin dat

Hamza:
Shut the fuck up.

This'll go on and on. Hamza's been denying it since the funeral, but Benit's sure he saw them out in Blanch together, when Benit was out playing basketball with the black lads. And some of Karl's Girls (as the group of fourteen- and fifteen-year-old flats girls call themselves) swore they saw Hamza down in Ringsend last week, with some young one with scarlet red hair. But when they shouted over to him, Hamza looked away, like he didn't know Karl's Girls (which Hamza definitely does). So maybe it wasn't Hamza after all. Karl doesn't get it. Not that he would. But none of the boys can. *Candy*, like?

He pushes open the outer door of the stock area. And that's when he hears them, inside in the room.

—No fucking way, you can't invite that pov. He'll probably bring a gang of those scummers with him. Remember the time they met him outside here? Jesus, Ton. United Colours of Knackeragua. Cop on.

—You're such an asshole, Damien.

—I'm warning you. I mean Karl's OK, but you don't know what you'll be getting if you ask him. Well, you do know what you'll be getting. Scurvy or something.

—Just shut up, Damien.

—But you know I'm right. You know what I mean, Ton. And then there's silence. Karl waits for Tanya to say something else. Anything. But there's nothing only the sound of the pair of them mooching around the stockroom. Karl's face heats up and it's like he has a massive stone in his belly. He turns and walks back to capri woman.

—Really sorry, no more size tens, he says. But we're getting an order in next Wednesday, if you wanna check back in.

Fuck it, she looks proper sad, and the capris are pretty good in the khaki.

—The fit's a bit different on the capris. Have you tried a twelve? Or an eight? Try them on, sure, he says, before turning away, his face still burning.

*

Out for lunch, he sits alone, poking at his noodles, thinking about Tanya and the party and the silence from the stockroom. There's Halloween—him and the boys have the bonfire sesh planned. And then, there's Hamza's eighteenth. So Tanya's gaff will probably clash with one or the other, in anyway.

On the afternoon tea break, he walks in to find Tanya and one of the girls from downstairs, trying on clothes.

—I don't think so. The blazer's too much. Deffo no jacket. And I think the pink is better, Tanya says, pursing her lips.

—Really? It's not just that you want to look better than me and you don't want me getting off with anyone? the other girl says, laughing.

Karl can tell she's only half-laughing but.

—What? Tanya says, kinda annoyed.

In fairness, Tanya's not the type of a one to do that kinda shit. Although …

Karl stares at his phone, ignoring the two girls. Messages from the boys, Deano and Benit are up for the kebab and the rest. Oisín going to his da's. And Hamza's not that keen. But they'll grind him down. Unless he really is getting his hole off Candy. Chief Karl's Girl, Amy, is on a buzz.

Amy:
You come mine. All the grlz comin. New PLL's 2 watch. Mam sez u stay over. Dominos?

He feels the pull of a marathon sesh of *Pretty Little Liars* in Amy's gaff. Him and the girls, jammies, Domino's, toasting marshmallows on the gas. Whatsup! Amy's ma never has a problem with Karl staying. The boys'll roast him but, if he pulls a Hamza. They'll start on about being a weirdo, hanging out with kid girls and *Pretty Little Liars* and *The Vampire Diaries*. And why is it that Amy's ma is OK with him staying and all. Like when Amy opened her big gob and told the lads that Karl had been round hers for a sleepover with the girls, when he'd told them he'd been in the scratcher, puking his ring and he couldn't go out with them.

Why she had to blab, he'll never know—probably sucking up to Deano or Hamza. Amy likes Hamza. Told him that he looked Spanish and then was fake-surprised when Hamza said he was Pakistani. Funny, cos in first year Hamza *had* pretended he was Spanish when everyone knew he was Pakistani. Hamza laughs about it now but he still says that no one *really* wants to be Pakistani when they're thirteen and in Ireland. Says he's happy enough now being Pakistani—Punjabi first—but Karl saw Hamza's smile when Amy said he looked Spanish.

Anyway, Karl knew what they meant, the boys, roasting him that time about the girls and PLL. Benit and Hamza asked him straight out, in fairness. Said they knew. Said he had to be. And Karl point-blank denied it. They'd have been weird with him otherwise. That was the end of it. That was last year.

—Right, Karl's here. Let's see what he thinks. Tell her, Karl. Blue dress or the pink flowy one? With or without that *jacket*? Tanya says, grimacing.

Karl tips his chair onto its back legs.

—Hold up the blue one again.

Rolling her eyes, the young one holds the rose chiffon skater dress under her chin. Karl squints up his eyes.

—Right. Now, stick on the jacket, he says.

A white blazer, gold chain detail. Karl's seen it. Came in last week. It's a mess.

The girl shrugs it onto her shoulders.

—No way! Karl says, averting his eyes. Take that yoke off you! And hold up the blue dress. Where's this yiz're going?

—Dunno, probs Tramline or somewhere, the girl says.

Jesus Christ almighty! It's that prosto bodycon one-shouldered midi in baby blue, from Boohoo. Amy got it in the post last week too.

—Okay, the pink's best. No heels. Wear them Converse you had on last week, the green ones, bare-look tights, hair in a high shaggy pony. Denim jacket. That yoke you've there makes you look like an aul one going to a wedding, yeah?

Tanya laughs and gives the girl, now standing with her mouth open, an I-told-you-so look.

—You are so good, Karlo! Tanya says.

—Yeah, I'm great, amn't I, Tanya? Tanya frowns a little, peering at him.

—You alright, Karl?

—Yeah, just dandy. Know what I mean, Ton? he says, as he gets up and walks out.

*

He drops home to change his clothes. Has another sorta row with his ma over when he's quitting that damn job and heads out to meet the boys. On the way down the stairs, the guards have a young fella up against a wall. Ach, poor feckin Titch.

—Youse can't do that. He's not eighteen, Karl shouts.

—You mind your own fucking business and head on there with yourself, the taller of the guards says, releasing his grip on Titch's throat.

—He's a kid, I told yiz. Garda brutality, that is.

Raging-guard charges towards Karl.

—What have *you* in your bag, hah, smart fella?

Karl turns and legs it down Marrowbone Lane, the guard only half-heartedly running after him. Titch's going to have to look after himself. Half-touched, he is.

Banjaxed after only a bitta running, Karl falls into a laneway, catching his breath, hands on thighs. The boys are right, gotta get back to the hurling. Clattering and banging from across the street.

Not young lads collecting, a woman. With a shopping troley loaded with a couple of huge, badly packed sports bags, picture frames and a lamp thrown on top. It's dark but, as she gets closer, there's something about her. Blonde hair dyed offa her head. Holy fuck, it can't be. He steps back into the shadows, in case she sees him. It is her. Looking better than the last time he saw her but that was years ago and she was having that scrap with some fella she was riding. She's struggling now to get the trolley up the rampy bit of the pavement. Deano's gonna go mental if she's back in the area.

Deano's already there, sprawled all over a bench. Good, they'll be on their own for a bit. The place is starting to fill up: Muslim families in for the dinner, bunches of country fellas in tracksuits, up from the boxing stadium, a gang of young ones on their way out for the night.

—Another day working for the man? How's Tanya? Deano says. Tanned Tanya, wouldn't mind a bit a that.

—Yeah, she wouldn't look at you, ya strap.

—Dunno about that. Some of these D4 birds like a bit of a real man, yeh know? All them fellas they have round them are gay as fuck. D'yeh see all them *Made-in-Chelsea* fellas? Benders, the lot of them.

—Why were *you* watching *Made in Chelsea*? Karl says.

—Me controller was broken. June was watching it. All these posh rats, staring at each other like they've had a bleedin stroke or something, I swear. There's these girls, right, and they're trying to get with these fellas. The lads are pretending they're all gagging to ride the girls. But they're *definitely* homos. Total fucking benders.

Karl laughs and whispers:

—Maybe keep it down a bit, yeah?

Deano looks around the room.

—What? Why? Not saying there's anything wrong with benders. Sure, I don't give a rat's. I'm only saying those girls won't get a decent ride from some gay-as-fuck posh fuck like that, yeah? No offence, buddy.

—What do you mean, no offence? I'm not posh.

Deano laughs.

—Nah, you're definitely not posh.

Their food arrives. Mixed Doner Meal × 2, naan on the

side, paprika chips, 1 × Coke, 1 × Yup yup 7up!

—Here. How come you've so much grass all the time these days? Karl asks. Yer not even working anymore. Where are yeh getting it?

—Confirmation money.

—I'm serious.

—So am I, buddy.

—Yeh spent all yer summer money on yer gaming gear and the holiday with Oisín and his ma. Not getting it from Lynchy in Charlo, are yeh? That yackball's in with Wino now, I heard. I'm not touching it if yeh got it offa him, right?

—No one's buying offa Lynchy, for fuck's sake! You retarded? Them two young fellas from York Street who threw the leptos after Lynchy's gear are still in Beaumont.

—And Philly Pig's ma. She's still in the nuthouse in James's after it. That's what I'm sayin.

—Lynchy's gear, like! D'yeh think I'm a doughnut?

—So where then?

—Cousin of shop Sadie's—she's like fucken seventy or sixty or sum. Selling small-time outta her gaff in Drimnagh. The grandson who normally does it is inside for robbing nappies and rashers outta Tesco's, fucken eejit. I go down on Sundays and roll her six blunts for the week. She takes Saturday night off, goes to the local instead. She's got arthritis or Parkinson's or some shit. Can't roll her own, in anyway. Gracie she's called. She gives me me green for the week. Good stuff. No funny shit.

—They're spraying it with something.

—Not this stuff. It's clean. Got some squidgy too. And a new pipe.

Karl looks at Deano. Could be true. He's heard some aul

one's selling alright. But squidgy and a new pipe? For rolling a few joints? And he's been bunking off school loads. More than Karl even. If his ma's back in town, he'll be fucked altogether.

The cooking lads, sweating behind the counter, wave over at Benit strolling in. Holding up two fingers, one of them nods. Benit gives him a thumbs-up and slides into the seat beside Karl.

—Where've you been till now? Deano says. Not like you.

—Yeah, soz, got delayed down at Marty's.

Who the hell's Marty?

—The aul soldier fella? What yeh doing with him? Deano says.

—Bringing him back a book about Congo he lent me. Then he had me cooking with him. Tried to get me to stay for dinner.

Typical Benit making friends with randomers everywhere he goes.

—No sign of Hamza then? Benit says.

—He really with her? says Deano.

—Dunno, Benit says. Says they're just friends.

—Friends with a girl? Like Candy? Hamza going like this fella here? Deano says, gesturing towards Karl. *Vampire Diaries* an all?

—Hamza has loadsa girl friends that he's not riding, says Karl.

—But they're mostly lezzers I think, Benit says. Or queers.

—Lezzers are queers, Karl says.

—Lezzers fuck women. Queers have blue hair and don't fuck anyone, Deano says.

—Like you then, Karl says.

—Is my hair blue? Deano says.

—There's the girls he knows from clever camp, yeah, Benit says. But they're not like Candy. Don't think he's with her tonight, fam. Think he's out with the Arabs.

—With that fucken skankbag, Mohammed? What's he doing with them? Karl says.

—Hamo's a man about town, Karlo, gotta hang with the Muslim Brotherhood sometimes.

—Mohammed and his mates are dicks, Karl says.

At least that was the agreed position last time Mohammed came up in conversation.

—Sure it's not just that they've better threads than you? Deano says.

—I'd say he's getting uck off Candy at the very least, Karl says.

—Candy's sucking off Mohammed?

—No, Karl says. Hamza, and you knew who I was talking about.

Deano and Benit turn to stare at Karl.

—If Hamza's with Candy, course he's getting uck off her, Karlo, Deano says.

Benit shakes his head, changes the subject, rubbing his hands together.

—So what are we on tonight, boys? I got nothing on me.

—Bumbles? Karl says. I can get some from the cousin.

—Bumbles, white man's food, fam.

The range of what's white man's food keeps getting bigger, soon they'll be limited to grass.

—What the fuck, Karl? Who's hitting yokes, when they're just chilling with their homies? Deano says.

—Just sayin, might help everyone be a bit nicer, Karl says,

shovelling rice into himself. Can't believe Oisín's missing this, boys.

—At his dad's, innit? Benit says. Man needs a father. *Definitely* does these days with weird spooks appearing to him, fam. Seeing your dead twin at the end of your bed every night is no good for no one.

—Is it Ruairí he's seeing but? Karl asks. Sounds weird to me.

Etem arrives with Benit's grub, slapping Benit on the back.

—How are you, my friends?

—Good bro. You alright? Benit says.

—Yes, yes, can't complain. You all still at this hurling? My son has started. He's very good.

—Yeah, *we're* still at it, Deano says, pointing to himself and Benit. Shitebag here hasn't been in years. Shows, amirite, Etem?

—Karl, my friend, you're a good man, don't listen to them, Etem says, and he puts down an extra tray of rice and three more chips.

Ah here!

—Compliments of the house.

—That rice's got my name on it, Deano says.

—For sharing, Etem says, as he walks away. You look after my boy at the hurling.

—Oisín shouldn't be missing this food though, Benit says. Probably eating hummus and carrot sticks all night long with his dad. White people and hummus, story fam?

—No hummus in my gaff! Deano says. Just Oisín and his faggy primary school mates. All their mas make them eat it.

—Yeah, not *your* kinda white people, Benit says. The

amount of it Oisín's ma has in the fridge. Like an addiction, fam.

Karl stands up. His head hurts and he suddenly isn't in the mood for whatever they're planning—white people's drugs or brown people's drugs, hummus or no hummus.

—Look boys, I'm in work tomorrow and I'm knackered. Gonna go home.

—What the fuck's wrong with you? Deano says, a bit concerned-looking.

—Nah, nothing. Be grand. Gotta headache, is all. Just don't wanna be up late like. Heading home.

He knows they're watching him through the window as he walks down the street, talking about him. It's starting to rain and he's only brought his light Harrington. Mistake. October, should always have a hood. He messages Amy, telling her he's in and he'll be round with popcorn in ten. His phone beeps.

> Tan:
> Didn't get the chance to say earlier I'm having a going away gaff. Wanna come? It'll be Halloween weekend or the next.

Karl shakes his head and smiles as he walks towards Amy's flat.

Kevin Barry
There Are Little Kingdoms {short story}

It was deadening winter, one of those feeble afternoons with coal smoke for light, but I found myself in reliably cheerful form. I floated above it all, pleasantly distanced, though the streets were as dumb-witted as always that day, and the talkshops were a babble of pleas and rage and love declared, of all things, love sent out to Ukraine and Chad. It was midweek, and grimly the women stormed the veg stalls, and the traffic groaned, sulked, convulsed itself, and the face of the town was pinched with ill-ease. I had a song in my throat, a twinkle in my eye, a flower in my buttonhole. If I'd had a cane, I would have twirled it, unquestionably.

I passed down Dorset Street. I looked across to the launderette. I make a point always of looking into the launderettes. I like the steamy domesticity. I like to watch the bare fleshy arms as they fold and stack, load and unload, the busyness of it, like a Soviet film of the workers at toil. I find it quite comical, and also heartbreaking. Have the misfortunes no washing machines themselves, I worry? Living in old flats, I suppose, with shared hoovers beneath the stairs, and the smell of fried onions in the hallway, and the awful things you'd rather not hear late at night... turn up the television, will you, for Jesus' sake, is that a shriek or a creaking door?

And there he was, by the launderette window. Smoking a fag, if you don't mind. Even though I was on the other side of the street, I couldn't mistake him, he was not one you'd easily mistake. Steel-wire for hair, a small tight mushroom-shaped cloud of it, and he was wizened beyond his years, owlish, with the bones of the face arranged in a hasty symmetry that didn't quite take, and a torso too short for his long legs, heron's legs, and he was pigeon-chested, poetical, sad-faced.

I walked on, and I felt the cold rise into myself from the deep stone centre of the town. I quickened my pace. I was too scared to look back. I knew that he'd seen me too, and I knew that he would flee, that he would have no choice but to flee. He was one of my oldest and most argued with friends. He had been dead for six years.

I didn't stop until I reached the river. The banks of the river were peopled with the foul and forgotten of the town, skin-poppers and jaw-chewers, hanging onto their ratty dogs for dear life, eating sausage rolls out of the Centra, wearing thin nylon clothes against the seep of the evil-smelling air. The river light was jaunty, blue-green, it softened and prettified as best as it could. I sat on a bench and sucked down some long, deep breaths. If I had been able to speak, the words would have been devil words, spat with a sibilant hiss, all consonants and hate. Drab office workers in Dunnes suits chomped baguettes. People scurried, with their heads down. People muttered; people moaned. I tried to train my thoughts into logical arrangements but they tossed and broke free. I heard the oompah and swirls of circus music, my thoughts swung through the air like tiny acrobats, flung each other into the big tent's canvas maw, missed the catch, fell to the net.

I was in poor shape, but slowly the water started to work on me, calmed me, allowed me to corral the acrobats and put names to them. A car wreck, in winter, in the middle of the night, that had done for him, and there is no coming back from the likes of that, or so you would think. The road had led to Oranmore.

I tried my feet, and one went hesitantly in front of the other, and they sent me in the direction of Bus Áras. I decided there was nothing for it but to take a bus to the hills and to hide out for a while there, with the gentle people. I walked, a troubled man, in the chalk-stripe suit and the cheeky bowler, and this is where it got good. A barrier had been placed across the river's walkway and there was a sign tacked up. It read:

NO PEDESTRIAN ACCESS BEYOND THIS POINT

Fine, okay, so I crossed the road, but the throughway on Eden Quay was blocked too, with the same sign repeated, and I thought, waterworks, gasworks, cables, men in day-glo jackets, I'll cut up and around, but there was no access from Abbey Street, or from Store Street, everywhere the same sign had been erected: Bus Áras was a no-go zone. I saw a man in the uniform of the State, and he had sympathetic eyes, so I approached and questioned him.

'I am sorry, sir,' he said. 'There are no buses from here today. There are no buses in or out.'

I stood before him, horrified, and not because of the transport situation, which at the best of times wasn't great, but because this man in the uniform was undeniably Harry Carolan, a.k.a. Harry Cakes, the bread-and-fancies man of my childhood. The van would be around every day at half three, set your watch by it, loaves of white and loaves of brown, fresh baked, and ring doughnuts and jammy doughnuts and sticky buns too. The creased kind folds of his face, the happy downturned mouth, eyes that in a more innocent era we'd have described as 'dancing'. Éclairs! Fresh-cream swiss rolls! All the soda bread you could eat, until 1983, when Harry Cakes had dropped down dead in his shoes.

I went through the town like a flurry of dirty snow. This is a good one, I said to myself, oh this is a prize-taker. Now the faces of the streets seemed no different. It was the same bleary democracy as before. Some of us mad, some in love, some very tired, and all of us, it seemed, resigned to our humdrum affairs. People rearranged their shopping bags so as to balance the weight. Motorists tamped down their dull fury as best as they could. A busking trumpeter played 'Spanish Harlem'. I took on a sudden notion. I thought: might a bowl of soup not in some fundamental way sort me out?

There was a café nearby, on Denmark Street. I would not call it a stylish operation. It was a tight cramped space, with a small scattering of tables, greasy ketchup holders, wipeable plastic table cloths in a check pattern, Larry Gogan doing the just-a-minute quiz on a crackling radio, and I took a seat, composed myself, and considered the menu. It was written in a language I had no knowledge of. The slanted graphics of the lettering were a puzzle to me, the numerals were alien, I couldn't even tell if I was holding the thing the right way up. No matter, I thought, sure all I'm after is a drop of soup, and I clicked my fingers to summon the waiter.

You'd swear I'd asked him to take out his eyes and put them on a plate for me. The face on him, and he slugging across the floor, a big bruiser from the country.

'What's the soup, captain?' I asked.

'Carrot and coriander,' he said, flatly, as though the vocal chords were held with pliers. He seemed to grudge me the very words, and he did so in a midwestern accent and as always, this drew me in.

I considered the man. A flatiron face, hot with angry energies, mean thin mouth, aggravation in the oyster-grey eyes, and a challenging set to the jaw, anticipating conflict, which I had no intention of providing. I looked at him, wordlessly—you'll understand that by now I was somewhat adrift, as regards the emotions—and the café was on pause around us, and he grew impatient.

'Do you want the soup or what?' he said, almost hissed it, and it was at this point he clarified for me, I made out the childhood face in back of the adult's.

'It's Thomas, isn't it? Thomas Cremins?'

Sealight came into the oyster-grey, he gleamed with recognition, and it put the tiniest amount of happiness in his face—even this was enough to put some innocence back, too, and thus youth. He clarified still further: detail came back for me. He'd been one of those gaunt kids, bootlace thin and more than averagely miserable, a slime of dried snot on the sleeve of his school jumper. I remembered him on the bus home each day, waiting for someone braver to make the first move at hooliganism. A sheep, a follower, no doubt dull-minded, but somehow I remembered kindness in him, too. He said:

'Fitz?'

We talked, awkwardly but warmly, and with each sentence my own accent became more midwestern, and his circumstances came back to me. I remembered the small house, on a greystone terrace, near the barracks. Sometimes, after school, I would have been in there for biscuits and video games, and I remembered his sister, too, older and blousy, occasional fodder of forlorn fantasies, and of course there was his younger brother, younger than me but… ah.

Alan Cremins had been killed, hadn't he? Of course, it all came back. It had been one of these epochal childhood deaths some of us have the great excitement to encounter. He was caught in an April thunderstorm, fishing at Plassey, and he took shelter in a tower there and was struck by lightning. I remember the shine of fear on us all, for weeks after. Hadn't we all been fishing at Plassey, at some point or other, and hadn't we all seen the weather that day, it could have been each and any of us. It was about this same time I noticed girls. I liked big healthy girls with well-scrubbed faces. We had any amount of them in the midwest.

Should I mention it?

'I remember,' I said. 'Oh God, Thomas, I remember the time with Alan. When he, you know…'

'Al?' he smiled. 'You remember Al?'

'Of course,' I said, though in truth it was vague. I remembered a slip of a child, a pale face, hadn't he, blue-veined I think, one of those cold-looking young fellas.

'Sure isn't he inside,' beamed Thomas, and he called out:

'Al! Come here I want you!'

Alan Cremins, in chef pants and a sweat-drenched tee-shirt, with a tureen's ladle in his hand, stepped through the swing doors of the kitchen and he smiled at me, a somewhat foxed smile.

'Fitz?' he said.

Grotesque! Horrible! A child's head on a full-grown man's body! I legged it. What else could I do? Away into the winter streets, these malignant streets, and I raved somewhat at the falling skies: you couldn't but forgive me for that.

By and by, anger overtook my despair. Frankly, I'd had enough of this messing for one day. I raised the collars of my jacket and dug my hands into the pockets of my trousers. I hunched my shoulders against the knifing wind. The sky was heavy with snow, and it began to fall, and each drop had taken on the stain of the town before it hit the pavement. Chestnut sellers huddled inside their ancient greatcoats. Beggars whittled the dampness off sticks to keep the barrel fires stoked. The talkshops sang in dissonant voices. Tyres squealed angrily in the slush. Black dogs roamed in packs. We were all of us in the town bitten with cold, whipped by the wind, utterly ravaged by this mean winter, but we stomped along, regardless, like one of those marvellously tragic Russian armies one reads about.

Of course, yes. The obvious explanation did present itself, and as I slipped along the streets, heading north out of town, I considered it. If the dead were all around me, was it conceivable that I myself had joined their legion ranks? Was this heaven or hell on the North Circular Road? A ludicrous idea, clearly—I was in far too much pain not to be alive. I soldiered on. I began to wind my way slowly westwards and the streets quietened of commerce and became small terrace streets, and toothless crones huddled in the sad grogshops, and from somewhere there was the scrape of a plaintive fiddle. A man with a walrus moustache came along, all purposeful, and he passed a handbill to me. It announced a public meeting the Saturday coming: Larkin was the promised speaker, his topic predictably dreary.

I made it to the park, and it was desolate, with nobody at all to be seen, and it calmed me to walk there. I came across some of the park's tame deer. They were huddled behind a windbreak of trees, and I stopped to watch them. The tough-skinned bucks seemed comfortable enough in the extreme weather, but the does and the fawns had to work hard at it—there were rolling shudders of effort along their flanks as they took down the cold air, and the display of this was a symptom of glorious life, and my heart rose.

Fawns! I was clearly in a highly emotional state, and I thought it best to make a move for home. Jesus' sake, Fitzy, I said, come on out of it, will you, before they arrive with the nets.

I went into the northwestern suburbs of the town, the patch that I had made my home, and I allowed no stray thoughts. By sheer force of will, I would put the events of the afternoon behind me. I made it at last to my quiet, residential street in my quiet, residential suburb. I rent there the ground floor of an ageing semi, and the situation I find ideal. I have a sitting room, a lounge, a neat, single man's bedroom, and a pleasant, light kitchen from which French doors open to a small, oblong garden, and to this I have sole access. I turned the key and stepped inside. I brushed the dirty snow from my shoulders, and I allowed the weight of the day to slide from me with the chalkstripe jacket. I blew on my hands to warm them. I went through to the kitchen area and drank a glass of water. I then pulled open the French doors and stepped outside.

I stepped into glorious summer. The fruit trees were full in bloom, and it was the dense languor of July heat, unmistakable, and I unfolded my striped deckchair and sat back in it. The transistor was by my feet and I turned it on for the gentle strings, for the swoons and lulls of the afternoon concert. I removed my galoshes and my shoes and stockings, and I stretched ten pale toes on the white-hot concrete of the patio. I unfolded my handkerchief and tied it about my head. I turned up the sleeves of my shirt, and opened the top three pearl buttons to reveal an amount of scrawny chest. I listened: to the soft stir of the notes, and the trills and scratchings of insect life all around, and the efficient buzzing of the hedge strimmers, and the children of the vicinity at play. They played crankily in the sun, and it was my experience that the hot days could make the children come over rather evil-eyed and scary, beyond mere mischief, and sometimes on the warm nights they lurked till all hours around the streets, they hid from me in the shadows, and played unpleasant tricks, startling me out of my skin as I walked home from the off-licence.

Drinks were all I was required to provide for myself. Since I had begun this lease, I found that the shelves daily replenished themselves. Nothing fancy, but sufficient: fresh fruit and veg, wholemeal breads, small rations of lean meat and tinned fish, rice and pasta, tubs of stir-in sauce, leaf tea, occasionally some chocolate for a treat. I had a small money tin in the kitchen, and each time I opened it, it contained precisely eight euro and ninety-nine cent, which was the cost of a drinkable rioja at the nearby branch of Bargain Booze. Utilities didn't seem to be an issue—no bills arrived. In fact, there was no mail from anywhere, ever.

The phone, however, was another matter. Sometimes, it seemed as if the thing never stopped, and it rang now, and I sighed deeply in my deckchair, and I lifted my ageless limbs. I went inside to it—summoned! The power of the little fucker.

'Uphi uBen?' said the voice. 'Le yindawo la wafa khona?'

'I'm sorry,' I replied, wearily. 'I have no idea what you're talking about. Didn't get a word.'

'Ngifanele ukukhuluma naye.'

'No,' I said. 'Not getting this at all. Thank you.'

I hung up, and waited, for the calls always came in threes, and sure enough, it immediately rang again.

'Chce rozmawiac z Maria! Musze powiedziec jej, ze ja kocham!'

'Please!' I said. 'Don't you speak any English at all?'

'For sure,' he said, and hung up.

The third call was promptly put through.

'An bhfuil Tadgh ann? An bhfaca tú Tadhg?'

'I don't know any Tadhgs!' I cried. 'I haven't seen any Tadhgs!'

I'd complained several times to the Exchange, for all the good it had done me, but I thought I may as well try again. I dialled the three-digit number and was quickly connected to a faceless agent. The Exchange was part of the apparatus of the State that seemed to be a law onto itself. I gave my name and my citizen tag-number.

'I'm getting the calls again,' I said. 'It's been a bad week, it's been practically every day this week and sometimes at night, too. Can you imagine what this is doing to my nerves? There's been no improvement at all. You promised it would improve!'

'Who promised, sir?'

'One of your agents.'

'Which agent, sir?'

'How would I know? I wasn't given the agent i.d., was I?'

'No you were not, sir. We are hardly permitted to enter into personal terms with citizens of the State. It would be untoward, sir. This *is* the Exchange, sir.'

'Well how can I tell if…'

'Please hold.'

A maudlin rendition of 'Spanish Harlem', on trumpet, and I whistled along, miserably. I had fallen into melancholy—the drab old routine of these days can get to a soul. But I was determined not to hang up. They expect you to hang up, you see, and in this way, they can proceed, they can get away with their thoughtlessness. The music faded out, and I was given a series of fresh options.

'If you wish to hear details of the Exchange's new evening call rates, please press one.'

I threw my eyes to the heavens.

'If you would like a top-up for your free-go, anywhere-anytime service, please press two.'

I refused to carry one of those infernal contraptions.

'If you wish to discuss employment opportunities at the Exchange, and to hear details of our screening arrangements, and of our physical and mental requirements for operatives, voice engineers and full-blown agents, please press three.'

I'd rather work in the sewers.

'If you seek an answer to the sense of vagueness that surrounds your existence like a fine mist, please press four.'

I pressed four. A happy voice exploded in my ear. It was the voice of heartiness. It was the voice of a resort manager at a mid-priced beach destination. It was a kind of stage Australian.

'Watcha!' it said. 'Feelin' kinda grooky, mate? What ya wanna do, ya wanna go down yar garden, ya wanna go down them fruit trees, and ya wanna find the ladder that's hidden there, right? Then what do ya do? YA BLOODY WELL CLIMB IT!!!'

The phone cut out—dead air. I proceeded directly to the garden. I put on a pair of plimsolls. I removed the handkerchief from my head. I walked down to the dense, summer tangle of fruit trees. I pulled back the hanging vines, parted the thick curtains of growth, and I could see nothing, at first, but then my eyes adjusted to the dappled half-light and I made out a dull, golden gleam, and yes, it was a ladder. I pushed my way through, thorns snagging on my trousers, and I began to climb. Slowly, painfully, I ascended through the thick foliage and I came to the treetops, and a view of my suburb, its neat hedges and mossy slate rooftops, and I climbed on, and I went into the white clouds and I climbed still higher, and the ladder rose up against rocky outcrops. I found that I was climbing past the blinding limestone of a cliff-face, and at last I got to the top, and I hauled myself up onto the salty, springy turf.

I walked. The marine breeze was pleasant, at first, after my sweaty efforts, but soon it started to chill me. It was a bright but blowy spring day, and the first of the cliff-top flowers were starting to appear: the tormentil, the early orchids, the bird's foot trefoil. A milky white sea lapped below, it had latent aggression in it, and I looked down the stretch of the coastline and oh, I don't know, it may have been Howth, or Bray, or one of these places. There was nobody around. Black-headed terns battled with the wind and rose up on it, they let it turn and throw them: sheer play. I walked, and I concentrated on clearing my mind. I wanted to white out now. I wanted to leave all of it behind me again.

Yes I walked, I walked into the breeze, and after a time I came to one of those mounted telescopes, the kind that you always get at the seaside. I searched in my pocket, found a half-crown, inserted it, and the block slid away on the eyepiece and I looked through. There appeared to be a problem with the telescope—it was locked in place, it wouldn't swivel and allow me to scan the water, the shore, the sky. It was locked onto a small circle of grey shingle, just by the water's edge, and I saw that it was a cold and damp day down there. It was winter by the tide-line, it was springtime on the cliffs.

I kept looking, and she appeared. She crouched on her heels and looked out over the water. She wore a long coat, belted, and a wool scarf about her throat. It wasn't a close-up view but even so, I could see that age had gone on her. I could see the slump of adult weariness. The view was in black and white, flickering, it was old footage, a silent movie, and I knew that the moment down there had passed, too, and that she herself was long gone now. If I was to find her again, it would be pure chance, a random call coming through the Exchange. And I would try to explain, I would. I'd try to tell her why it had happened the way that it did, but my words would sink beneath the waves, where shock-bright colours surprise the gloom: the anemones and starfish and deadman's fingers, the clam and the barnacle, the brittlestar.

The eyepiece blacked out and I walked back the way that I came. I descended the ladder to an autumn garden. Russets and golds and a bled, cool sky: turtleneck weather. My favourite time, the season of loss and devotion.

Niamh Mulvey
Stringing Up The Brides {short story}

It is a good day to buy a bed because it's Tuesday and the shops are quiet. It's also nice bed-buying weather: it's grey and blustery, but it's not raining and I can smell the earth stirring beneath the grass as if it's being touched. It feels like you could peel away the clouds to reveal a purer, bluer kind of morning, if you knew how. As we walk to the second-hand furniture shop, John turns his face to the wind and breathes in and says, You can smell the spring coming, can't you? My stomach twists, it's only three months now and I'm still a stone away from target and I wish that were the reason I am sometimes so terrified.

It's an important thing, to have a good bed, like good, proper people, I say to John and he laughs at me, as usual. I am joking, in a way, but our bed has been tormenting me for some time now. Springs poke into my back and I get hot and sweaty from tossing and turning while John lies sleeping like a big hairy baby. I've been phoning the council's furniture recycling scheme and looking on websites for people giving away beds for months now. But I can't seem to find anything. And then last night I couldn't sleep again and when I eventually did, I dreamt I had really long, claw-like fingers with sharp, lethal fingernails, like in *The Witches*. I dreamt that I ripped through the mattress with my claws, plucked out the bed springs one by one, and chewed on them, as if they were spare ribs. I woke with the feel of the springs splintering meatily in my mouth.

John says, Let's try find a big, old, oak four-poster that we can restore and talk about when we are featured in the *Style* supplement. I laugh because I'm always imagining being featured in a newspaper about my 'lifestyle'. John thinks that's hilarious, and it is. But it would be nice.

We go to the second-hand furniture shop and there is not a bed to behold. People use up beds. John goes up to the girl at the desk to ask if they expect to get any beds in. She should tell him they never get any and even if they do they are bound to be banjaxed, but she doesn't. She giggles and says no, but if he leaves his number, she'll be sure to call him if they do get anything in. She has hair that is blonde and messy in a complicated way. She is about eighteen and beautiful and working part-time in a charity shop to observe human nature as she writes her first poetry collection. Probably. She should write a poem about me. I'm good at being written about.

'C'mon my bedfellow.'

John pulls me by the hand out of the shop. He bounds a lot, my mother once pointed that out.

'What next?' I say, smiling, but I am also firm, like a really nice teacher.

'Noooo,' John is laughing but I know he's not happy about this.

'It's time, we need to own our own bed. I want our bed to be our own, at least.'

I am surprised by how rational that sounds. But really, it is not unreasonable to want to own one's own bed.

'Okay, I suppose, it's okay.'

'You could write about it, John.'

'I wouldn't want people to know. I hate buying cheap crap in these places.'

'Oh don't be such a snob.'

'I thought you loved my pretensions.'

'Not more than sleep.'

I am a bit cross with John. I feel bad for not earning half as much money as he does and he knows that. But one of the rules of Things One of Us Always Feels Bad About is that the other person should never mention any of those things in an insensitive way and should always pretend such things are Not a Big Deal. I also feel bad for being shit at restoring things like beds.

We sit on the upper deck of the bus to the furniture superstore. The blustery spring freshness has moistened to misty rain. The city is grey and the sky dog-eared. There is no one on the bus so there are no conversations to listen in to. John is listening to music. I start thinking again about how I tried to avoid this trip, how I checked out all those recycling websites for people giving away beds and rang the council waste scheme and everything. I feel better when I think about this because I know that I tried, at least. Then I stop thinking about furniture because we're going in the direction of Howth, and this reminds me of going out there a couple of years ago with John when I was just after finishing my post-grad and I'd won a prize for my exhibition piece. We drank cheap red wine out of Ribena bottles on the way and we were so tipsy walking around the Hill of Howth that at one stage I thought we were both going to fall into the sea. I remember thinking how silly that would be, to fall into the sea when everything was so fantastic and the day was so gorgeous and blue. The heather was purple and it was August and I made John laugh by sticking my face in it to smell it, even though it smelled of pretty much nothing and was prickly.

It's full of fat people, this shop. The beds don't look as if they were made for fat people though: the mattresses are cheap and some of the boards don't look like they would stand up to much in the way of strain. The light is too bright and the floor is dirty. But it's all quite funny, in a way. I look at John, smiling, and say, Not exactly what *Modern Brides* would have in mind, but he frowns. I then feel guilty for laughing at these people.

We approach a salesman. He's middle-aged with a round, neat belly and a stubby pencil behind his ear. He looks like the kind of man who dreams of getting into training greyhounds.

'Yis lookin for a bed, is it?'

We nod. I smile.

'Well, yis have come to the right place, so.'

I keep smiling.

'Are yis movin in together or lookin for an upgrade, so to speak?'

He laughs uproariously. They are enviable, these moon-faced, middle-aged men who slap their thighs at the hilarity of their own jokes.

'Well, actually, we've been living together for some years now, but we're getting married in May and we need a new bed. We want to see the best you have.'

I sound like a lady of the manor picking out a hat. Or a horse, maybe.

The man looks delighted and slightly worried.

'Well now, that's great. So the matrimonial… eh… nest then… so to speak. Well, we're proud to help.'

John is quiet. He's thinking about the gig tonight, I know. Or the feature he's working on for next week. He takes my hand as the salesman leads us to a corner of the warehouse.

'It's not so bad, I suppose,' John says. 'We might find something half-decent. Don't feel bad about it.'

The salesman shows us the cream of the crop, the most expensive bed in the warehouse.

It's a perfectly ordinary bed, without a headboard, an ordinary plastic-shrouded mattress on top of a polyester covered base. It's exactly the same as the bed we have at home, the bed belonging to the landlord, the bed we've slept in together for four and a half years, the bed with the springs that poke me in the small of my back. Even the pattern on the base is the same—a sort of blue and red check, like a tablecloth in a picture book.

I can't believe it.

'John, look!'

'What, I am looking. It seems alright.'

'*Look.*'

'I am.'

I clamber onto the bed. The salesman wanders off, quite tactfully, I have to say. The seat of his trousers is very tight and the material very shiny. John gets onto the bed beside me.

'*Well?*' I'm aware my voice is shrill. I feel a bit hot.

'*Well*, it's grand. Do you want to get it?'

He looks at me, confused.

'John, this is the exact same bed as the one at home. Even the pattern on the mattress is the same. And the base.'

I expect him to laugh.

He frowns.

'Well that's a bit shit, isn't it? Waste of time coming out here if this is the best they have.'

I don't say anything. I feel very tired, all of a sudden. John gets up. Change jangles in his pocket.

'Let's go so. We'll get a bed after the wedding, when I've a bit more cash.'

He holds out his hand to help me off the bed.

We wait for the bus in the rain. It's getting dark. John is humming one of the songs from his set. He doesn't seem to feel the cold.

I don't go to the gig. John is surprised but I don't feel like it. If I go I will get drunk because getting drunk makes me extremely happy. But in the mornings, after drinking, I wake with fear and dread and guilt. I used to think it was because it reminds me of all the times I've woken up after drunken nights beside different men in strange beds. But I think I'd *like* to think that is the reason, when the truth is I don't feel one bit guilty about all that. Sometimes, when me and John aren't getting on, it makes me feel better to think that I have had way more sexual experiences than he has.

I sit in the apartment, quietly, with a pile of bridal

magazines on the table in front of me. A bride to be, on an evening like this, should lie in the bath with glass of wine, flicking through magazines and picking out pictures for her scrapbook. I read somewhere that when you begin planning your wedding you should cut pictures that inspire you out of magazines and stick them in a scrapbook, as this will, over time, give you an idea of what you want for your wedding. I really liked that idea. Scrapbook is such a cheerful word, and cutting things out and sticking things in is a lovely activity that people should do more often. So I started, but I never really got into it, and my scrapbook only has about four pages filled.

We should have a lovely quirky wedding as I am arty and John is music-y but I can't think of anything arty to do that doesn't feel fake. We're not getting married in a church and already that feels like I'm turning my wedding into an adolescent political statement. My mother said, Why can't you pretend, like everyone else? Not me and John, I thought at the time, our wedding is going to be an authentic expression of our love, and our love doesn't involve the Catholic church. But now I wonder if I was right. A church is such a nice, stable building. And even the pre-marriage course bit probably would have been okay: John would have charmed the priest and the two of us could have had great fun eating bourbon creams and pretending to be virgins.

I look at the pile of magazines. They make me anxious because they're full of stories about people like Cathy from Bray who set up her own wedding invitation company using organic toilet roll and I always start thinking I should use my wedding to happen upon a business opportunity.

And I could then be featured in a bridal magazine, smiling and looking artful.

I look at my phone. John hasn't rung or texted me. They'll be finished their set by now, he'll be having a few pints. I make myself some tea and look out the window. The night is so beautiful, the way it is when grey, full-bellied clouds push across a black sky. I breathe in the damp, warmish air and feel guilty. I should be busy making lists and ticking things off other lists or lying in the bath with a vibrator or any of the other things you're supposed to do when you're twenty-nine and about to get married.

The brides on the magazine covers stare at me, cheerfully. They have white teeth and perky tits. They almost seem to be goading me, daring me to ignore them. So I pick up a magazine and start to flick through it. I pick out my favourites, the brides who look like they might be good craic, and I cut them out. I make a neat pile of cute, fun-loving brides. I then cut out my favourites from all the other magazines. When I've done this, I just keep going, cutting away, cutting out every bride from every magazine I can find. I'm surprised at how many I have, they're all over the flat: under the bed, on top of the wardrobe, in the bathroom. As I work, I'm reminded of cutting out bits of felt in Arts and Crafts summer-camps with those awkward kiddy-scissors that hurt your hand. I remember weak diluted orange and soggy biscuits and the pride of finishing something that you could show your mam.

The ground is soon littered with bits of shiny paper: jagged bits of dream-honeymoons, mother of the bride hats, fat sleek cars. I cut out romantic brides, glamorous brides, classic brides, modern brides, bohemian brides, beach casual brides. As I cut, I imagine what kind of women these brides are. I imagine them as 'sporty', 'slutty', 'intellectual', or 'career-driven': clean-cut, comprehensible characters, like in a TV programme. In this way, I grow rather fond of them. When there is not a bride left in any of the magazines, I make a small hole in each of their pretty little heads and I loop them onto a long piece of twine which I find in the bottom of the kitchen drawer. I then hang this across the living room, like a Christmas decoration. I tie one end to the curtain pole and sellotape the other end to the ceiling by the door. The brides hang across the living room, a dangling row of pretty whiteness. All of this takes some time, a few hours maybe. When I finish, I feel tired so I go to bed. I am so tired that the springs in the bed don't bother me much and I fall asleep quickly.

'What the fuck?'

The next morning. John has just noticed the brides. He mustn't have turned on the light last night when he came in. I am still in bed.

'What were you *doing?*'

John doesn't sound amused. John sounds annoyed. I stumble out of bed and into the living room.

He is standing in the middle of the room waving his hands towards the ceiling, the way cartoon characters do when they're admonishing God for a terrible fate. The floor is still littered with bits of magazine pages.

'What were you doing?' he says again.

I don't say anything for a minute. I look at all my lovely

brides swaying slightly in the breeze from the open window. Last night, under the harsh yellow light of the kitchen, the brides were garishly white and a little threatening. But in the daylight, as the sun streams into the room picking up all the dust on the floor and on top of the telly, the brides are muted, harmless and friendly. 'Sporty' almost seems to wink at me. Looking at them, at my brides strung up in the air, I suddenly feel I can do anything. I feel the way I used to feel, way back in art college, way back before it all became so serious. I feel light and amused, and full of fun and hope.

John's face is a picture of utter confusion. He looks helplessly from me to the brides. It's actually quite funny.

So I laugh. I feel sorry for poor John, but it's all so funny that I can't stop laughing. I laugh the way children do, the way you do when you know you're not supposed to, when knowing that you're not supposed to makes it impossible to stop.

'What are you laughing about? Is this a joke?'

'No... well, yeah... yes a joke. That's what it is, a joke.'

'Well, I don't get it.' He's sulky now, which is understandable. It's not nice to be laughed at.

I try to explain. 'I was just... I was just... bored. And looking at the magazines annoyed me. So I decided...'

'You decided to decorate our house with brides.'

'Yeah.'

'And you think that's a normal thing to do?'

'I just felt like cutting up some brides. What's the problem?' I'm still laughing.

'The problem. The problem is that that's nut-job behaviour.'

He says this quietly, like it's a hard fact, as if in an important book somewhere, someone has written down: *Cutting brides out of magazines and stringing them across the living room equals nut-job behaviour.*

I say nothing. John turns around and heads out the front door. I know he's not really angry, that he's just confused and tired, and that he'll be back soon with some coffee. I go back to bed to wait for him.

But the springs poke me in the back. I get out of bed. I go to the kitchen and find a clean, sharp knife. I go back to the bedroom and whip the sheets off the bed. They raise up a cloud of dust which looks lovely as it swirls in the bright morning sun. I take the knife and shove it into the mattress. I pull my hand down, making a big groove in the middle of mattress. It's difficult, and I can't go deep because obviously you can't cut through bed springs with a crappy old kitchen knife. But I manage to make a big rip in the surface of the mattress. It's hard work but I manage. I then go over to the other side of the bed and cut a line down the other way. Destroying a bed seems like an impossible thing to do, until you do it. And anyway, I don't really destroy it, the cross is really quite neat. Our bed, our springy nightmare bed, now looks like a hot cross bun. A hot cross bun bed. Or a crusader bed. It's quite funny, really.

Sean O'Reilly
Levitation {short story excerpt}

One day when his mother was out Valentine took the spare key from behind the clock and borrowed her car, a two-door Fiesta.

    He stuck to the terraced streets of Crumlin at first, Kildare Road, Clonard Road, Raphoe Road, all more or less the same. Growing in confidence, he came down Bangor Road to the crescent and the parade of shops, and onto Sundrive Road. He waited at the junction, turned left. Mount Argus. Harold's Cross. The R137 now. He hit another red at the canal, behind a silver '03 Mazda with two dogs in the back, big ones. He added up the numbers on the registration. The light turned green and he followed the Mazda across the canal bridge. Easy. He pressed the button on the door to bring the window down. It often didn't work but today it obeyed. Good sign, he hoped. Now he was moving downhill to the junction with the South Circular, R137 and R811. This was the one he was afraid of. Three lanes going each way, turns left and right, buses, lorries and the taxi drivers who never gave you a chance. The Mazda switched lanes. In front of him now, a Fiat, the same colour as the car he was in, a cinnamon red.

Was that another good sign? The important thing was not to think about the other drivers, that's when he got stuck. Don't look at them. Count the number plates. Dream of the open road. The toot of a horn behind him. Green. Release the handbrake and he was away.

Clanbrassil Street welcomed him like a victorious king. He should give people a wave. Dublin city centre was what lay ahead, however, and he didn't want that, too hectic, so he went left into the Coombe. On Francis Street he saw a spot to park, and that too went smoothly. Sitting on the bonnet, he had a victory smoke. The world had secret rhythms. He got back inside the car and nearly surrendered to the temptation to call Mr Wells. No, first, he had to do it again, in reverse now. He poked the nose of the Fiesta out into the street, checked the mirror again and saw a good gap. He took his foot off the brake, turned the wheel, touched the accelerator and was almost clear when something hit him from behind.

It was an Audi, tinted windows, white as a new fridge. The driver, a blonde lady, accepted responsibility for the damage, a broken light and a dent. The cost didn't matter, she said, as long as nobody was hurt. She was a Dublin woman in her fifties, he guessed, heavy on the make-up and hair freshly blow-dried. He stood in the cloud of her perfume at the door of the Audi while she searched in the glove box for her details. The back seat was awash with folders and papers. A box of business cards had spilled out on the front seat. Lauren Musgrave, he read, some kind of PR work.

You know how it is, Valentine said, maybe we could avoid the paperwork some way? Sort it out between ourselves like?

The lady looked out at him with soft, shining eyes that

seemed much younger than the rest of her.

Is it stolen?

Valentine took a chance, a big one, and said, Not quite.

No insurance?

No licence either, he confessed. Just the provisional.

The lady's long, tinted eyelashes fluttered hectically. The big face on you, she said. Like the dog ate your homework.

It was kind of her to agree. She gave him one of the business cards and he was to contact her with the bill. Valentine thanked her and then happened to ask who did her hair and it turned out that he not only knew the salon but the man who generally looked after her.

Tell him you ran into Valentine. Valentine King—I mean Rice.

The girlish flutter of eyelashes again. A strange man who has to think twice about his own name, she said disapprovingly, and smiled.

Rice. Valentine Rice. Maybe it's whiplash, he said and as he put his hand to the back of his neck to feign a discomfort, a very real pain shot up his arm, and he roared and sank to his knees on the tarmac.

It was his wrist. He must have damaged it against the steering wheel when the Audi struck. The lady seemed devastated by what she had done. She parked the Fiesta for him and insisted on taking him to A&E. Luckily, it wasn't far. They almost had another accident on the way up Thomas Street, rashly trying to overtake a bus. He was relieved to get out of the car.

Thanks again for your discretion, you know with the insurance stuff, he said, but the lady shook her stiff hair and said, You go on in and I'll park the offending beast.

Valentine had a last smoke, wondering how long she would stick around. Inside, a nurse asked him to wriggle his fingers, which he could just about manage. She told him to take a seat. There were all sorts of casualties to observe in the waiting area and some with nothing visible wrong with them. Wrapped in a kind of pink shawl, Lauren appeared with a bottle of water for each of them. He told her there was really no need for her to waste her day and again she shook her head in that way she had, slowly east and west and back again. For a while, then, they told each other hospital stories; she wasn't half bad either, he thought, she knew what was funny and what wasn't.

Maybe we're done with that subject now, he said.

You're some gas, Valentine, you really are. The ladies must be dying about you. And, by the way, I'm still wondering about that name of yours, whatever it is.

Coincidentally, his mother had done some research on the history of his surname so he took the opportunity to sound intelligent about it for a few minutes and prove he was one of them, the Rices of Munster. Lauren responded in kind with some odd facts about the Musgraves, not the least being that her mother and father shared the same name before they were married. Her eyes grew moist as she spoke about them and their love of the horses, Punchestown, Listowel, Cheltenham, and yes, they had taken her to the Grand National as a kid. Luckily, there was bit of a commotion in the waiting area. Somebody thought another human had died in a yellow plastic chair, but then they woke up. Next, Ms Musgrave's phone rang. Her nails were done professionally. Three expensive rings on her hands, but the significant finger was unsheathed.

Whoever it was on the other end, she was cutting strips off them by the lifts. She was a posh, confident lady with a soft centre, he thought. Divorced most likely. Children: doubtful. He also had time to wonder whether it would be possible to return to the front gate in Crumlin before his mother got home and claim total ignorance of the damage. In heels and shawl, the lady businesswoman hurried across the hospital tiles towards him, as if she were late for a meeting.

The pool cleaner? he enquired.

An utterly hideous man, she said. Ugly to the very core, I'm sorry but he is. You know when you get a chill? I don't like to talk ill of people but I sometimes think he might be missing some human DNA. Behind his back, they call him Doctor Gonzo.

Does he live in Dublin by any chance?

Lauren Musgrave thought he was being funny and laughed and smoothed her skirt as she resumed her seat beside him. So, anyhoo, where were we, Mister Valentine Rice? Oh yes, you were telling me about your parents.

He most certainly was not. Instead he told her a story from the shop. She was laughing by the end of it, but she was soon talking about parents again and how her own two doted on each other. Not wanting to appear rude he offered a few uncontentious glimpses of his mother, that she had once run over a hare in her '92 Fiesta and when she stopped the car and looked in the mirror she saw another hare in the road beside the body and the hare was glaring at her and she panicked and drove off, that she had arthritis in her left elbow and probably should be driving an automatic, she made lots of lists and never threw them away, she had an amazing sense of smell, spent most of her time these days on demonstrations against the war in Iraq, had a mild phobia about scarves, struggled to be a vegetarian, and that, recently, she seemed to have developed some moral objection to adoption.

Maybe we're done with this subject now, he said, and he launched into another story from the shop, one he thought she would appreciate, about a man who ferried the tourists around in a horse and carriage.

I think I would prefer a different one, Lauren Musgrave interrupted, gentle but resolute.

The horse saves the day, Valentine protested, but the moment was gone. Across the way, there was an elderly man with a bruise on his head and beside him a younger man in a suit and tie holding a bucket he might get sick into. Three doctors in their white coats came bursting out of the lifts. Valentine turned to Lauren and said she was entitled to her opinions about show jumping, but when he was a kid he had seen a miracle on a Dublin street.

I was in town with the parents, he began. Embarrassed as hell. I needed to get a new pair of hiking boots. I'd deliberately mislaid my other pair in a hole in the grounds of Stanaway Park, but that's another story. So there we were, the three of us, crossing the hump of the Ha'penny. A smelly aul drunk pushes past us, knocking the father up against the railings. The mother is for getting stuck in but the father as per usual prefers to let it be. They start into an argument about it. I can see the aul drunk up ahead. He's pushing people out of his way, waving his fist at the sky. It was funny in that sad sort of way, you know. So we cross onto the northside. Liffey Street. And I see the drunk vanish around a corner. I'm curious to know where he's bound, who's going to bear the brunt of the anger. And then we reach where he vanished. Strand Street Great, it's called. And I see him there, with his fist raised. And right before my eyes he's lifting off the pavement. He's rising into the air. About two feet in the air. Like superman, yes, but just stuck there. Hovering. The fist up. This truly terrified look on his face. We're looking at each other. Thirty seconds, a minute max. Suspension. The parents see it too. Then, bang, he hits the ground. Ultan his name is. He comes into the shop. Likes a cup-a-soup. And he's been sitting on that same spot every day since.

Lauren's mobile phone rang again at this point. It wasn't the hideous man this time but she had to take it. The same as before, she paced up and down in front of the lifts. He liked this lady, he decided, she was good company but it was a shame she wasn't his type. He was only a two-bit barber and she seemed to have a taste for expensive things. And she was older than him. Maybe they could be friends though. Sex wasn't the only thing in the world. Yes, maybe they could be friends. It was then he heard his name called from the desk.

After they had fixed him up with a bandage and a sling, and he left the hospital building, and saw it was dark, and the traffic was clogged up, and he managed to get his fags out and light one with one hand, a text came in from Lauren. To be continued was all it said.

Belinda McKeon
For Keeps {short story}

Nobody looks at her anymore because she is ugly.

A woman—she is that woman—walking down Exchequer Street without a single pair of eyes latching on to her. Without that thing; that thing she used to take for granted. When it had stopped, for the first while, it had seemed to her that people were somehow distracted, that it was just another aspect of the business that was pushing in on everything by then; that people had so much on their minds that they could not even look at one another on the footpath, could not even register other people as they passed. And then it hit her. That it was not the economy, stupid. That it was the years.

You are not *ugly*, Elizabeth; that is Philip's voice. Philip, is not with her on Exchequer Street just now; he is in his office in a building on the other side of the city. He is getting ready to leave. To meet Elizabeth for a drink in the bar she has chosen for their conversation, the bar in the Central Hotel, where she usually stays, now, when she is in Dublin, since she can hardly stay where she always stayed before. She can hardly stay in the house she chose with Philip; the house she left. You are not *ugly*, Philip's voice, says in Elizabeth's head, and he sounds irritated. Tired of her. Tired of her stories. For a moment, Elizabeth is reassured.

Then Philip speaks again. This time, he starts as though from the beginning. You are not *ugly*, Elizabeth, he says, and then he pauses, and she hears a little laugh. A silent laugh; a breath, really, an exhalation, finding its shape in a smirk. You are not ugly, Elizabeth, he says again, in exactly the same tone. You're just unremarkable. And Elizabeth can see his face, then, and his gaze slides away.

This is how she knows that she was right to end things with Philip. Because she is capable of imagining him saying such things to her. Philip would never; Philip would never say to Elizabeth, you are just unremarkable. Not even after what she has done; not even after all the things that have, after all, already been said. But in her head, she hears him, and that is enough. That may as well be the same.

Earlier today, she thought she saw him. It was in Kilmainham; she was coming from the gallery, nowhere near to where Philip, on a working day, would be. Philip, or the man who was Philip for a mistaken second, was driving a Volvo estate, heading out of the city. It was a new model, or a newish one, not one of the older Volvos which trundled contentedly around the streets of Greenpoint these days, wearing their dirt and scratches proudly, dogs and children and found pieces of lumber propped up in their backseats. A bright yellow 1980s model had been the car of Elizabeth's childhood, its form as familiar, as folded into the family unit, as the forms of her parents, of her siblings. And fueled, it came back to her as she blinked after the not-Philip Philip, by a bass cylinder in the boot; by an actual, Calor Kosengas cylinder, in matching yellow. *I couldn't take that risk*, she had overheard her father say to her mother, once, when there had been some problem with the cylinder, some danger—what danger, with a tank of gas in the back of a car, could there possibly be?—and Elizabeth, nine or ten at the time, had been dazzled, intensely moved, by his obvious concern. Her father, sounding like a TV father, hectic with the drama of what was happening, puffed up with regard. *I couldn't take that risk; I couldn't take it*—and probably, Elizabeth sees now, he was only annoying her mother's head.

And anyway, that was not Philip, in the Volvo, driving west.

There are shops on Exchequer Street that seem as though they should not be here; as though they should not be surviving. This city has become funny that way. The shops, for example, selling little flecked slabs of soap, and glass jars of cream, and bath stuff in glass bottles with stubby glass stoppers. They are everywhere in New York, these things, as well, these imitation apocatheries. As though you would wander in, with your wicker shopping basket, and someone would weigh the grains for you, or pour the tonic for you, or cut for you the brown paper and the brown length of twine. And in the windows of the cafes, all the cafes, are women who have their mothers' mannerisms, who watch each other, who talk to each other, raising their eyebrows, tilting their chins, thinning their smiles, in precisely the way a mother must have done, in a sitting-room somewhere, thirty years ago. In a kitchen, or in a garden, or at a school gate, or in the forecourt of a shop that sold milk, and bread, and Super Splits, and gas: that same way of nodding, *Ah, yeah*. That same way of frowning. That same way of taking some absent person down. *Sure, doesn't she—sure, she knows damn well. Sure, I heard—wait till you hear what I heard—*

At least you weren't married, Elizabeth's mother has said. At least that. Marriage would have made the end of everything so much more difficult. Marriage would have piled on the details. Marriage would have—*sign here—and here—and here—oh, and also just here, thanks—*and it is good that there has been no need for that. They did not marry, and they did not buy, and thank the gods of jitters and long fingers and downright uselessness for that.

They rented. It was a nice house. Off the South Circular: red brick and scrag-grass and a chilly kitchen extension in which it did not make sense to linger too long. The sitting-room was cosy. The bedroom curtains were always drawn. The couch was shabby—not shabby-chic, just shabby—and the television was ancient, and in winter the peat briquettes cost €3.50 and in summer you could sit in the back yard by the bikes and the washing-line and the noise from the Montessori came across the wall. It is the one part of Dublin now that is capable of yanking her into a deep pool of nostalgia; it is not a good idea to walk there, not a good idea to visit that place in her dreams. It is not a good idea, either, to zoom in on the street corner on Google Street View, which is something you can do at any time; which is something you can do from anywhere. From your kitchen table in Greenpoint, for instance; from your desk in Varick Street. From your bed; Jesus, from the toilet, if the notion takes you. And once a notion takes you, it has you in its hold.

Everything was fine with Philip. Everything was fine.

But then everything was not fine, which was Elizabeth's fault, of course, and she could not very well stay in the house off the South Circular after that. And New York was an opportunity, and Elizabeth took it.

Do you know what you're doing at all? her mother said.

And no, Elizabeth said, in a tone of voice that implied that the insane thing, the unstable thing, was not when you did not know what you were doing, but when you did, or thought you did. And something else came into her mother's eyes, then—a kind of fear—and her mother turned away.

The Central is cheap, or cheapish, and it is close to everything, whatever everything is. Some of the rooms smell of burned meat, and at night, the noise from Dame Lane keeps her awake, but Elizabeth has long since decided that she likes this noise. It is the noise of the Stag's, after all. It is the noise of Rí-Rá. It is noise like the noise of a July night, once, when she sat on the kerb, with Philip beside her, and tucked under the strap of her vest was the head—not much more—of a flower he had pulled for her off a bush in the Green, and tucked into her mind was the certainty of him, and the beginnings of some kind of shape on some kind of future. Eight years; it is astonishing, what you can do with eight years. How you can crash on through them without ever, really, looking around. How you can use them up, that way.

How you can blunt the heart. She knows this now. How you can take the edges off it, so that it cannot catch itself on things the same way. It does not hurt the heart, to do this to it. It does not bother it. The heart is almost mockingly resilient. It works out its own, new terms, no matter what you do.

Philip is not in the bar when Elizabeth arrives, although she is late; although she has made sure of this much, to be almost fifteen minutes late. She pushes her way in, through the crowd already there, already almost filling the place, at half six on a Thursday. But then, why should they not be here? They've finished work. This is how it goes; Elizabeth remembers that. She walked past her old office on the way here, and she remembered that feeling; work done for the day, and there is someone who wants the pub in the same way as do you. Enablers, yes; enablers, you might call them, if you were so very awful and so very serious and so very dry.

She sits at the bar. She has a book with her, and she intends to read it while she waits for him to arrive, but instead, she takes out her phone, and she dives into the tiny moments of other people's days, and this is what she is still doing when something tells her that Philip has come in the door.

Maybe after years with someone, it just gets like that. That you can sense their presence; that, even with your eyes directed elsewhere, you can see them move. That your eyes will always go to them. The way, in a block of text, without even reading it, you can see your own name.

Or maybe this is just Elizabeth. Maybe this is just how Elizabeth is about the words that make up her name. About the people that have made up her life.

She waves. He waves. The mortified choreography of it; the smiling, the eyebrows, the looking away, pretending to have something else to see, the looking back, the inability to hold on to one another's gaze. They hug, and it is too quick to feel like anything, to feel like his arms around her, or her arms around him, to feel like body close to body, or warmth pushing in on warmth. He is thinner, she thinks, as he stands back from her, lifting the strap of his bag away from his chest and over his head. Thinner; is that because of her, or is that to spite her? Visceral fat; that had been one of the things, late on, far into the trouble, that she had added to the snag list. Visceral fat, and what it could do to you, ten, fifteen, twenty years down the line. Which was about as dishonest as Elizabeth could get. About as disingenuous. To rag at him, to needle him, about something that might happen years from now, when now was the problem; when the problem was what she was doing to the now.

'Hi,' he says, a long 'Hi', and she knows that he is nervous. He is not really a *Hi* person, Philip. Though does this make him a *Hello* person? Is *Hello* the kind of thing that Philip used to say? She cannot remember. She has found this; this whole experience has been made up of moments like this. What is he like? What, from him, is likely? And does all of that have to shift, for her, into the past tense now, as well? Because it is hardly, really, any concern of hers, now, what he is like, what kind of greeting he is most inclined to use. *How's it going*; is he a *how's it going* kind of guy? She can hear it, in his voice; she can quite clearly imagine him saying the words, but then, that does not seem right, either. It's the new thinness; she decides; the new thinness throws everything off. The new thinness makes the suit look sharper, and the eyes look colder, and it is no longer possible to be sure. *Hi, Hello, Alright?* She is staring at him, trying all of them out, as he sits on the barstool.

He nods. He nods at her; nods down at her body, it seems to Elizabeth, though she realises in the next moment that he is nodding at her clothes. Her new coat with the structured shoulders, the coat she had not wanted to take off until he arrived, so that he would notice how good she looked in it—

how thin, or pretend-thin, actually—how pretend-devoid of fat visceral or intellectual or of any other kind. 'You're looking well,' he says, and he instantly looks away.

'Oh, God,' Elizabeth says, 'I don't know about that.' And a doubtful little laugh, and a wince, and it must, surely, be complete now, the thing that is happening to them, whatever it is; whatever kind of bringing-down or humiliation this is. She has lived with this man. She has done the furniture thing with him. They have opened bank accounts together; those bank accounts which, it occurs to Elizabeth, really ought already to be closed. They have done together—*done?*—her mother's illness, her father's illness, his mother's illness, his father's death; she can recall very clearly the look in his eyes as he stepped out of his father's hospital room afterwards, the way he reached, so desperately, for her. And grief sex, which is something so good that Elizabeth is not at all surprised that it is something you are not told about, something you are left to discover all of yourself. All of this, she has done with this man. She has walked in front of him naked at night and in the mornings for years now, her flesh soft where it is, according to the websites, a matter of slovenliness and failure to be soft; her hair overgrown where it is a matter of the same things, of still worse things, to be overgrown. She has cried in front of him and she has cried with him and she has cried over him. She has ignored him; she has grown so accustomed to the fact of him, sitting in the same room, sleeping in the same bed, breathing in the same air, that she has forgotten about him, in the way that it is fine to forget about someone; in the way that could be thought of, actually, as love.

And now it has come to this; one maiden aunt talking to

another. Now it has come to this rote bit of nonsense, this *lie*; that she is looking well.

Which means that she will have to sleep with him tonight. That this will have to be done. One last time, to spread the balance of things back over itself; the room is just upstairs, just on the floor, actually, right over this bar, which cannot, she now realizes, be coincidental; which cannot have nothing to do with the fact that she asked Philip to come and meet her here. She needs it; needs to hear him say things to her, say things about her body, about her skin. About the absence of her, and the things it has put in his mind; she wants them out on the bedspread, wants them laid out between them like things brought home from abroad.

'How are things?' he says, and he leans an elbow on the bar.

'Grand,' Elizabeth says, and she lifts a hand to get the attention of the girl. 'Pint?' she says, because that is what Philip always has to drink, and in fact she has already, now, called the name of it out to the bargirl.

'Oh no,' Philip says, not to her but to the girl, who pauses now, tap in hand, a frown of quizzical vexation on her brow. 'Just a Coke for me.'

Elizabeth stares at him. 'Just a Coke?'

He nods without looking.

Elizabeth already has a gin and tonic in front of her; Elizabeth, in fact, is already on gin and tonic number two. It is past seven o'clock in the evening now, so it is not as though she needs to feel bad about this; but she does.

'Are you on antibiotics or something?' she has said, through an attempt at laughter that sounds only like panting, before she can stop herself. 'Having just a Coke,' she adds, and she feels how the blush splays itself on her face. His gaze tracks it, as though it is an insect hiking a trail across her skin.

'No, no,' he says mildly, accepting his drink with a nod of thanks. He slides a fiver across the bar.

'I'll get your drink, for Christ's sake,' Elizabeth says, reaching for her wallet.

'No, no,' he says in the same tone, and he pours out the Coke. The ice-cubes crack and settle; he slugs it slowly, neatly. Elizabeth glances at her glass; the naked, lonely lemon. She is ready for her third, but that, now, is hardly an option. The bargirl raises an eyebrow. With a rapid shake of her head, Elizabeth sends her away.

Nobody looks at her anymore because she is ugly. On Exchequer Street, the cafés are closing now, but the restaurants are busy, which is the thing you are not meant to comment on, not if you are a visitor, not if you are a returned whatever-you-are; do not say that thing, Elizabeth's sister said to her, the first time she came home, about how the restaurants are all busy and the pubs are all full, and about how the place does not seem to be doing so badly after all; do not, do not dare say that thing. Yesterday morning, when she said goodbye to her parents, when she told them that she would see them on the next trip back, whenever that might be, there was a scene of sorts, a little farce that she had imagined herself and Philip laughing about this evening, maybe over the second or third pint, maybe upstairs in her single bed. Her father wanted her to take a piece of heather—a clump of rust-coloured stuff actually tugged, that morning, from the bog—back to New York with her. The returning yank, that was how he insists upon seeing her, even though it has been only a year, even though she has been back to Ireland, within that time, twice.

'Can't you take it, Elizabeth?' her mother said, saying something much more forceful with her eyes, and Elizabeth sulked, and Elizabeth caved, and now the bloody thing is in her suitcase, getting its gnarly dried pubes all over her clothes, and in the morning she will probably be stopped and humiliated at Customs, and now she will not even have the memory of this evening—not even the memory of Philip—to ease her on her way.

'Alright, *alright,*' she said to her father, taking the damp lump, but that was not enough, either; that was not, she knows, the correct etiquette, the proper way in which to behave in these circumstances. She should have been emotional. She should have gazed at the heather wistfully, should have announced that it would always make her feel connected to home. She should have hugged. She should have hugged all and everyone around her; hugged her father, hugged her mother, hugged the heather, hugged the dog. Her father would have nodded, would have been unable to speak. Her mother would have had tears in her eyes.

'For fuck's sake, I took the bloody thing, that should be enough for you,' Elizabeth says now, and too late she realizes that she has spoken aloud. Someone, some woman, is staring at her.

But she does not live in this city anymore.

Sarah Gilmartin
Service {novel extract}

One Saturday in the middle of June, when I'd been at the restaurant about a month and was starting to shirk the new girl tag, Daniel summoned me to the kitchen. I'd come in early to get in Christopher's good books before he gave out the sections. I was still in civvies, a loose top and jeans that were so far past distressed they could have been committed. I ducked by the industrial slicers, hoping to get to the lockers for my apron.

'Oi!' Daniel appeared in the glassless, rectangular space in the wall that existed solely for the purpose of shouting abuse from the kitchen to front of house. It was a hot day and he didn't have his coat on. In his faded Joy Division T-shirt, he looked almost human.

'Hi, Daniel.'

'*Hi, Daniel*. Nice uniform.'

'Sorry,' I said. 'I'm going—'

'Want a lesson?' He beckoned impatiently and returned to the burners.

I came down the steps into the muggy, eerily quiet kitchen. The large grid on the whiteboard had yesterday's covers, the red ticks and crosses of plates delivered. Alongside Daniel there was the whirlwind seafood chef Shin, and Timmy the stoner sous, who was fine, except for the bouts of vaguely psychotic middle-distance staring. Utensils in hand, they barely acknowledged me. Shin was shucking oysters with the sharp point of a knife. Skilful or suicidal, I couldn't decide. I passed by them carefully. Entering the kitchen as a waitress was a dangerous business. We were used to vulgar comments, tickles, shoves, whistles and grunts, the occasional perplexing *miaow* that seemed, in my estimation, to be tied in some nebulous way to Tracy.

'Over here, sweetheart,' said Daniel.

He was spooning half a block of butter over a freakishly small chicken. There were spriggy things in the melting sauce. He took his hand off the pan, pulled me in by the wrist, pushing his thumb into my palm. I felt a rush through my body, like I was on the edge of a height, the threat or promise of gravity making itself known.

'Tonight's special,' he said. 'What do you think?' He stuck his head over the pan and inhaled. 'Identify the sauce.'

I leant in, sniffed deeply. 'Onions. And something sweet.' Another sniff. 'Like a burnt sweetness?'

He continued to douse the bird, the skin starting to blister. 'Not bad,' he said. 'Go again.' I went closer, so close he had to move back. All I could get now was the sprig. It smelled of trees, and faintly of regret. I started to laugh.

'What?' Daniel smirked.

'Notes of tree.'

He laughed, turned down the gas, and with a spoon delicately skimmed the sauce. I half-expected him to feed me, was almost ready, but he held it out, our fingers touching as I took the handle and tasted.

'Nice.'

His shoulders relaxed. 'Why, thank you, Miss Hannah Blake.'

I smiled.

'You can't rush a sauce,' he said. 'You cannot rush it.'

An oyster shell flew down the counter.

Daniel did a vicious spin. 'Careful!'

'Yes, Chef,' said Shin. 'Sorry, Chef.'

'Right.' He folded his arms. 'Last chance, Hannah. I'll give you a hint—it's a herb.'

'Obviously.' I went back to staring at the chicken. 'A green herb, in fact.'

'Hannah, Hannah. It's thyme.'

'I was about to say that.'

'Were you now?'

'Yes,' I said. 'And by the way, you should get a new chicken dealer. The ones in Dunnes are twice that size.'

'That, sweetheart, is no chicken.'

'Duck?'

'Wrong.'

I stuck my fingers into the belt loops of my jeans. 'Pigeon,' I said. 'Final answer.'

He took the mystery meat from the pan and rested it on a board. Through the hole in the wall, I saw Eve at the swing doors, already in uniform.

'I have to go.'

'Oh, yes, the vital prep,' Daniel said, breaking the mood.

I looked away.

'Come on now,' he said. 'I'm teasing.'

'Yo.' Marc came into the kitchen, stubbly and hungover-looking. Daniel turned his attention to the bird. He pressed the flesh with his fingers, cut me a slice. My mouth watered,

I had it gone in seconds. Daniel ate his portion slowly. 'Quail, Hannah,' he said when he was finished. 'In Madiran wine sauce. A little something I picked up from Alain Ducasse.'

I nodded as if I knew who that was.

'Might make it onto the menu proper. What do you think of the sauce? The perfect nappe.'

Though I didn't have a clue what he meant, I decided to be brave. 'Honestly? It's a bit sweet.'

Daniel picked up the knife, nostrils flaring. Time stilled. He cut another slice, tasted it. 'Interesting,' he said, before dismissing me.

As I walked off, I heard him repeat the word. *Interesting*. Well, I thought, there were worse things to be.

A few days later, the girls and I fled to the alley in the midst of a chateaubriand catastrophe. Even outside, through the noise of the evening traffic, we could hear the rebukes, profanities, the threats of castration for whichever hapless sous had turned off the convection oven by mistake.

'It's not Marc,' said Tracy, offering cigarettes from her squashed packet.

I took one but Eve declined. She tested the step with her hand, before laying a napkin across it and beckoning me to sit. 'How do you know it's not him?' she said.

'I just do,' Tracy said mysteriously. She turned the packet upside down and tapped until a half-smoked joint fell into her palm with a rancid whiff of burnt weed. She lit the thing, took a long drag, then offered it to me. I hesitated, the choreography of service seemed unsuited to the marshmallow-like effects of the drug, but I reasoned that one puff wouldn't kill me. I checked left and right before a quick acrid inhalation.

Eve produced a stolen brioche roll from her apron and began to take small, delicate bites. I felt a drop of rain on my cheek. The alley was full of small puddles, slick and shimmery like tiny urban lakes, a reminder that the world outside the restaurant continued to spin.

'Here,' Tracy smirked. 'I have one.'

'Go on,' I said.

'Pascal or Flynn?'

'Ew!' said Eve. 'I'm eating.'

We laughed at the disdain, so blatant on her heart-shaped face. This was a continuation of a game we'd been playing all week—the lesser of two evils—which could be done with staff, customers, food, drink, whatever prep tasks we hated most. Anything, really, but it was Tracy who came up with the good ones. In this instance: the ancient French pastry chef or the Neanderthal from the bar.

'Pascal,' Eve said.

'Same,' I said, a friendly wooziness burrowing through my brain.

'Creepy grandad?' said Tracy. 'He's like ninety-five.' She finished the joint in three impressive tokes and stamped it on the ground.

'Better than Flynn,' I said. 'Anyone but Flynn.'

'The tattoo,' Eve shuddered. 'Imagine waking up beside it.'

Tracy hopped up on the railing by the stairs, nearly kicking Eve.

'Hey!'

'Sorry,' Tracy said, lighting a cigarette. 'Now, I don't mean to freak you out here, girls.'

We looked at her, expectant.

'But I think I'd have to pick Flynn.'

'You're disturbed,' said Eve.

'Mentally unwell,' I agreed.

'Well, who would you pick, Hannah?' Tracy rounded her eyes.

'I told you. Pascal. He might make me a cake afterwards.'

'Unlikely,' said Eve. 'Unless you paid him.'

We laughed.

'But out of everyone,' Tracy said. 'All the men in the restaurant.'

I shrugged, less easy outside the confines of the game.

'Come on,' she said. 'You both know who I'd pick.'

'Obviously,' said Eve.

'Your turn,' Tracy said.

'Jack,' said Eve.

'He's gay!'

'So,' said Eve. 'He's still a ride.'

We concluded that he was. Tracy stubbed out her cigarette. She had it gone already, and I hadn't finished mine. The drops of rain quickened to a patter.

'Let's go,' I said.

'Not until you answer,' said Tracy.

'Christopher?' said Eve.

'No,' I grimaced. 'I couldn't. He loves himself too much.' I flicked ash beyond the steps. 'And I wouldn't do that to Mel.' They had been an item, for years apparently, until the previous summer when he'd left her for a girl my age, a classical pianist from Foxrock, who—of course—didn't work in the industry. The restaurant was full of these titbits, gleaned, whispered, divulged in alcoholic bursts. Other learnings to date: Vincent had four children; Zoe owned a house in Swords; Jack had shagged a well-known, heterosexual Irish actor in the presidential suite of Dublin's swankiest hotel; and last but not least, Flynn was Daniel's cousin, which for me was a lightning bolt moment that explained a seemingly unanswerable question, namely how a man without looks, charm or intelligence had managed to swing a job at T.

Tracy was getting ready to leave. She pivoted towards me. 'Timmy?'

'Please.'

'Daniel?' she said. 'What about Daniel?'

'Too old,' I said.

'But if you had to. Out of anyone. Those eyes,' she said. 'Those *arms*.'

We laughed at her display of masculinity, the way she tried to inflate her slight shape.

'OK,' I said, relenting, because the woozy feeling had an edge to it now and I wanted the interrogation to be over. 'I'll pick Daniel.'

And just like that, I swear it wasn't a second later, we heard the inside shutter latch and the sound of footfall receding.

'No!' said Eve.

'It wasn't anyone,' said Tracy, far too quickly. 'It was only the wind.'

Later that night, I was helping Mel with her final table, both of us waiting at the bar for trays of dessert cocktails, confident that the end of the working day was in sight. The door to reception opened and Rashini's demeanour changed entirely as she welcomed into the restaurant a trio of women who looked dressed for a wedding. By now I'd learnt that our hostess's infinite supply of good humour came largely from the bumps of cocaine she did in the lull between sittings, but even this didn't account for the over-the-top greeting that was currently underway at the gilded stand.

Under her breath, Mel cursed, turning her back to the bar. She scanned the almost empty dining room. Watching her every move, as was my tendency back then, I jolted a tray of whiskey sours, one foamy top sliding over the rim of a tumbler. Mel was already holding out a napkin, anticipating my mistake.

'What's wrong?' I wiped the glass. 'Why did you—'

'Quarter past ten and they're only sitting down.'

'Who are they? Are they famous?' Which was a forbidden question, but one she sometimes allowed.

'It's the wife,' Mel said.

'Whose wife?'

'Daniel's.'

I set down the tray and studied the women. Two blondes, one brunette. I guessed the brunette, tall and svelte, with shiny, shoulder-length hair.

'She's pretty,' I said.

'She's dead late,' said Mel.

But when I looked left, Mel was smiling, her trademark rose-coloured liner still perfectly in place. I wondered if she took a break at certain points to reapply it. I felt like I would know if she did, though she had that quality particular to great waiters—omnipotence—so perhaps, as I was tracking her across the dining room floor at any given point, there was another version of her in the bathrooms doing up her face, another outside smoking, another at each table, keeping everyone happy in her inimitable way.

'Julie,' she said now.

'Hello!' Julie stopped at the bar. Rashini led the others up the mezzanine stairs, to Table Ten I suspected, the one at the front, looking out on the Green. 'Melanie,' Julie said,

'I love the hair.'

'Easier for the job.' Mel touched her plait.

'Très French,' said Julie.

'Très classy,' Mel laughed.

I smiled vacantly, wishing I could fix my messy bun, but I was, at least, no longer stoned.

'This is Hannah,' said Mel, presumably to stop my gawking. 'The newest waitress.'

'Of course.' Julie extended a hand. 'How are you finding it?' She gave me a sympathetic look, and I liked her for pretending to care.

'Getting there.'

'I hope everyone is being kind'—Julie's eyes flickered—'front and back of house.'

We all smiled then, I was in on the joke. 'It's great,' I said. 'I love it here. I really do.'

'Wonderful,' said Julie.

'We better let you sit down,' Mel said.

'I'm sorry,' Julie smiled. 'I know we're late. My sister.' She shook her head, her long earrings shimmered. 'Can't leave a pub. A terrible affliction.'

I laughed out loud. I hadn't expected her to be funny. She was like the popular female tutors in college, clever and generous with it, knew how to court her audience.

'We'll only have mains,' she said. 'I promise. Lovely to meet you, Hannah.' She smoothed her silk dress and set off for the stairs. I looked at my tray, the foam on the cocktails had started to flatten.

'Jack!' Mel said. 'Four more.'

Jack appeared, and in a couple of swift movements, tossed sixty quid's worth of booze down the sink. 'What about the ports?' he said.

Mel put her pinkie against the middle of a glass. 'They're fine.' She slid the tray to me. 'Apologize for the wait.'

I did her bidding, returning quickly, hoping she would ask me to serve Julie while she closed out her eight-top. 'Christopher's up there,' she said. 'See if he needs help. And Hannah?' Already striding off, I reluctantly turned back. *Tranquillo.*' Mel made a wave motion with her hand. 'Nice and easy.'

At the table, Christopher was talking them through the wines. One of the blonde women had a lot of questions. When she was finished, she folded her arms under her chest so that her breasts rose above the square neckline of her dress. Christopher didn't seem to notice. He was too caught up in his role, full of preening charm.

'Now, Julie,' he said. 'I don't want to overstep here, but I have the most beautiful Pouilly-Fumé from the Loire. Earthy, buttery. You'll love it.'

'I think we'd prefer the Marlborough,' she said. 'It's a favourite.'

'Oh, absolutely. Great choice. So versatile.'

She gave a thin smile and reached for a bread roll.

'Hannah,' said Christopher. 'Isn't that a great choice?'

'Delish,' I said, to take things down a notch.

Julie grinned. 'And some sparkling water, Hannah. If you don't mind.'

'Do you want to take them through the specials first?' Christopher said.

'Of course.' I confidently relayed the mackerel, sweetbread and red mullet dishes we'd learnt earlier that evening. While I was still a novice about the drinks, the wines, the endless varietals, I knew the intricacies of the regular dishes, and

I'd watched Mel enough times to know how to upsell the specials.

Christopher elaborated on the food, essentially repeating what I'd just said with fancier phrasing. As I left to get the drinks, Julie raised an eyebrow in a quick, comical peak. I smiled the whole way down the stairs. At the bar, I asked a runner to sort a wine canister and a sparkling Voss, the expensive bottled water we imported from Norway. I borrowed Jack's corkscrew, which was better than mine, and returned to the table, carefully puncturing the top of the wine and easing out the stiff cork, half-listening to the ongoing pleasantries as I poured.

'What are the boys at for the summer?' Christopher said.

'Oh, the usual circus of camps,' said Julie, buttering the other half of her roll. They began to talk about a tennis camp in Dun Laoghaire, part of a club where Daniel was a member. I paid more attention. I was keen to know about his life outside work. I'd never met his children, I don't think anyone had. Two boys, the elder just in school. The restaurant wasn't a place for children. You couldn't imagine them there, not even for lunch. There was something too transgressive about the environment, like a child might disappear if left untended.

Julie finished her roll, reached for another. I could see she was hungry, and I knew that the kitchen would want the docket, yet Christopher seemed oblivious.

'Would you like to order?' I blurted, knowing there was no good way to outrank him, except to do it, and deal with the fallout later.

'Is Mel not?' Christopher did his multifaceted smile.

'Still busy with Thirteen.'

'You mean, busy with our *guests*, Hannah.' He clicked his tongue. 'No shop talk on the floor, please.'

'We don't mind,' Julie said. 'I could do with a spy in here, actually, see if that fella works as hard as he pretends.'

The women laughed, Christopher joining a beat too late. I took their order—one filet mignon, one duck, one lobster, a couple of sides, a glass of Merlot for square-neck, who had decided to switch to red—and hurried off. Christopher followed me downstairs into the throughway, where Marc was waiting. 'At bloody last,' he said. The other chefs were wiping down, getting ready to leave. I couldn't see Daniel anywhere.

'Two *frites*, one spinach, one duck, one lobster and an eight ounce,' said Christopher, as if he was the hero of the day.

'Just mains?' said Marc, with a little hoot.

'Don't get too excited,' said Christopher. 'Well done on the filet.'

'For fuck's sake.' Marc slammed the double doors and left.

'What?' I said.

'Forty-five minutes for a cremated steak.' Christopher tutted. 'They may as well have ordered starters. And you watch what she does with the lobster,' he said in a quieter voice. 'The last time, she didn't even know to crack the claws.'

It took me a second to realize that she was Julie. I looked wide-eyed at Christopher, the blasphemer, his mouth puckered in disdain. Then it passed and he was his congenial self again, off to find Daniel so that he could say hello.

Tracy came through on her way to the kitchens. 'Big guns on Ten,' she said. 'Can you handle it?'

'Of course I can,' I said, though the table wasn't even mine.

'Ooh,' she said. 'Cranky. I'm only messing.'

'Sorry, I'm tired.' As soon as I said it, I realized how true it was. I'd done the double shift, was nearing twelve hours.

'Will I sneak you an espresso martini?' She held up a plastic beaker, which was not, as it turned out, her usual Diet Coke. 'Jack's been doling them out all night.'

The last to know again. Things like that were starting to irk me.

'Whatever,' I said. 'OK.'

'If you had to lose,' Tracy smiled. 'Sight or sound?'

'Sound.'

'Arm or leg?'

'Arm.' I thought about the cocktail trays. 'Hmm, maybe leg,' I said, with the callous indifference of youth.

'Your phone or your virginity?'

'Game over.' She was always trying to get the goss on my sexual history. We knew her tally, she wore it like a badge: fifteen and counting. Eve had a long-term relationship with a guy from Athlone. I had three and a half, which had seemed perfectly adequate, until I met Tracy.

Christopher swung round from the dining room. 'Earth to Hannah?' He snapped his fingers. 'The Merlot?'

'Crap!' I made to rush off but he took hold of my arm.

'It's done.' He didn't release his grip.

'Thank you, Chris!'

'Not a problem,' he said. 'But don't ever interrupt me when I'm talking to guests. That's not what we do here. Is that clear?'

'I'm sorry,' I said automatically, because the second time is always easier. I didn't like that Tracy was still there, that she'd heard me say it twice.

'Look,' said Christopher, relenting. 'You're still a newbie, really. Service is an art form. And like all great art forms, it takes time.'

'Please,' said Tracy. 'Save me from the sermon.' She left through the swinging doors before he could rebuke her.

'Can I close out?' I said. 'I'll transfer to Mel.'

'Stay on them,' he smiled. 'It's your table now.'

I went to protest.

'Julie asked to keep you.' He tapped me on the nose. 'So the newbie has done something right.'

I was thrilled, even if I was wrecked and it was a tricky table to tend. I couldn't hover around the mezzanine, pretending to be busy, because the surrounding tables were empty. I went up once to check their wine, noted full glasses. I went up exactly six minutes later and the glasses were drained.

'We're parched,' said the blonde of the questions.

'Don't mind her,' Julie said. 'But we'll have another.'

'Is the food on the way?' the third woman said. 'I'm starving.'

This was the same woman who had ordered the steak. I could have given her the reason, Tracy or Zoe wouldn't have hesitated, but I didn't want to be rude. I tucked a strand of hair behind my ear and told her I'd check with the kitchen. 'Sometimes they just get behind,' I said.

'Who gets behind?' The booming voice filled the mezzanine, the soft orange lighting blurred. Daniel stopped at Julie's chair and folded the brilliant white arms of his show-coat. He stared at me, nostrils on the go.

'Um,' I said. 'No one. Just—'

'Leave her alone,' said Julie. 'She's doing a great job. Isn't she, girls?'

Daniel bent to kiss Julie's cheek. Her friends sat to attention. The cleavage was back in the square, the steak woman crossed and uncrossed her legs. If this was a regular table, these details would be reported to the kitchen, relished and ridiculed by the chefs. They all did this, I'd learnt, Daniel was no exception. In that long, hot room that was fuelled by aggression and banter and occasional lines of speed, everything was sexualized. Customers, staff, even the food. There was the obvious—cucumbers, aubergines, the bananas that were peeled and defiled then used for the award-winning toffee dessert—and the more abstract. It takes a certain kind of mind to look at a plate of grated cheese and think *cock curd*. Kitchen repartee, extra points for vulgarity. *If it bleeds, it breeds. If there's grass on the pitch. If it flies, floats or fucks.* (Answer: rent, don't buy.) How quickly we got used to it, or worse, enjoyed it, learnt to laugh and smile with the pack. As I watched Daniel caress his wife's hand now and tell a story about a famous footballer that enthralled the table, it struck me, possibly for the first time in my life, that people were capable of being many things at once.

'Hannah, bring a new bottle,' Daniel said, proving my point. He looked through me, like I had already gone to fetch it. There were none of the withering smiles I'd started to associate with me and him. No winks, no concessions at all.

'Yes, Chef.'

'Cobwebs,' I heard him say as I went downstairs, and once more, the chorus of laughter.

In the dining room, a whistle came from the direction of the bar. Flynn, standing there with his maudlin, cartoon-dog face, a wine bottle in his hand. 'I figured they'd need another,' he said when I got there. 'You can thank me later, babe.' He puckered his lips.

I suspected it was Jack who'd had the foresight to prepare the wine, but I didn't have the energy to argue. Tracy had never brought me the cocktail. I felt the lack of it, like blood draining from my veins.

My buzzer chose that moment to go off, typical, just as I'd another task in hand. I grabbed Eve, who was about to sit down for her shift drink, and pleaded my case. She took the wine, ushering me across the floor. Between the pair of us, we served the booze and main course, petits fours with coffee, a round of sambuca to finish, and then they left to go to a party in Ranelagh, which even in my exhausted state, I found disappointing, for I'd hoped they—or Julie, really, I didn't care about the others—might stay for staff drinks. I wanted to talk normally to her. I wanted her to see I wasn't an idiot. She was another one, like Mel, an older woman who had thrived, a person to look up to, who you wanted on your side.

After they'd gone, I went to clean the table and pick up the bill, which I knew would be comped—the cost voided entirely. Mel had told me not to expect a tip, but I still had to close out the table, that's how the system worked. It wasn't until I was in the throughway that I opened the leather holder to find a fifty, and a note on the receipt thanking me for the service. Classy, I thought, très classy.

Niamh Campbell
We Were Young {novel extract}

It's after eleven when Cormac walks home. He takes the route from North to Southside: follows the tramline down Abbey Street, under the sad yellow sign for a mid-century employment agency, to turn at the Gin Palace and cross the Ha'penny Bridge. Some of these outlines or the script of vestigial shop signs make him remember colophons, bosses, met in earliest life.

He has thought before of a fantastic walking tour that would cause holograms of intimate inscription to pop up over corners and buildings, like a computer; so instead of the Google logo, you might have the state publisher *An Gúm*—detail from an illustration glimpsed in a textbook, nineteen-eighty-seven—or the emboss of a scout medal for bike repair, *bí ullamh*; do you see? A button click would cause the past to cascade as contextless images, flat: time itself revealed to be circular after all.

This would be clever, but you worry that other people don't experience the environment in the same way. That it wouldn't resonate.

It's getting late now and the streets are loosening. On the bridge, a man in a blanket breaks into action and holds out a cup that is bitten at the edges like a lip.

Spare change for a hostel, he calls.

Do you want, Cormac asks, something in the shop? He nods towards the Centra blazing like a shrine on Merchant's Quay.

The man considers it, then says, Not really to be honest now.

Cormac enters the dazzle of the shop and dials for a twenty from the ATM and, as he waits, thinks, I hope it has twenties left. There were years—years ago—when everything was fifty notes only, idiot agape of the city's cash machines. He breaks the twenty up and crosses the bridge again, jiggering with chill by now, to poke a folded note into the cup.

Ah, says the man. Good man.

He does this periodically. Say every six weeks. It buys karma and some distance; it measures time. Two years in the city centre now. Did not expect to stay this long.

Cormac continues along the quay, the suicide strip of low wall and the light on the river ribbing and recomposing. The quaint boxy burgher building on the corner of Essex Street. Crowds.

At first, he thinks there's another homeless person crouched in the doorway to his building, then wonders if it's one of the loiterers who routinely pretend to be lost as they pace before the laneway to the gay sauna. Up close, though, he realises it is Patrick, sitting on the step.

Heya, Cormac hails.

His older brother slides to his feet with great reluctance, as if in pain. Even out of his work suits, Patrick always looks formal and handsome and funereal; he holds himself languidly, stooping from the spine.

What's up? Cormac asks.

No less than three lads, Patrick drawls, in the last half-hour have asked if I want to go into that fucking sauna.

Did you consider it? Cormac puts his key into the lock.

I was starting to think that at least I'd be warm. I was wondering where you were. I've been ringing you.

My battery died. Cormac pushes the door to. The windowless hallway smells of trapped air and, on the floor, a layer of news-sheets and menus have become coloured mulch. Were you out in town? He asks this without looking at Patrick.

I went to Brogan's for a while. Where were you?

Theatre. Alice.

I see. *Theatre*, Patrick says.

Cormac knows by his mood that Patrick has been put out by his wife again and decides to be gracious.

You should try it sometime, you might get civilised.

I'll have you know, says Patrick, standing now by the barricade of bicycles, Deloitte have been sponsoring shit for years and given us tickets many times. I will have you know I am not unfamiliar with the theatre.

He asks, What floor are you again?

Three, Cormac reminds him. Very top.

The men begin to climb, and as they do, the building stretches and tightens around them audibly. The steps are hollow and the walls hollow. A child, perhaps, has dragged a pencil against the paint, consistently, a faint fault-line. Their bodies trip the sensors so the lights wake up, wetly, like eyes.

I'll have you know, Patrick continues, that I saw *Anna Karenina* in the summer and it was like looking into a fucking mirror, let me tell you, of my life.

Cormac lets them into the flat, where a window slightly open in the kitchen-living room spreads the sound of the street. The air smells fresh from rain, and potent in its coolness, like a wild thing. It's November, but the *Weltgeist* since September has been climate-catastrophe mild. The apartment looks onto a square of slippery paving slabs and benches, in the shadow of City Hall. In daylight, tourists and addicts sit on the benches; by night, revellers expelled by Dame Lane pause there to fraternise or hail taxis or buy pills from a well-dressed, banker-looking guy who always meets with a rougher man for the midnight rush. The banker is the face of the operation and the rough one takes a seat, on a news-sheet spread with care, in front of the Castle gates.

Patrick slaps the switch, but Cormac reverses this and turns on table lamps. The place feels welcoming now, even though the kitchen chairs are broken and the recycle bin overflowing. Patrick looks around for something to comment on and then, inspired, asks, How's Alice?

Good I think, Cormac says. He raises the blind of the opposite window, closes the open window, and dims the more vigorous lamp.

Still getting divorced?

I presume. Cormac pauses to judge the atmosphere, the angle of coffee table and irascible shag, the ceiling with its bulb like a drop of ice.

What is the husband like again?

Garrett—oh, he's just a prick really. Beat up his own hole. Aren't you all?

Well yes, but this one more so, Cormac says. The thing is, he explains, Garrett and Alice edit this journal together, they run it, you know about that? They've been doing it for years. They are still business partners.

Nightmare. Patrick has lost interest.

Last year, when an edition of the journal came out without any of the visuals Cormac supplied, Garrett sent him an email from the editorial account that read: Dear FILL, thank you for your interest. While we liked your work we have not found a place for it this time. Please feel free to submit again in future.

The sound of the street, now, is the sound of the ocean or a storm outside. Patrick sits on the sofa, on the morass of throws preserving the sofa, and sinks into it quickly; annoyed, he hauls himself to the harder edge. Can I smoke? he asks through a cigarette.

Cormac reaches for the plastic ashtray that he keeps on top of a press. Putting it before Patrick, he says, So, wine or something? Whiskey?

What do you have?

Just that.

Whiskey then. No beer?

Hang on. No, no beer.

The Jameson is Senan's and the flat is Senan's too, although Cormac has been renting it so long ownership has become, intuitively if not legally, muddled. Senan, a composer, is either on tour or on residency or in Berlin. Sometimes he stays with his parents outside Edenderry, recording samples and playing piano in a soundproofed cowshed. Cormac has not seen him since June, when he came by one weekend and stayed, picking guitar and leaving a half-read novel open everywhere—the couch, the table, the toilet—like a witless hint.

Senan bought the apartment with his brothers. There are five of them altogether. Senan is last and *the shakings of the bag*: he is slight and precise, tow-headed into adulthood, darting through a crowd in an auditorium or lobby or party or street always, hood up, head down, onto something or out to meet someone. Even now he comes and goes with little warning. He took Cormac out to Edenderry once: in the bedroom that had been Senan's, there hung equestrian rosettes faded by sunlight and a framed picture of Snoopy the Dog. The place was a self-built bungalow and about the melancholiest thing Cormac had ever seen. His mother was small like Senan and placed her hands on her son's shoulders as if blessing him, or compressing him, singing, My little pal he was, my little pal!

Whiskey can make a man mean, Patrick remarks, looking at the bottle.

There's always tea.

I'll put water in it. Patrick stands and sees to himself at the sink. The kitchen is a strip of linoleum in country dun. Each of the glasses has a county crest on it. They remind Cormac of holidays to the north-west in childhood, of turfsmell and ginger ale, a bath of well-water drawn for him in a house on sand and gravel overlooking the lough. This was their cousins' house, the farm with its sunken and guttered pigpen, the bath of yellow well-water without bubbles or foam.

He, Cormac, at four or five years old, backed up crying out and refused: What is that, what is it, what? He remembers Thomas sitting in the bath, leaning out—Thomas's face, at nine or ten, intact.

Cormac's glass, in his hand, wears the crest of Tipperary. He thinks, I know absolutely nothing about Tipperary. I couldn't even place it on a map.

The well-water looked dirty: he had not wanted to get into it. The well-water had been the colour of beer.

When Patrick returns to the sofa he smokes for a moment before saying, So, tell me all your news. Cormac laughs, as he knows he is expected to.

How's Ursula? he parries back. Patrick reacts with a private twitch of the eyes.

I'm lying low, he says, tonight.

Well, I didn't think you were here for the craic.

Patrick looks sharply at him. Yeah, no, he says, I can just go, Cormac, like, I'll find somewhere else, OK?

Cormac swallows a mouthful of the Jameson and shakes his head. Not, he coughs, what I mean.

It's not a problem, right? I can go to Kehoe's.

Don't be stupid, stay.

Cormac thinks: And anyway, seriously, Kehoe? But then he feels sorrow on Patrick's behalf—a surge of loving dread—which becomes pity, and thrilling.

And how are—the kids?

They're asleep, Patrick answers gruffly.

How much calmer he felt, Cormac thinks, with Alice, just a small time ago. How calm in her company. And how he had shone in the ten-minute attention of Nina, who was tipsy but also chaperoned by some guy and dipped in queenly conspiracy to Cormac, whispering fiercely, It's been so long since we hung out! How happy, he thinks, I was. A mere hour ago.

It's lively out there, Patrick says.

Friday night.

What play? Patrick asks suddenly, fixing his eyes in a resting gaze on the pane. What theatre?

Cormac frowns. He must feign a degree of simplicity to avoid making Patrick feel stupid. It was—you know, immersive?

Huh?

You go into the play, like; you are part of it.

Oh right.

It was about Magdalene laundries, he explains.

Patrick looks taken aback at this, but then smiles with faint wickedness. Oh, he says.

So it was dark.

What, did you, like, have to wash sheets or something?

Just watch mostly. But, Cormac sits up and twists towards Patrick in his chair. Get this, at one point I'm just standing or whatever, in this room, with a coffin.

What? Patrick barks. A coffin? With a body?

No. I mean, I presume not. It was shut. It was a prop. So anyway, I am just standing there and this girl comes in, dressed normally—like, the actors and actresses are all in either this, period costume, or nude. But she wasn't. I thought she was a member of the audience.

She was a plant.

Cormac begins to nod vigorously. Yes! he says. A plant!

Did she talk to you?

She starts saying, *What, what, what?* Like, as if I'd been staring at her.

Were you?

I don't think so.

Was she hot?

Cormac feels a flutter of shame but answers anyway, Little bit.

Sounds stressful, Patrick commiserates.

You know what? It was very fucking stressful.

Stay away from them theatres. Patrick shakes his empty glass. Stay away from them *actresses*.

Help yourself.

Patrick pours another whiskey and lights another cigarette. He does not dilute the drink this time.

So you went to a play with a naked woman in it? When Cormac nods, Patrick asks, And where can this play be witnessed?

It's an old bank. Not a theatre. They had it set up inside—Cormac shapes this with his hands—like a bar and a parlour and then cells or something. It's empty. It's been boarded up. Probably the National Assets Agency, like, owns it now.

Patrick smokes thoughtfully for a moment and then says, We're backing a data analysis intervention, with academics, on vacant properties in Dublin. He refers to Deloitte. Making a database, he continues, to categorise them as derelict, habitable, private, probate, protected, things like that. So it's humanitarian. He speaks this technical language fluently. It is one of his registers: the others are bawdy, boyish and profound.

Humanitarian?

It's towards solution-based approaches to the housing crisis. It's, you know, co-funded by UCD.

As opposed to what, destruction-based approaches?

To what? Oh, right. Patrick says: As opposed to nothing at all. It gets results.

It gets profit, I'm sure.

Same thing, darling, Patrick says. But, you know, your shtick is always cute.

My shtick?

Noble. He drains his glass. *Beautiful soul.*

This makes Cormac laugh. Fuck you, he says. He stands up, feigning casualness, and continues, I'm going to have tea and I'll make you one.

No tea for me, Patrick objects, but when Cormac places the mug before him he picks it up and sniffs.

What's on in the window? he asks. He raises a hand and points to it. It's like a TV, that window. Especially since you don't actually have a TV. Every time Patrick comes into the apartment he makes this point as if he has only just thought of it.

I can stream on the laptop, Cormac drills.

Both rise, bored, and move to the window and watch the street. The crowd has diminished and everyone is wasted now; two men hanging onto each other try to hail a cab but are distracted by women with heels in their hands walking zombie-awkward down Dame Street. A road-sweeper grinds along the kerb, grazing the pavement with its brushes. These buff the shoes of the men and cause the men to leap back, shouting abuse.

You want to go to bed?

Yeah, but I'll shower, Patrick says.

When Cormac lies down, Patrick lies next to him, smelling wet, and passes into sleep immediately.

Cormac watches headlamps calculate across the ceiling, preoccupied by the constipated awkwardness of sharing a bed with someone who is not a lover. He has known Patrick for longer, of course, than any lover—he has known Patrick all his life—but time and ascension into identities have made them strange. Patrick will not sleep on the couch. Cormac suggested it once and Patrick laughed. This is because he is tall: tall and an arsehole. Cormac knows that to sleep in the living room himself would be a sin of capitulation and so when this happens, and it happens lately with more frequency, they lie side-by-side like boys again.

Thomas Morris
all the boys {short story}

The best man won't tell them it's Dublin until they get to Bristol Airport. He'll tell them to bring euros and don't bother packing shorts. The five travelling from Caerphilly will drink on the minibus. And Big Mike, the best man, will spend the first twenty minutes reading and rereading the A4 itinerary he typed up on MS Word. The plastic polypocket will be wedged thick with flight tickets and hostel reservations. It will be crumpled and creased from the constant hand-scrunching and metronome swatting against his suitcase—the only check-in bag on the entire trip. He'll spend the journey to the airport telling Gareth, and anyone who listens, that Rob had better never marry again, that he couldn't handle the stress of organising another one of these.

'You should see my desk in work,' Big Mike will say. 'It's covered in notes for this fuckin stag. It's been like a full-time job.'

Gareth will nod and Gareth will sympathise. He'll just be glad to get out of Caerphilly for the weekend; he's been waiting months for this, has imagined how it all might go. He'll take a swig of his can, and look to Rob's father. Rob's father will be fifty-four in two weeks and will think there's something significant about the fact, about being twice the age of his son. He had two kids and a house by the time he was twenty-seven, and he'll think about that as he listens to Larry telling the story about the woman he picked up at the Kings. She'd taken Larry back to her place, and in the middle of the night he'd heard sex noises coming from the room next to hers. Larry said to the woman, 'Your housemate's a bit wild', and the woman replied, 'I don't have a housemate, love. That's my daughter.'

Hucknall and Peacock, travelling from London, will arrive at Bristol before the others. They'll sit in the bar getting drunk and studying departures screens. Hucknall will have spent the whole morning moaning about the fact they're flying from Bristol, and why couldn't Big Mike have just told them where they're going?

'Bet you it's Dublin,' Hucknall will say, leaning back in his chair, his knees spread wide, his hands smoothing his tan chinos. 'Bet Big Mike's too scared to book somewhere foreign.'

'Don't make a difference to me,' Peacock will say. 'I'll clear up wherever we go.'

When the Caerphilly boys join the now-London ones at the airport bar, Big Mike will confirm that it's Dublin they're headed to. And he'll loudly declare the weekend's drinking rule: pints must always be held in the left hand. If you find yourself holding two drinks, your own drink must be in your left hand. Failure to adhere will result in a forfeit, as decided by Lead Ruler Larry. The boys will all say that's easy, and start suggesting additional rules, but Big Mike will be defiant: the left-hand rule is king.

'You sure no one here's a secret leftie, though?' Hucknall will ask.

'I've done my research,' Big Mike will say. 'Rob's dad is left-footed, but he's definitely right-handed. I made him write his name out earlier.'

When Peacock—with perfect stubble and coiffed hair—goes to the airport bar, everyone will laugh at his shoes that seem to be made of straw.

'Couldn't believe it when I met him at Paddington,' Hucknall will say. 'Doesn't he look benter than a horseshoe?'

'I've seen straighter semicircles,' Rob will say.

Gareth will shout to Peacock: 'Mate, why don't you do yourself a favour and just come out?'

Peacock will stand there, between table and bar, and kiss his own biceps. He'll accept the jibes, and say none of the boys has any idea about style. He'll take the piss out of Caerphilly's clothes shops, and say David Beckham wore a pair of shoes just like these to the *Iron Man 3* premiere. And that will be it: Peacock will be called Iron Man Three for the rest of the trip.

When they board the plane, Larry will tell the air stewardess that Peacock's ticket isn't valid, that his name is Iron Man Three.

When they get to the hostel in Temple Bar—and Hucknall has finally stopped going on about the ten-minute wait for Big Mike's suitcase, he'll ask if Iron Man Three has a reservation.

And in Fitzsimons on the first night, to every girl that Peacock talks to, one of the boys will come up and say, 'Don't bother, Iron Man's gay.'

Peacock will laugh. 'They're just jealous,' he'll tell the

girl from Minneapolis or Wexford or Rome. 'They wouldn't know fashion if it woke them up in the morning and gave them a little kiss.'

Gareth, meanwhile, will be at the bar ordering shots. He'll have his arm around Rob and he'll tell him that he loves him, that he's really happy he's happy. He'll make Rob do shots with him—sambuca, whiskey and vodka—and Rob will say he can't handle any more after the apple sours.

'Who's for shots?' Gareth will say, looking around '*Shotiau?*'

He'll order shots for whoever's beside him at the bar. He'll buy randomers shots. And he'll persuade the English barman to have a shot with him. He's not meant to, but he'll do one just to shut Gareth up.

At a table, Rob's father will have his arm around his son.

'I love Rachel, you know,' Rob will say, his eyes ablaze. 'I really love her.'

'Just pace yourself,' his father will say quietly. 'The boys are getting wrecked. They won't even notice if you don't drink the stuff they're giving you.'

He'll offer to drink his son's drinks; he'll get wasted so that his son may be saved.

Big Mike will be careering around the pub making sure everyone's alright. He'll always have a pint in his left hand. And he'll be going from boy to boy, just to make sure everyone's okay. This first night he'll be torn between keeping steady and getting absolutely bollocksed. He'll decide on ordering half-pints but asking the barman to pour them into pint glasses.

'Dun want anyone thinking I'm gay,' he'll say, and he'll

order another pint for Rob, and place it down at his table without saying a word.

And Larry? He'll be getting attacked by an English girl for calling her sugar-tits. When her friends pull her off, he'll retouch his hair and say, 'Fair play, my dear, that was lovely. Can we do that back at yours?'

The night will become an ungodly mess. All the boys will be pouncing on each other for holding pints in their right hand, and drinking shots as forfeits, and drinking faster as the night slips by. They'll make moves on girls on hen-do's from Brighton and Bangor and Mayo. By eleven, Hucknall will be puking in the corner of the dance floor, and Rob's father, after a quiet word in Big Mike's ear, will take Rob back to the hostel. Peacock will go missing, talking to some girl somewhere, his deep V-neck shirt showing off his tonely chest and glimmering sunbed tan. And Rob, the groom (lest we forget), will be flat-out on the hostel bed, fully clothed, but shoeless, his father having taken them off while his drunken twenty-seven-year-old son lay half-comatose. He'll send a text to the boy's mother: *'all gd here, back at the hostel. Rob's safe and asleep.'*

Outside McDonald's, Larry'll coax the boys to take turns hugging the Polish dwarf in a leprechaun costume.

Larry will say: 'Cracking job this would be for you, Mikey-boy.'

Big Mike will laugh and grab at his own hair. He'll slur, 'I'm small. I know I'm small. But at least I'm *not* fucking ginger.'

Gareth will ask the Polish dwarf if Big Mike can try on his hat, but the man will decline.

'No hat, no job,' he'll say.

So they'll take turns to photograph each other hugging the Polish dwarf in a leprechaun costume. They'll ask a passer-by to take photos of them hugging the Polish dwarf in a leprechaun costume. And when the Polish man points at the little pot-of-gold money box and asks for two euro, Larry will say—actually, Larry won't say anything the leprechaun will understand. Larry will be speaking Welsh. When abroad, all the boys slag everyone in Welsh.

At Zaytoon, Gareth, Big Mike and Larry will queue for food while Hucknall sits on the pavement outside, his head arched between his legs, his vomit softly coating the curb and cobblestones like one of Dali's melted clocks. A blonde girl will ask the boys if they're from Wales. She'll say she loves the accent, and Larry will say he likes hers too—where's she from? But when she answers, she'll be looking at Gareth, not Larry. She'll say she likes his quiff.

'Cheers,' Gareth will say. 'I grew it myself.'

She'll be asking about the tattoo of a fish on Gareth's arm when Larry will tell her that Gareth has a girlfriend called Carly, that they're buying together a house in Ystrad Mynach. The girl will lose interest, not immediately—she won't be that obvious—but she'll allow herself to be pulled back into the gravitational force of her friends who lean against the restaurant window.

'Cheers,' Gareth will say to Larry. 'You're such a twat.'

'Any time,' Larry will say. 'Have you seen *Iron Man Three*?'

Big Mike will have his hands on the glass counter, his head resting like a small bundle in his arms. Gareth will be looking at Big Mike's tiny little frame, his tiny little shoes against the base of the counter, and Gareth will think he should text Carly back.

'I ain't seen Peacock all night,' he'll say. 'Probably shagging some bloke somewhere.'

Larry will smile. 'Aye,' he'll say. 'Wouldn't surprise me.'

all the boys

Saturday, the hostel room smelling like sweated alcohol and men, heavy tongues will wake stuck to the roofs of dry mouths. Set up a microphone, and this is what you'll hear: waking-up farts and morning groans; zips and unzips on mini-suitcases and sports bags; the library-*shhhhhhh* of Lynx sprays; and the sounds of the bathroom door opening and slamming, its lock rotating clockwise in the handle. Pop your nose through the door, and this is what you'll smell: dehydrated shit mingling with the minty hostel shower gel in the hot, steamy air. And back in the room, more sounds now: the beginning of last night's stories, the where-did-you-go-tos, the how-the-hell-did-I-get-backs and Larry inviting the boys to guess if the skin he's pulling over his boxers belongs to his cock or balls.

Big Mike will be first to breakfast, the others dripping behind. All the boys will be scrolling through iPhones for photos from last night, with Rob's father doing the same on his digital camera. There'll be sympathetic bleats for headaches and wrenched stomachs, with paracetamol handed around like condiments. Big Mike will be urging the boys to get a move on or they'll never make it to Croke Park. Hucknall will ask why the hell are they going there anyway? And Big Mike, tapping the inventory in its polypocket, will say: 'Culture, mate. Culture.' Fried breakfasts and questions:

how's an Irish breakfast different to an English? When you buying the house then, Gareth? And seriously, Peacock, where the hell did you end up last night?

Peacock's story will be confusing and confused. He got in a taxi with a girl, and she was well up for it—he was fingering her in the backseat. ('Backseat?' Larry'll say. 'Up the arse, like?' and Peacock will go, 'No, the backseat of the taxi, you dickwad.') Anyway, when they got to her place she realised she didn't have her keys ('Sure this wasn't a bloke?' Rob will say.) So Peacock and the girl walked for like an hour to somewhere—Cadbra or some random place—and when they arrived she told him he couldn't come in because it was her nan's house. She just went in and closed the door on him. When he finally found a taxi, he didn't have enough cash so the driver dropped him off at some random ATM in a 24-hour shop, but Peacock got talking to some random guy about London for ages ('Oh yeah, bet you did,' Gareth'll say) and when he came out, the taxi had gone, so he—('He's holding his glass in his right hand!' Rob's father will say. 'It's orange juice,' Peacock will say. 'It don't matter,' Larry will say. 'Down it!')—so he found the tram stop and—

'Gay Boy Robert Downey Junior,' Hucknall will say. 'I'm bored now. Worst Man, when we going to Croke Park?'

Big Mike will be glaring. He'll say: 'As soon as you've finished your fucking breakfast.'

All the boys will be surprised and impressed by Croke Park's size, by the vastness of the changing rooms, the way the training centre gleams. When the guide takes them out onto the edge of the pitch, he'll point to the stand at the far end, and tell them about the Bloody Sunday Massacre in 1920, how the

British army opened fire on the crowd during a Gaelic football match. Fourteen were killed, he'll say. Two players were shot. There'll be a silence. Rob's father will be nodding—he'll have read about all this in the guide book he bought at the Centra in Temple Bar. Three of the boys will be wearing Man Utd shirts. And the guide will go on, explaining how Gaelic football and hurling—he'll just call it GAA, and it'll take a few minutes for the boys to fully get what he's talking about—are not sports, but expressions of resistance. But they're also more than that, they're not just reactive things. It's in the blood, he'll say. And Gareth will be sort of startled. Something the guide says, something of its tone, will resonate. Though resonate isn't quite how Gareth would put it; he won't even know what he's thinking. He'll just be looking out to the far stand, trying to picture how it all happened.

'They were boys,' the guide will say. 'The ones who fought for independence, they were younger than all you.'

The sky will be white, and there'll be silence and rapture. When the guide leaves them at the museum, Hucknall will say to the boys, 'Fucking hell, I thought he'd never shut up.'

And Larry will put on an Irish accent and go: '*GAA is in the blood.*'

And Hucknall will laugh and go: '*And they killed all our boys* . . . Yeah, nice one, Worst Man. Most depressing stag do in the world. You got any other crap trips in that suitcase of yours?'

Big Mike will be quiet, he won't know what to say.

'I enjoyed it,' Rob will say, and his father will thank Big Mike for bringing them.

Gareth will send a text to Carly. '*Miss you too*', it'll say.

Peacock will be using his iPhone to check his hair.

*

They'll get a taxi back into town, then they'll walk around and look at things. Larry'll be in hysterics when he sees the place called Abrakebabra, insisting that one of the boys take his photo next to the sign. They'll walk in a group, taking up half the width of Westmoreland Street, wondering what the hell goes on in the massive white building with the huge columns that look as if they belong in Rome.

'It's a bank,' Rob's father will say, and Big Mike will go, 'No wonder things are so fucking expensive.'

When they pass Trinity College, Rob's father will say there's meant to be a nice library in there, he read about it in his guide book. And Gareth will point ahead at Hucknall and Larry as they eye up a group of Spanish-looking tourists, and he'll say: 'I've got a feeling the boys aren't really in the mood for a good read.'

Before they know it, they'll be in Temple Bar again. In Gogarty's they'll order bouquets of Guinness, and Hucknall will insist that they should have gone to the Guinness Factory instead of Croke Park.

Big Mike will say: 'If you know so much, why dun you be fucking best man?' And the boys will do a handbags-*oooooh*, and laugh until their already-aching kidneys hurt. A greying man on a guitar will sing 'Whiskey in the Jar' and 'The Wild Rover' ('The Clover song!' Peacock will say), and when the boys request 'Delilah', he'll oblige, and all the boys will sing-shout along, all the while pushing more pints in front of Rob. Rob will be singing loudest now. He'll have decided that tonight's the night he's going to properly go for it. Leaving Croke Park, he'll have felt something stirring, and he'll have told his father he was ready to have one more final night of going nuts.

Gareth will sing along too, but he'll be thinking of his small bedroom at home, of the journey back to Wales tomorrow night.

'By the way,' Big Mike will tell the group when talk turns to eating, 'before we go for food, we've gotta go back to the hostel.'

'How come, Worst Man?' Hucknall will say.

'Costumes for tonight, butt. And if you call me Worst Man one more time I'm gonna knock you out, you ginger prick.'

'Sorry, Worst Man.'

The boys will be awkward-quiet, and Rob's father will ask where they're gonna get the costumes from. And Big Mike will smile now. He'll say, 'Why the hell do you think I checked in a suitcase?'

'A fucking potato?' Hucknall will say. 'Are you fucking serious?'

They'll all be back at their room, and Big Mike will have his suitcase open on the bed, the bag bulging with bumpy, creamy-brown potato costumes.

'Aye,' Big Mike will say. 'Got a problem with that as well, have you?'

Peacock will take a costume from the suitcase and place it over himself in the mirror. 'These gonna make us look fat, you reckon?'

'No way am I wearing a potato costume,' Hucknall will say. 'We're in Ireland, for fuck's sake.'

'Exactly,' Big Mike'll go. 'They love potatoes. *Dirtytree potatoes.*'

And the boys will shake their heads, will say all sorts.

'Are they all the same size?' Larry'll go.

'All the same,' Big Mike will say, 'except for Rob's. He's wearing something else. Oh, and you all owe me fifteen quid.'

Rob will beam, his teeth visible, a smile in his voice. 'What the fuck you got me?'

A plunging arm into the suitcase depths and Big Mike will pull out something black in cellophane.

Wordless, he'll hand the package to Rob.

Rob will tear at the cellophane. There'll be some kind of dress: green-and-orange and hideous. It'll take a moment for Rob to click: he's been given a woman's Irish dance costume. There'll be white socks to go with it too.

'*Rrrrriverdance!*' Big Mike will scream, doing an odd, high-kneed jig on the hostel floor.

And all the boys will laugh, and Hucknall will say fair play, that's a good un. And once they see that Rob looks the biggest tit, they won't mind dressing up like potatoes. At least we'll all be warm, Rob's father will say.

They'll drink the cans left over from last night, and Gareth will find himself at the point of drunkenness where he wants to fight. He'll offer arm wrestles to everyone. Using Big Mike's suitcase for a table—and at Gareth's insistence—they'll take turns to lie on the floor and arm-wrestle each other. And when he's not competing, Gareth will come up behind Larry, give him a bear hug and lift him off the ground. He'll do the same to Hucknall and Peacock and Rob. They'll be laughing at first, but by the end they'll be properly pushing him off.

In Temple Bar, with the boys dressed like potatoes, and Rob dressed like a female Irish dancer (but wearing his own brown Wrangler boots), they'll argue over where to go for dinner. Foreign girls with dark hair and dinner menus will approach, trying to coax them into their restaurants. Passers-by will cheer and laugh, and tourists—German, American, Chinese—will ask for photos with all the boys. And they'll begin to get into it, begin to feel like Dublin's central attraction.

'We should start charging,' Larry'll say, as Rob poses for a photo with a girl from Cincinnati. 'Two quid per photo, whadyou reckon?'

At some point in the night someone will say that the euro feels like Monopoly money, and everyone will agree.

After forty minutes of wandering and arguing, they'll land on Dame Street, at an empty Chinese restaurant.

'Never a good sign when it's empty,' Rob's father will say, but they'll have been walking around for too long, and will be too hungry to go elsewhere.

Before they've even ordered, Hucknall will suggest they split the bill. Hucknall is an accountant, Hucknall can afford to say such things. And for reasons beyond them, to save hassle perhaps, everyone will agree. They'll order pints immediately, but the food will take deliberation. They'll all ask each other what they're going to order, as if each boy's afraid of getting the wrong dish, of getting the whole eating-out thing wrong. They'll wind up the waitress who takes their orders, ask her if she'll be joining them for starters, and then they'll make her stand at the table for photos with them all.

The potato costumes will be chunky and clunky , so the chairs will have to be set some distance from the tables, and Gareth will find that to eat he has to lean forward, his back arched like a capital C. His arms will be free, though—he'll have that at least.

'When you buying this place with your missus, then?' Larry will ask.

'We'll see,' Gareth will say, taking a swig of his pint. 'No rush, is there?'

'I heard she wants somewhere by the summer,' Big Mike'll say.

'Carly talks too fucking much,' Gareth will say, and the table will laugh, giddy. Gareth'll say: 'What? It's true. She shouldn't talk about stuff like this with other people. I dun know what's wrong with her.'

Peacock will be smiling like a bag of chips, brimming over, as if he can't believe they're allowed to slag off their partners publicly. He'll think he could handle having a girlfriend if he could just slag her off all the time.

Gareth will finish off his pint and call to the waitress for another. Rob, his arms beginning to itch in the dance dress, will be watching Gareth's left leg. Under the white tablecloth, it'll be shaking.

The boys will chant football songs as they eat. They'll recall stories from school, from holidays, and from other stag trips. And all the boys will laugh as Larry pretends to cry and goes *'I'm soooooo hungry!'*—in imitation of the time Hucknall passed out in Malaga and woke to find his wallet had been stolen. When the boys found him, he'd been walking the streets for three hours and he was a quivering, starving mess. At some point, some food will be thrown at someone. A man and a woman will sit down at a table across from the boys, then promptly leave. Of all the boys, Rob's father will be the only one to notice. But the restaurant manager won't mind the noise because the boys are buying so many drinks and extra portions of egg-fried rice and chips.

'Alright then,' Rob will shout across the table, raising his glass. And it'll take Big Mike and Hucknall to quiet everyone down. 'I should have done this earlier,' Rob will shout, 'but I just wanna say thanks for all this. I know you're all wankers, but I've known you all so long —'

'So he's gonna dump Rachel and marry us!' Gareth will yell, and the boys will cheer.

'Dump the girl,' will come the shout from Larry, and Gareth will shout it too, and they'll both chant the words, banging the table. Hucknall will tell them to shut up, and Big Mike will be annoyed because that's his job, really, not Hucknall's.

Rob's father will smile and tell his son to go on with the speech.

'If I could,' Rob will say, 'I'd marry you all.'

'A toast to us!' Gareth will shout. And though his glass will be empty, he'll raise it anyway. And Rob won't realise he never said what he wanted to say.

In Gogarty's, Gareth will be doing his bear-hug-picking-up-mates routine again, but the place will be packed and he'll be banging into everyone. It won't help matters that they're all dressed like potatoes. Big Mike will take Gareth aside and tell him to calm the fuck down.

Upstairs, in the smoking area, Larry and Rob—neither smoke—will be reminiscing.

'Getting older's mad, innit?' Rob will say, taking a swig of his pint. He'll almost have forgotten he's dressed like a woman, and he'll be repeatedly confused by all the looks he's getting.

'Yeah,' Larry will say. 'I can't believe we're twentyseven.

Innit sad thinking about all the things we'll never do? I was thinking about it the other day. Like, at this age, I will never be the victim of paedophilia.'

Rob will laugh and bury his head in his hands. Between his fingers, he'll see the cream foam collecting on the inside of his glass. He'll take a swig and look at Larry. 'Incredible,' he'll say.

'It's not real, though,' Larry will say. 'I reckon we're in *The Matrix*. We're gonna wake up and we're gonna be five years old and it's gonna be the end of our first day at school again and—'

'Yeah,' Rob will say.

'But back to the issue,' Larry will say. 'Any pre-match doubts?'

'What, about Rachel?'

'Yeah. Any niggles?'

'Nah, all good, mate. All good.'

'I dunno how you do it,' Larry will say—and he'll mean it now, he'll be sincere. 'My record is three weeks and four days.'

Downstairs, Rob's father will be standing on a table with a Welsh flag around his head, singing 'Don't Look Back in Anger'.

'I'm telling you,' Gareth will shout at Hucknall at the bar, 'I'm not buying a house.'

'You been with Carly five years now, though, mate.'

'I know, but I'm not buying a house.'

'Look, you bender,' Hucknall will say, 'you can't live at home all your life. I'm spending shitloads on rent in London. I know that. But at least I'm not living with my fucking parents.'

'I know,' Gareth will say, and when Hucknall turns to fetch his pint from the bar, Gareth will put his arms around Hucknall's potato waist, pick him up, and launch him into a group of French guys in the corner. Pints will be knocked over, and Hucknall will be winded. He'll get up, confused, and make apologies to the jostling French men. He'll push his way through, smile at Gareth, and gesture for him to come back. And when Gareth takes a step forward, Hucknall will smack him square in the nose. Gareth will feel the cartilage snap, the muscle tear from the bone, and he'll be buckled over when he sees Hucknall lining up another.

He'll bound for the doors then. He'll leg it out, down the lane, down Merchant's Arch. He'll dodge and weave through the traffic, and lunge up to the bridge. He'll put his hand to his nose and there'll be blood wetting his fingers. He'll keep running until he's on the other side, on Lower Liffey Street. He'll take a seat at the bench.

He'll be sat there, watching the boardwalk, seething and lost, when a girl who's smoking outside the Grand Social will come sit beside him.

'Have a chip on your shoulder, do you?' '

What?' he'll say.

'You're a potato,' she'll say. 'Chips. Potatoes.' She'll look at him, see the nose. 'God, you're bleeding.'

'I know,' he'll say.

The taxis will be piling up beside the Liffey, glowing. Gareth will be staring at them, at the thin whistle of white lights, at the dark night, at the starless sky, at all the people on the boardwalk, and he'll think that only yesterday morning he was leaving his mother's house to get on the minibus. He'll feel small now, as if he's shrinking even, as if he's been dragged down from that vast sky and put here in Dublin, with his past and everything he knows about himself left behind. It's as if they've just brought the shell of his body over to Ireland, as if the rest of him might still be on the plane. He'll realise he hasn't looked up at the girl in some time.

'You alright?' she'll say.

He'll pause for a moment, unsure if he'll actually say it. This isn't how he imagined it. This isn't how he thought it all might go. But he'll look down at his bobbly potato body and think *fuck it.*

'I'm gay,' he'll say, and he'll feel there's no returning now.

'Good for you,' the girl will say. 'I was just asking if you're alright.'

He'll shift over on the bench, put a hand on her shoulder. 'No, you don't get it. My friends don't know I am. No one knows.'

'Oh God,' she'll say, watching the blood dribble from his nose, past his lips. 'I bet you're having a long night.'

'Yeah,' he'll say, getting up. 'I've got to go tell the boys.'

He'll leave the girl then, he'll rise, and he'll cross the bridge, and he'll wait at the beeping traffic lights before crossing the road. He'll wipe the blood with the sleeve of his potato costume—red streaks on the creamy-brown. He'll walk through the arch and over the cobbles to Gogarty's. The bouncers won't let him back in because he'll be too drunk, so he'll sit outside on the pavement and ring the boys. He'll call and he'll text, and Larry will come out and Gareth will go to say it, will go to tell him everything. He'll look at Larry, his fringe gelled upwards, and Gareth will open his mouth, he'll go to say how it's been like this since he was fifteen—

but Larry will speak first.

'You alright?' he'll say. 'All the boys are off to find a strip club now—are you comin or what?'

There'll be a pause, a moment of nothing.

'Aye,' Gareth will finally say, 'I could probably do with seeing some tits.'

all the boys

They'll wake late on the Sunday. They'll be rushing to check out of the hostel. They won't all have breakfast together because the London boys will have an earlier flight. All the boys will hug and high-five, and the Caerphilly boys will say bye to Hucknall and Peacock as the two leave in search of a taxi.

Big Mike still won't be talking to Gareth and there'll be a tough silence in the group until Rob tells them to sort it out cos it's getting depressing. Gareth will apologise for 'ruining Gogarty's', and say he was wrecked, he doesn't remember any of last night now. He'll buy Big Mike a make-up pint and Big Mike will accept.

'Don't get me wrong,' Big Mike will say, 'Hucknall's a prick, but you don't go chucking your mates around a pub.'

Big Mike will say there's still time for them to see a little bit more of the city, but the boys won't be up for it. They've got their bags to carry, and Man Utd are on at 12.30, and can't they just watch the match at Fitzsimons? They're sure the place has Sky.

So they'll watch the United game at Fitzsimons, and they'll nurse slow pints, and they'll keep looking at their phones, sending texts to their girlfriends and wives. They'll decide to leave earlier than they need to because they're just killing time now, aren't they? There's no point waiting around here, they're better off getting to the airport than staying around here. At least they know they won't miss the flight then.

So they'll get the taxi, and they'll wait at departures, and they'll board their flight, and they'll sit there as the plane carries them over the water, over from Dublin to Bristol, and they'll wait at Bristol Airport for their minibus to pick them up, and they'll get on the minibus, and they'll tell stories about the weekend to each other, and they'll try and clear up some details that are hazy, like how much did it actually cost to get into the strip club? Did anyone else see Rob Senior on the table in Gogarty's? And Gareth, where did you get to last night, mate? What happened to you?

And when they cross the Severn Bridge, and see the *Welcome to Wales* sign, all the boys will cheer.

Róisín Kiberd

The Night Gym {essay extract}

It's 2 AM, and I am coming up on my 700th calorie burned. I'm on a stationary bike that rattles, sweating from the hoodie I've forgotten to take off. At 666 calories I pause and take a picture of the screen with my phone: workout of the beast. As well as displaying my distance cycled and calories burned, the screen offers reassuring messages. *Remember to stay hydrated*, says the bike. *Take long, smooth strokes*. It tells me, *Remember: this is your ride.*

I joined the low-cost supergym in the autumn of 2015, to flatter myself into thinking I was the type of person who went to the gym. It was also a bid to impose order on my life. I didn't know if I could even afford to live in Dublin, the city I'd grown up in, but which was rapidly transforming into one meant solely for the rich. I was freelancing, writing mainly about technology, and while I was happy with this work I harboured a fascination with people who got up every day to go to an office. The idea of predictably sleeping, waking, dressing and seeing other human beings seemed enviable compared to my own unstructured existence, with its mood swings and deadlines and multiple breakfasts. Looking through my wardrobe of freelance slob-wear, I realised I had become the very thing I wrote about: an internet weirdo, a basement dweller, one acquainted with the night Twitter.

When I first joined the gym I went there in the morning, like a normal person. I figured if I could get up every morning and work out, I'd set myself up for a productive day. Membership cost just €32 per month, including access to classes with names like 'Rockin Rebound', 'Ass and Abs', 'Battlebells' and 'Fight Club'. They promised 24-hour opening, every day of the year except Christmas.

For a while I was entertained by it. I liked it for people-watching, studying the coders and lawyers and marketers. I began to harbour dreams of meeting a heartless libertarian tech millionaire and marrying him. I bought discount designer workout wear in TK Maxx. I bought a phone holder from Tiger that looked like a black Velcro tourniquet. I shopped around for a gym mascara. The gym occupied the fringes of the corporate world, one I could infiltrate and observe. To join its denizens here struck me as a common test of will and dedication: could I be as hardworking, as employable, as they were?

At 7 AM, I attended a spin class held in darkness with ultra-violet disco lights. The promise was that you would burn 700 calories, with an arm workout built in alongside the frantic pedalling. At intervals we had to stand up on the bikes and manipulate the handlebars through left and right turns, an awkward waltz with a partner that was lifeless and heavy, and fixed to the ground. Meanwhile the sound system blasted a track by David Guetta and Kid Cudi, with lyrics about and late nights and hedonism. After the class I took a shower and went home, and fell instantly back to sleep.

*

I began to overthink the gym, worrying about the correct amount of time to use machines, or how to behave in the locker room, or how to dress. I was unsettled by the degree to which some people dressed up for the gym; I counted around me the number of tiny lower-back logos for Lululemon, the activewear brand which prints quotes from *Atlas Shrugged* on its shopping bags, and which charges over €100 for yoga pants. Around this time, Beyoncé's line of athleisure wear, Ivy Park, debuted at Topshop. I went and looked at it, thinking this was how people are meant to dress for the gym, but I just didn't understand. I wondered if this made me the 'Becky' discussed in online think-pieces: Beyoncé's suburban white nemesis, a girl too basic to pull off high-cut bodysuits and logo leggings.

My problem was not gym clothing. My problem was too much watching, and proximity to people who, I felt, were achieving more than me. The anxiety I experienced in standing and waiting for a treadmill was greater even than that produced by running on one while being watched by the next person in line. Worst of all was when someone using the treadmill or stationary bike before me failed to press the 'stop' button when they disembarked, leaving behind a screen displaying their miles and calories burned as a challenge for me to match.

Throughout the spring of 2016 I grew volatile and fearful; I took on more work, saw my friends less, and felt myself retreating from the world outside. The gym no longer offered respite from these feelings; I entered a state of paranoia, watching the gym-goers and wondering if they were watching me. I began to fear the judgement of women in the changing room for being too naked, or not naked enough. I was becoming scared of other people: the more I went to the gym, the greater my conviction was that they and I were not the same. I measured myself against these 'normal' people and failed. I felt like an alien, using weight machines to work on my human suit.

The day I finally gave up going to the gym in the daytime was the day of Dip Belt Man. He was tall and broad, and had a *Dumb and Dumber* haircut, a vest top and ill-fitting shorts. He was wearing a thick black belt, which gave him the appearance of a 1990s WWF superstar. I noticed him because he'd been standing in the same place for fifteen minutes. I knew this because I had been on the bike that long, wondering who the fuck this guy was, who was staring and making me nervous.

As the podcast about serial killers I was listening to wound up, Dip Belt Man finally started to move. I watched as he took one of the largest weights from the rack in the corner, unclasped the belt and hooked it onto his waist. Slowly he swung it around to the front, until it dangled from his crotch like a cast-iron codpiece. Then he went back to staring and standing in the same place.

Bodybuilders use this method for weighted pull-ups, when lifting the mass of their bodies isn't enough. The belts resemble devices from a medieval dungeon, fashioned from chains and neoprene. But it wasn't the belt that disturbed me: it was Dip Belt Man's eerie stasis, and his utter lack of self-consciousness.

I concluded that day that the Day Gym—as I later came to think of it—was for people who were prepared to be put on display. It had not escaped my attention that the word 'gym' comes from the Greek verb γυμνάζειν, a verb meaning 'to train naked'. I wanted to work out among basement dwellers and freelancers, like me. I wanted to be an odd fish among clams.

I knew that the gym was open twenty-four hours, and that unlike the rest of the working world my life had no rhythm, no obligation to wake in the morning and sleep at night, when I could have the gym almost entirely to myself. So, I would give the Night Gym a try.

On my first trip to the Night Gym, I arrived at midnight and noticed a nu-metal and hip-hop soundtrack: Eminem, Limp Bizkit, Crazy Town, Red Hot Chili Peppers. Nearing 1 a.m., the music stopped entirely, along with the air conditioning, and the screen that normally played old Popeye and Mickey Mouse cartoons went dark. The lights dimmed on those of us who remained: a solitary weightlifter, a woman on the stair climber and a man sprinting on the treadmill, set to its fastest setting.

I liked the darkness: it felt like cover. I returned every night of that week and the week after that, staying later with every visit.

My favourite part of going to the Night Gym was going to the Night Gym—which is to say, the walk from my house. The air was cool; the lights of Custom House Quay glimmered on the river. The McCann FitzGerald building, a giant square made of glowing neon blue cubes, seemed safer by night when the lawyers were gone. If I timed it right, the streets were empty of cars and late-night drunk people, too. On the streets I caught glimpses of a nocturnal economy: the flight crews pulling suitcases on wheels, and drowsy staff pouring out of the bars and restaurants around CHQ.

At the Night Gym, I began to notice the regulars. There was the late-middle-aged man doing weight machines to build up his skinny arms. There was a group of young Asian guys who I imagined worked together somewhere on a late shift. One weekend night there was Drunk Guy, wearing a tight shirt and dad jeans, bootcut, over leather loafers, one of which fell off his foot as he crossed the floor. His eyes were half open. His feet dragged and he dropped his wallet as he made his way to the machines. In one hand he held a bottle of Budweiser, which he set down before beginning a set of chest-presses. Nobody stopped Drunk Guy, and everyone watched him. What drove him from the night that he was dressed for, and into the gym? Why were the rest of us here sober? Deep in the lizard brain, would we all remember how to use a chest-press machine, even during a blackout?

The year 1995 marked the first mention of Ireland as a tech hub; in an interview with the San Jose *Mercury News*, a Harvard business professor named Rosabeth Moss Kanter described us as '"the Silicon Bog'. By 1998, *Wired* magazine was calling us the Silicon Isle, and by the early years of the new millennium we'd established the Silicon Docks, a term still used today to describe Dublin's tech district. Google played a role in its creation; in 2004, after courtship by Ireland's Industrial Development Authority, they set up their EMEA headquarters on Barrow Street, and eventually spent €250 million on four office buildings. Rents in the neighbourhood climbed, other tech companies arrived, and gradually the docklands transformed from a neglected inner-city suburb into a Silicon Valley outpost.

Years ago I did some freelance writing work for an Irish venture capital firm, helping to create a guide to Dublin and its tech scene for visiting entrepreneurs. I remember it featured a series of maps of Dublin; the first, dated 'Pre-2000', featured Oracle, Microsoft, Dell, IBM, HP, Intel and Sun Microsystems, dotted mostly around the outer suburbs in campuses and business parks. The next map, for the early 2000s, saw Facebook, Google, eBay, PayPal, Amazon and Salesforce set up in Dublin too. Finally, between 2010 and 2012, there was a rush of new arrivals: Twitter, LinkedIn, Dropbox, Etsy, Airbnb, Zynga. Almost every well-known name in tech had established a base in Dublin, most often in the docklands.

I worked on and off within this self-declared 'tech ecosystem', mostly writing blog posts and web copy, and occasionally running social media accounts. I was expected to downplay the low Irish corporate tax rate of 12.5 per cent, and emphasise our 'high-quality local talent' instead. Occasionally I'd go to meet-ups and start-up launches. There was always a free bar with a corporate sponsor, and speeches extolling the virtues of entrepreneurialism, of burning through funding and, ultimately, of failure. 'Fail again. Fail better,' I heard repeated on every occasion. I had just graduated from an MPhil in literature. I fantasised that one day the Beckett estate would catch on to these start-up people, and sue them for everything they had.

I often wondered if this was a bubble. The nation was marketed abroad as 'Innovation Ireland'; a land of *céad míle fáilte* filled with English-speaking, overly qualified potential customer service agents. Very little tech IP was created in Ireland; a large number of the jobs were in marketing, customer service and content moderation. Our time zone, Greenwich Mean Time, was eight hours ahead of Silicon Valley's, and suited the idea of 24/7 business. One Industrial Development Authority (IDA) print ad published in business magazines read 'Facebook found a space for people who think in a certain way. It's called Ireland.'

The new wave of tech companies in Dublin were assigned a category, 'born on the internet', meaning they relied on ubiquitous connectivity to remain in business. Their founders, programmers and customers were very likely born on the internet too. As in California, the Silicon Docklands fetishised youth; throughout my twenties, I watched as casually tech-minded acquaintances founded start-ups and attracted funding with little more than a hoodie, a pitch deck and a LinkedIn account as qualification. Money was thrown around with a fervour not seen since the Celtic Tiger, but under the guise of something less frivolous: an investment in Ireland's future.

I remember being brought on a tour of a new start-up accelerator in the Docklands in order to write about it; a former wine cellar, dating back to the Georgian era, had been turned into an underground business hub. Dim, cavernous halls the size of football pitches lay dormant under the Silicon Docklands. Technology had colonised this space; already it had covered the surrounding area, reaching into the sky with ambitious, oddly shaped towers. Now it was clawing downward, digging up history, and finding it fertile ground for 'growing' more businesses.

Eventually I stopped doing marketing, and began to find work as a freelance journalist. I mostly wrote for international websites, earning a small and precarious living. I was never really sure where I fit; I had a middle-class South Dublin accent, a good education and very little money. A steady stream of articles was published about the rental crisis, about mortgages and zero-hour contracts and how young people could no longer live in Dublin. Money felt like a joke to me; I would put in long hours, staying up all night researching stories, and in the daytime I carried my work around in my pocket, on my phone, and with my laptop in my bag in case I suddenly needed to work on edits. I didn't have work hours—I simply worked until it was done, and then took on more work—and often the pieces I wrote paid a set fee of €100. Mostly I lived on savings from years before, when I worked on commission selling make-up in a department store, earning considerably better money.

The shared house I rented a room in was on a street just off North Strand, a historically neglected area of north inner-city Dublin. During the Second World War, in which Ireland was neutral, it was famously bombed by the Luftwaffe, but these days drug addiction was a far more significant problem, with a memorial nearby on Sean McDermott Street featuring a 'flame of hope' in memory of local people who had died due to heroin addiction. Down the road in Ballybough, a feud was accelerating between criminals allied to a local figure known as 'the Monk' and the Kinahan gang, an international drug cartel.

From these streets you could just about see the effects of tech-driven urban regeneration, a ten-minute walk away. Towers and odd neon geometries lit the night sky; the blue bands of light on the Convention Centre; the uneasy curve of the Samuel Beckett Bridge. I pictured the trajectory of a tech executive, arriving at Dublin Airport—doubtless at the new, shiny Terminal 2 rather than Terminal 1, which was run-down and only used by Ryanair. They would be driven along the Liffey to a newly built hotel in the Docklands, before meetings in one of those towers, from which they would see other shiny new start-up headquarters and hotels. It was a version of Dublin designed to be seen from a boardroom: tall buildings, surrounded by other tall buildings, air-conditioned and clinical and gleaming.

I would walk out the door, and then under an old train bridge where I occasionally saw people passed out with syringes in their arms, past the rumoured IRA pub and the defunct mattress shop, then past the bus station and into the Docklands, moving from former tenements into new architectural complexes more suited to Dubai. Online one night, I read about Silicon Valley's 'hour-glass economy': the concentration of very rich and very poor people, with few residents falling in between. Something similar was happening in Dublin; house prices and rents had skyrocketed, as had the number of homeless people.

One night I walked in the dark along North Strand, and paused at the railway bridge to watch a group of teenage boys gathered around a bonfire in the trainyard. There were scraps of wood, furniture and old tyres burning in front of them. Behind them, across the water, was East Point Business Park, a campus I had once visited for work. They stood in a loose circle, staring into the flames, and facing an enclave of a new and stratified Ireland; Astroturf greens, car parks, bright cafeterias and the offices of Cisco, Citrix, Oracle and Enterprise Ireland. I watched them a while, then continued on my way to the Night Gym.

Peter Sirr

Noises Off: Dublin's Contested Monuments {essay extract}

If you're a statue with any ambition the place you want to be is O'Connell Street, the biggest theatre of all and the most contested site. The street opens and closes with high drama: at one end the domineering solemnity of John Henry Foley's O'Connell, at the other one of Augustus Saint-Gaudens' masterpieces, the Parnell Monument, an obelisk of Galway granite at whose base, startlingly close to us, is the statue of Parnell in full oratorical flight. Saint-Gaudens is an interesting figure. He was born in Dublin to a French father and an Irish mother who immigrated to New York when he was six months old. At nineteen he travelled to Paris where he studied at the École des Beaux-Arts. His first big commission, and the one which established his reputation, was a monument to Civil War Admiral David Farragut, in New York's Madison Square. Other commissions included the Standing Lincoln in Lincoln Park, Chicago, and the Robert Gould Shaw Memorial on Boston Common. Shaw was the colonel in command of the African-American 54th Regiment of the Union Army and was killed in a failed attempt to capture Fort Wagner in South Carolina. Robert

Lowell gives a brilliant description of the relief in 'For the Union Dead':

> *Two months after marching through Boston,*
> *half the regiment was dead;*
> *at the dedication,*
> *William James could almost hear the bronze*
>   *Negroes breathe.*

'Their monument,' the poem continues, 'sticks like a fishbone / in the city's throat...' There were undoubtedly many for whom Parnell's monument performed the same function. Shaw said once that one Englishman couldn't open his mouth without offending another; in the same way, at least half of a city is likely to be offended by a new monument. How many love the great silver needle of the Spire towering over O'Connell Street where Nelson's Pillar used to be? Many cities seem to need a phallic gesture in the centre. For a hundred and fifty-seven years the phallus was Horatio Nelson on top of a column one hundred and thirty-four feet and three inches high. A hundred and sixty-eight stone steps led up to the parapet from which, on a clear day, you could see, as well as the spread of the city and its bay, as far north as the Mountains of Mourne. The city had rushed to celebrate the fallen hero years before he appeared in Great Yarmouth and Trafalgar Square, and the unveiling was another of those days when official Dublin put its best foot forward with the obligatory procession of horse and foot yeomanry led by the Lord Lieutenant, the Duke of Richmond, with the Provost and Fellows of Trinity College, and a host of sailors, officers, sheriffs and aldermen.

To some, even then, it was an eyesore. The Wide Street Commissioners didn't want it in what was then Sackville Street, because it effectively divided the street in two and ruined the vista of the city's major thoroughfare.

Throughout its history there were many proposals to remove or relocate it as it was an obstacle to traffic. Maybe the most memorable suggestion was that made by the waspish Anti-Parnellite MP Tim Healy that not only the Pillar but also all the statues should be removed from the street: 'If it is desired to commemorate the dead, the statues ought to be placed somewhere where they will not be in the way of the living.' The end, or at least the beginning of the end, came at 1.32 am on Tuesday morning, 8 October 1966, when a massive explosion, the work of a group of former IRA volunteers, blew the Pillar in half, leaving seventy feet of truncated column and pedestal. The Irish Army had to be called in to finish the job, a pretty thankless one and one they made something of a meal of, causing more damage to the surrounding area than the original explosion had done. This was the ignominious end of one the most famous of all Dubliners, thirteen foot of Portland stone — if a hundred and fifty odd years of leaning on a capstan high above the city is enough to qualify you as a Dubliner. Nelson's head underwent further indignities, being leased by a group of Dublin art students to a London antique dealer to raise funds for the students' union, taking part in an ad for ladies' stockings shot on Killiney beach and even appearing onstage with The Dubliners in the Olympia. It now lies untroubled and at peace in Dublin City Library and Archive, Pearse Street.

*

Blowing up statues is not for the fainthearted. Nine years before Nelson was toppled from his column the IRA had assaulted another of John Henry Foley's works, the fifteen-ton equestrian statue of Field Marshall Viscount Gough (1779–1869) in the Phoenix Park. Gough was depicted in his uniform of Colonel of the Guards reviewing his regiment, field-marshal's baton in his right hand. The IRA had brought over a plastic explosives expert from France to help them accomplish the job, and Gough and his horse were hurled efficiently from their base. In his recreation of the event in *Foley's Asia*, a dramatization of the sculptor and his subjects, Ronan Sheehan has the bombers retire to Chapelizod for a post-explosion meal of tagliatelle and pesto. The statue ended up in storage at the Royal Hospital in Kilmainham; an old photograph shows Gough's severed head in a cupboard. The base remained intact and stayed in the Park. No one can have been entirely surprised at the assault. The hero of the Peninsular War and 'Hammer of the Sikhs', even if he was from Limerick, was never likely to be a popular virtual citizen of the city. It's something of a surprise that the statue was commissioned in the first place. When he died in 1869 his friends had tried to persuade the Corporation to erect a monument in a prominent city location. Carlisle Bridge (O'Connell Bridge), Foster Place or Westmoreland Street were suggested, all of which were vetoed by the Corporation. Having him on Carlisle Bridge would have meant having two Foley sculptures of ideological antagonists staring each other down across the Liffey. Foley was less concerned with the politics than with the opportunity to have a go at another big equestrian commission after the success of his

Lord Hardinge outside Government House in Calcutta and Sir James Outram, also in Calcutta, often considered his masterpiece. 'I need scarcely repeat how gratifying the task would be to me,' he wrote, 'and how willing I am to forgo all consideration of profit in my desire to engage myself upon it. I feel that the time has arrived for our native country to add to the memorials of her illustrious dead an Equestrian Statue, and that Lord Gough at once presents a worthy subject for such a memorial.'

His enthusiasm for the commission contrasts strikingly with the lack of interest he showed in the work for which most Dubliners know him best, the O'Connell Monument. When Dublin Corporation ran a competition for the project Foley didn't enter it. When the competition failed to produce a winner the Corporation appealed to the Dubliner who was the Empire's leading sculptor, who had produced the statue of Prince Albert in the Albert Memorial in Hyde Park, and whose Dublin work included Goldsmith and Burke outside Trinity College, and Henry Grattan in College Green, and eventually he accepted the commission, much to the displeasure of many who thought him too deeply implicated in Empire to appreciate the achievement of the Liberator. But the model was enthusiastically accepted when it was exhibited in City Hall in 1867. In the event Foley died before either the Gough or O'Connell statue was completed and both were finished by his pupil Thomas Brock. The O'Connell Monument wasn't unveiled until 1882. Meanwhile the Corporation found a site for the Gough statue at a discreet distance from the city, in the Phoenix Park, but the inauguration was a nervous affair, packed with soldiery in case the citizens got out of hand. It was so much an icon of Empire that it was in fact subjected to repeated attacks. On Christmas Eve 1944 Gough was beheaded and his sword removed. Twelve years later the right hind leg of the horse was blown off, and the following year the final blow was struck. After nearly thirty years in storage it was eventually sold off to Robert Guinness, but only on condition that it leave the country. Guinness gave it to a descendent of Gough, Sir Humphrey Wakefield, and it's now in Chillingham Castle in Northumberland, England, having been painstakingly restored by Newcastle blacksmiths.

And that would have been the end of it, another minor saga of unloved imperial statuary, but Gough, or at least his horse, reappeared in Dublin, replicated by artist John Byrne for his sculpture *Misneach* (the Irish for courage), unveiled in Ballymun in September 2010. The dimensions are the same, and the pose is the same, head down to the side, right leg pawing the air, but this time the rider is a young girl in bronze track suit and Velcro-fastened runners, and she's riding bareback. The image was problematic for some in the local community; the tradition of children riding horses bareback in Ballymun and other working class suburbs isn't appreciated by everyone and many in Ballymun are weary of the image, perpetuated for the world to see in *The Commitments*, where a horse is seen being led to a tower block lift because 'the stairs would kill him'. Byrne's sculpture was commissioned by Breaking Ground under the Per Cent for Art scheme that was part of the redevelopment of the area (under the terms of the scheme, one per cent of development costs must be spent on art). Byrne wanted to subvert the tradition of equestrian statuary in Ireland and Europe, and when he found out that the Gough statue had ended up in

England he went to Chillingham and got permission to copy the horse. The figure for the rider is a local girl, Toni Marie Shields, chosen from open auditions. She was scanned with 3D software to make the mould, which was then combined with the mould from the model of Gough's horse to make the bronze sculpture. Byrne then distressed the bronze by applying a green patina at the end of the process, to make it look as if it had been standing out in the weather for a century or two. It's now in a school in Ballymun and may be transferred to the Main Street if the Metro rail project is completed. Wherever it ends up, it seems entirely fitting that Foley's Arab deconstructed and re-imagined stallion should be prancing in the city again.

*

All these illustrious dead. Part of me sympathizes with Tim Healy's impatience with them. What are they doing here, in the middle of the city with their frozen gestures? They inhabit their alternative city, their pigeon space, above the living, Kelly's Larkin, Father Mathew, Jesus of the Taxi Drivers, Hibernia, Fidelity and Mercury looking down from Francis Johnston's GPO, Oliver Sheppard's dying Cúchulainn in the ground-floor window. Sheppard's bust of James Clarence Mangan is in Stephen's Green, and I never go into the park without going over to inspect it, drawn by its sharp clear lines and the expression somewhere between gentleness and ferocity, with just the single word MANGAN on the base. That's been there since 1909 but in recent years there's been a rush to commemorate the city's writers on the streets. Here, in North Earl Street, is Joyce, swaggering in bronze outside the Kylemore Café. There's always something strangely literal about statues of writers. Writers, after all, live in their heads; they don't ride horses or inspect troops, they don't lift up their arms and orate, unless in the privacy of their bedrooms. Marjorie Fitzgibbon's bronze is based on a photograph of the author, but for all the jauntiness of the pose, the cane and the broad brimmed hat, it still looks odd and stilted. It was commissioned by the local businesses, presumably to add a bit of lustre to the street, but North Earl Street doesn't really need Joyce or anyone else to stand like a sentinel at its gateway. It's not as bad as the lurid kitsch of Oscar Wilde in Merrion Square. Kavanagh sitting on a bench by the Grand Canal, or Brendan Behan at a safe distance on the other side of the city, on the banks of the Royal Canal, work better because they at least depict the writers in a plausible attitude and occupation, staring into water and hatching plans.

The city doesn't stop at replicating writers, but also attaches their names to new bridges across the Liffey: The Sean O'Casey Bridge, The Samuel Beckett Bridge, The James Joyce Bridge. I'm not sure if this really works either. A street maybe, or a square. A modest plaque in the brickwork. Rue de la Poésie . . . A bridge, though, seems grandiose, a kind of monumentalization the writers themselves, you feel, might well resist if they had any say. There have been other attempts to represent writers in the cityscape. The city's first attempt to bring a writer into the circle of official celebration was the James Joyce Museum in the Martello Tower in Sandycove, the building where the opening of *Ulysses* is set. Apart from its spectacular location in Sandycove, I think this museum works not least because the building has such a strong imaginative resonance. Joyce only spent a few troubled days there but the fact that the opening scene of *Ulysses* is set there, with Buck Mulligan and Stephen Dedalus gazing down at the waters of the bay, the snotgreen and scrotumtightening sea, makes it a more real place than many carefully preserved writers' houses with their kitschy appeal to the literal. The museum has a very specific and selective brief: to focus on the life and works of Joyce, only displaying original material from Joyce's own time. There are information panels and photographs; in the gunpowder magazine various items are assembled: the death mask, a piece of Nelson's Pillar, a Clongowes pandybat, a photo of Throwaway, the twenty-to-one outsider which won the 1904 Gold Cup, an empty Plumtree's Potted Meat pot like the one Bloom finds when he eventually gets home, its contents eaten by Molly Bloom and Blazes Boylan. Samuel Beckett presented the museum with Joyce's famous family waistcoat; Maria Jolas donated his last cane, Sylvia Beach brought photographs, a prospectus for *Ulysses*, notes in Joyce's hand. The opening, on Bloomsday 1962, was a gala drink-fuelled Dublin occasion with a huge crowd in attendance, including Maria Jolas, Frances Steloff, Joyce's sisters, Louis MacNeice, Mary Lavin, Brendan Behan, Anthony Cronin. One of the first curators was the poet Michael Hartnett from whom Paul Durcan bought his first copy of *Ulysses*. Many volunteers helped to staff the tower, including the actor Eamon Morrissey, who used tell the more credulous visitors that Joyce was imprisoned in the tower by the British for his seditious activities. This museum was followed many years later by the privately run James Joyce Centre in North Great Georges Street and the ill-fated James Joyce House of the Dead in Usher's Island, and the recently opened MoLI (geddit?) Museum of Literature Ireland in Stephen's Green.

And, of course, there's the annual Bloomsday celebration, a jolly middle-class fancy-dress party with a few lectures and performances thrown in. The statue is a further attempt to integrate a writer who spent most of his adult life in exile from his native city into the bustle of its commercial life, but his gaze is upwards, away from the commotion of North Earl Street, and he doesn't look like a willing participant in the tourist industry. I try to imagine him at the meeting I attended, hosted by the tourism industry, whose main object was to discover ways of monetizing 'the literature product'.

One institution which tries to do just that is the Dublin Writers' Museum. Again, the notion of a 'writers' museum' is problematic. It tries to construct a product out of the idea of writers by assembling books, busts, objects: letters, portraits, typewriters, Oliver St John's Gogarty's driving goggles, Brendan Behan's Painters and Decorators Union membership card. 'Did you know, for example, that Oscar Wilde was a promising pugilist during his days at Trinity College, and that Samuel Beckett, had he not turned out to be one of the most influential writers of the twentieth century, would also have made a name for himself in the TCD cricket first eleven?' It attempts to compress centuries of literary achievement into an easily digestible narrative that can be read off the walls and listened to on the handset that comes with the admission ticket. There is a library, but it consists of locked bookcases, so that what is really on display is the idea of a library, a virtual representation of reading. The Gallery of Writers is a sumptuous Georgian drawing room with an ornate ceiling by Stapleton and portraits of dead writers. Living writers are outside the frame of the narrative. The museum wants fixity and certainty, the stasis of the past unruffled by new pretenders; once the panels and objects and audio guide are in place there will be no need for the tourist industry to revisit the exhibit or revise the narrative. It's the Dead Zoo model: the main work is in the collecting and the installation, but once that's done you only have to polish the cases occasionally. MoLI is more sophisticated. A partnership between UCD and the National Library of Ireland, housed in the freshly imagined space of the Aula Maxima of Joyce's old university in Newman House, it makes much of the Joyce connection, proudly displaying 'Copy No. 1' of *Ulysses*. It also features changing exhibitions on contemporary literature and it has already established itself as a challenging addition to the city's literary culture.

How should a city represent its writers other than by organizing festivals, events and exhibitions or displaying their ephemera in museums? One way is to find a way of stitching their texts into the fabric of the city. In 1988, as part of the Millennium celebrations, Robin Buick placed fourteen plaques in city pavements, tracing Leopold Bloom's movements through the city in the eighth chapter of *Ulysses*, Lestrygonians. The texts were chosen by Robert Nicholson, the curator of the Joyce Museum. Each plaque, about the size of an A4 sheet of paper featuring a bowler-hatted Bloom and brief quotation, is set at a point on Bloom's lunchtime route from O'Connell Street to the National Museum via Davy Byrne's pub.

There's something attractive about this mapping of the imaginary onto the literal, this plantation of an imagined journey onto the streets of the city. Maybe it's also attractive because it makes no obvious demands on the citizens, it doesn't come into their line of sight, it's almost secret. Just to see them you have to shuffle along the street, head down to the pavement, looking for the plaques between the feet of hurrying citizens.

A much louder, though of its nature temporary, attempt to map Joyce onto his city was undertaken in 1999 by Frances Hegarty and Andrew Stones when they placed nine fragments of Molly Bloom's soliloquy rendered in cerise-pink neon at a series of locations around the city. The neon was lit both night and day, but it was only at night that the project came alive as Molly's thoughts came out from Eccles Street to blazon themselves from prominent locations in the city. '… I hate an unlucky man…' was placed above a bookmaker's; '… it'd be much better for the world to be governed by the women in it…' looked down from its prominent site on City Hall, while on the side of Trinity College appeared '… I wouldn't give a snap of my two fingers for all their learning…' The quotes chosen are all humorous, sceptical of men and their self-importances. One might be taken as a sly critique of the way cities commemorate themselves and their dignitaries: '… a stranger to Dublin what place was it and so on about the monuments and he tired me out with statues…'

What was maybe most attractive about it was its projection of the private into the public space, the sense that the city could reflect back the private life of its citizenry through the words of one of its most memorably imagined citizens. It was a reminder, precisely, that a city is the sum of the interior life of its citizens and that one of the functions of art, even public art, is to attempt to represent that. The neon ramblings didn't want to improve us or set before us a massive icon of nationhood or historical memento. 'We hate poetry that has a palpable design on us,' Keats said, and this can also be true of public art. As I walk up O'Connell Street I pause to admire another creation of light, Julian Opie's LED panel on the central median, 'Walking Down O'Connell Street'. Each side of the panel shows an animated figure walking down the street, electronic shoppers taking their place in the pedestrian life of the city, mirroring the street's activity, blending in with it. Opie apparently came up with the idea for the LED panels when he noticed that LED taxi meters in South Korea display a small galloping horse when switched on. His figures in bright orange light, here on the street and in front of the Municipal Gallery, The Hugh Lane, in Parnell Square, which commissioned them, are elemental, childlike, yet they move with a fluid sensuousness. They go about their business just like the rest of the city, except that their motion is without destination, circular and repetitive, nothing but motion. How jealous they must make the rest of the street's figures, frozen forever in a single gesture.

Nuala O'Connor
Jesus of Dublin {short story}

I'm the O'Connell Street Jesus; I have a granite plinth and a glass case so swanky it could have come from the National Museum. My old box had a pitched roof—draughty—and I nearly passed out inside the PVC yoke some nut-job from Irishtown threw together. But this new box is the business: bulletproof glass, no less. Solar panels and LEDs for light.

The glass gets a bit foggy on a warm day, as if I've been hawing on it, but that gives me a rest. I let my arms down and shake them out. I normally only do that by night—4 AM-ish, when the last madsers are on the Nitelink back to wherever.

They hawk at me sometimes. Well, at the windows of the case. They fall around outside, wagging a finger and telling me how poxy the church is. I had one here last night.

'I can't stand priests,' he roared. 'Do ya know what they do to little kids? Do ya?'

He had a single from Cinelli's in one hand and a can in the other. He went deep down into his throat and sucked up a massive gollier to spit at the glass. Snort and *fwuh*; it landed, it slid, and your man staggered off, feeling like he'd done something big.

The mother's down the Bull Island doing her Stella Maris thing, watching over the sailors; it's peaceful there, she tells me—gulls and boats and wind. But I like the bray of the city; the thrum and swagger of it. Give me sirens and buses and neon any day. I'm high on the hog here, all right; Parnell behind me, the Spire before me, and Daniel O'Connell himself down the other end, standing proud.

I'm taking a long rest tonight; the auld pins aren't the best. Once I step down off the starry stone I do a few stretches, then park myself in the corner, back to the glass. Ah, I've a great life, really; there's not a bother on me apart from the stiff shoulders and legs.

'Arthritis,' the mother says. 'I knew that'd happen the minute they cut down those trees. You're too exposed.'

'Would you stop?' I say, not wanting her going on. 'I'm grand.'

She puts on the face then. You know the face they make, all holier-than-thou and don't mind me. She doesn't mean to be getting at me, but; she just worries.

Anyway, it wouldn't do if I was caught slumped in the corner dossing, like some laxadaisy idler. No, up I get, red robes straight, golden heart a-glimmer and arms cruciform. I have work to do, a city of people to watch over, because I'm the Jesus of taxi man and traveller; of Garda and gambler; Jesus of the pissed and the pioneer. I'm Jesus of culchie and jackeen; brasser and nun. Jesus of Nigerian and Pole; of wino and weirdo. Jesus of soft rain, December snow and rare sun. I'm the Jesus of O'Connell Street. Jesus of Dublin.

Stephen James Smith
Dublin You Are {poem}

Dublin you are grey brick upon brick,

full of tarmac and hipster pricks?

Just face it all other places pale in comparison,

you are more than some former Saxon garrison

Dublin your warmth came too late for John Corrie

Dublin are you even sorry?

Dublin you are divided by more than the Liffey,

You said YES to equality

and it's about Blooming time.

Yet Dublin you always Proclaimed to cherish all!

Dublin your Panties are on Capel Street

compromising any Papal feats.

Dublin Jedward, awkward…

Dublin you are more than a settlement on the Poddle,

But Dublin what's the craic with coddle?

It's shite, why don't we just admit it!

DUBLIN, WRITTEN IN OUR HEARTS

Dublin you brought back Sam again, but
Dublin when did you go from,
the clash of the ash, to exchanging gold for cash?
Dublin, Dyflin, Eblana, Baile Átha Cliath,
and 180 other tongues your citizens are using to name ya…
So céad míle fáilte to all.
Dublin where power is held by too few in the Dáil
Dublin when will you revolt again?
1988 wasn't your true millennium
despite the 50ps & milk bottles.
Dublin you're mine, but I'm happy to share you.
Dublin from RTÉ, TCD, UCD, U2, SIPTU, IFSC
and acrimonious Temple Bar STDs, ODs & OMGs!
No longer the 2nd city, yet you play 2nd fiddle
to Google & Guinness,
to Facebook and unsociable twits.
Dublin look at yourself.
Dublin your tower blocks & tenements
are an excuse for a solution.

Dublin c'mere 'til I tell you can be more than,

rapid dirtbirds & banjaxed bowsies,

alrigh' story bud & yeah sure it's all good,

jaysis that's scaldy,

Why Go Baldy,

I'm excira & delira,

Dublin I cry for ya!

Dublin you're a tough bastard,

yet full of the softness of all of the people on your streets

Margaret Dunne dancing on O'Connell Street,

The Diceman Tom McGinty miming on Grafton Street,

Pat Ingoldsby with his poems on Westmoreland Street,

and your Mollys, Malone, Ivers & Bloom.

To Daily-Sally-Sandy-Mounts…

From the gospel of Kelly, Drew, McKenna, & Sheahan,

to Borstal Boys like Brendan Behan

Two Gallants reJoycing, and Eveline looking out to sea.

Snow falling slowly on The Dead in Glasnevin

Glen & Markéta *Once* strolling,

to Christy Brown willfully controlling a foot

to paint pictures & poems,

to your heroines.

Brenda Fricker the city's mother,

Maureen O'Hara an enchanting other.

Dublin you are boom & bust,

running Wilde & Swift

Dublin can I trust you?

Dublin your true blue is Harry Clark's cobalt

Dublin from a Thin Lizzy, Dicey Reilly,

to a floozie in a jacuzzi God fearin',

Dublin shooting down Veronica Guerin.

Dublin you are Bang-Bang, 40 coats,

Zozimus a blind street poet,

Dublin you are all of us,

and all who are yet to come,

so let's go to the Gravediggers and have a pint

Dublin remember Stardust and all your waltzing lovers

Dublin Big Jim's arms are outstretched to a Risen People,

yet are we under the thumb again?

Dublin your GPO columns are scarred from The Crackle of gunshots.

Dublin your CCTV will never yield your essence like the shots

of Arthur Fields Man on Bridge.

You are the Poolbeg Towers,

and the poor shower

begging on Bachelor's Walk.

Dublin you're all talk, yet you have my attention,

from Robbie Keane to Paula Meehan.

Dublin's Calling, ohh ahh Paul McGrath, while some say Up The RA

Dublin bridging caps with Joyce & Beckett

and finally to Rosie Hackett!

Dublin Paddy Finnegan was forced to sell

The Big Issue on your streets,

while Daffodil Mulligan was played to bodhrán beats

Dublin you say delish,

Dublin you are full of Polish

and Brazilians speaking Portuguese,

and now the Chinese

have turned Parnell Street into Chinatown,

Dublin don't let them down.

Dublin don't forget 'no blacks, no dogs, no Irish',

Dublin perish the thought of you being racist.

Dublin Cú Chulainn has fled the GPO, and heading for Monto

Dublin your bay embraces despite the Sellafield Sea,

and your mountains frame all your natural beauty,

Dublin a wailing banshee stricken with T.B.

Dublin you're European, but could be Craggy Island in disguise?

Gabriel Conroy is heading west because of an epiphany.

Just sayin' Dublin you only painted your post boxes green!

Is The Abbey doing all you'd dreamed?

Dublin you are notorious for clampers, Senators & seagulls,

to Celtic Tiger & septic tanks

to singing High Kings & rampaging Vikings.

Dublin come here,

take me for a Teddy's and a romantic stroll down the pier…

Dublin you are

a dancing place, a sprawling space

of villages and many faces on the edge

of an island that's eroded by the Atlantic,

battling with being romanticised,

Dublin are you dynamic?

Struggling with identity?

Changing for the better?

Changing for us?

Stephen James Smith

Dublin don't be scared

to change.

Don't be

scared!

We're

with you.

Always.

Dublin.

My friend.

My home.

Mentioned

50 times

in this poem.

We live in you,

My city,

Mo chroí,

I love you,

Most of the time,

You see…

Dublin You Are,

Me!—

Réré Ukponu
Famine Days {short story}

My dad and I are sitting in the same seats we always choose, the blue and orange and green-flecked grimy ones at the front. There's ample room for his knee, room against the wall for his cane and room enough for me to cross my legs and arms, rest my head on the streaky bus window and ignore him. When the bus swerves, I peel another strip of skin from my fingers, snap my gum and hunch my shoulders even closer to my ears.

'Adanna?' Dad says.

I flick a look vaguely in his direction. Make sure he's mostly fuzzy before I sigh: 'Yeah?'

'I was talking to Mummy this morning and I—we—are both so proud of you for deciding to go in today. *So* proud. Of course, I know how scary doctors can be, but this is a good first step, the first of many steps but by the grace of God...' He takes a stabilising breath. 'We'll get through this, won't we?'

I give an infinitesimal nod. Dad waits until I mumble 'Yeah'. I think: if I have to spend another second listening to him, I will die, I will literally die, and then my corpse will spring up from the floor and kill itself again.

'Adanna Kamsiyochukwu,' he repeats, all heart, all wobble. 'My special girl.'

I tap each of my teeth with my tongue and look at his eyebrows. Their rebellious squiggle, the grey shoots.

These days, the way Dad says my name makes me furious. The lack of hesitancy to hide the real hesitancy. Like the way you plunge into a swimming pool.

He catalogues me, the ticking of my jaw, the half-mast eyelids, the way I hold my neck.

'*Kedu?*' he says, mouse quiet. I think of butcher blocks, knife sharpeners and cheese traps.

'I'm fine,' I say. I will not speak Igbo to him.

'Then why are you looking so annoyed?' He scans my face, his eyes misty, mouth like a downturned umbrella. 'My gloomy child.' He bumps my leg with his and pulls a face to try and make me laugh.

'I'm literally not even annoyed.' I bare my teeth, making sure he can see each incisor and canine. 'This is a smile, like.'

Dad's eyes go big and wide. *Oooooh*, he says, voice warbling like a cartoon ghost.

He stops quickly when my jaw tightens even more.

This fury is so new to me. I've never held it like this before. I've never been excited about the taste of blood in this way. I think it's the only thing that keeps me from shivering at this moment.

My mum says Dad lets me get away with everything. The growling in my stomach and the gum in my pocket. The hunch of my shoulders and the *ata uhie* chewing stick. The self-inflicted baby craters on my thighs.

(A teenage girl is a landmine.)

'We can do dinner after the doctor's appointment,' Dad suggests. 'What do you want to eat the most right now?'

The Igbo words sound like a lullaby. Like something I loved a long time ago. Like a note stretched too long.

I squish close to the wall, pig snout my nose on the window and wish for a tapeworm.

'Ate already,' I say.

We both note the absence of a time frame.

Outside, there are boys walking, drenched in bravado. They take up the whole footpath. Their hips low, legs wide-set, looking for what the world owes them. Carbon copies fading into each other. Grey hoodies, grey trackies against a grey sky. Hair licked back, saliva gel, a razor line on the side. I watch them laugh in sync, their mouths perfect ovals.

The bus pulls gently to a stop, scattering them like pigeons. In the space they leave, two women manoeuvre a buggy onboard. They pay the driver and move down the aisle, stopping when they get to our seat, waiting for dad to shift his leg out of the way. The older lady has corkscrew curls; I can almost see them vibrating with impatience. I smile apologetically at her, and nudge Dad, hard. He shifts with effort.

They sit close enough to hear dad's mini sermon.

Dad rhapsodises about God. About how he never gives us anything more than we can bear, and how much he loves me. He knows what fear is, Dad stresses. Knows that even Jesus wept, so not to shy away from feeling, not to be made up of icicles and knives—

Mhmmm, I say. 'Yeah, I know, I promise, I'm listening— Amen Amen Amen.'

My dad liked to believe me, even when all odds

were against my being truthful. Selective blindness, Mum called it. Favouritism, my brother called it. I used to call it being loved.

Lately, he's decided to see through my lies and I'm learning to detest him almost as much as myself.

He looks at me for a long time. '*Ka'idi nwata ina-enwe anwuli shinne,*' he sighs. You were such a happy child.

I blink slowly.

Each time the bus moves, our shoulders touch. I think about venom, the sweet sizzle of cooked meat, of splitting and clawing off my skin, revelling in pink.

I think of detonation.

My schoolbag is on the floor of the bus and my bouncing leg keeps whacking against it.

'When you tell a story,' Ms Clarke said, in primary school. 'You start with an action. You show, not tell. Start with an empty cup and top it up. Known to unknown,' she said.

'Make up words,' Ms Clarke said, in the next class. 'Lewis Carroll gave us the word "chortling".' Inside my head, I counter, He also gave us 'galumphing'. When we did *Alice*, I liked the bottle and the cake. How easy it was for her to grow and shrink by 'Eat Me' and 'Drink Me' alone. I liked the thought of being tiny enough to sleep in a snail house, the thought of also being big enough to crush the shells myself. I liked the thought of shapeshifting, of being invisible and smiling.

'Tell your own truth,' she said, at the last class. 'Your own special truth.'

Okay. I'll start at the toilet and sink and slap and citrus.

No. Before that.

Start at Adanna, start at the beginning. Start at ten fingers and toes, the wonder of learning things for the first time.

No, don't rewind that far. Start at—

I start at four.

[Play]

I come here with milk teeth. The first taste of Ireland is salt and fizzy syrup, Mickey Mouse plastic toys shoved into my hand at the drive-through window.

They wave us on, and my starfish hand flashes once, twice in reply. It's dusk, and the sky is soft. My mother says, 'Don't eat too quickly.' I slow down so I don't choke, but my eyes are busy gobbling up. The cold, the scarves, the milky skin. The first stars. We pass under tunnels, and every second we are in the dark I hold my breath.

The first day of school, Bambi-blinking, the one-two shuffle onto polyester carpet. Dad's voice while I bite my thumb. Him saying, 'Do well, be good.'

Standing in front of the class, I raise my head and look at the twenty-nine pairs of marble eyes looking back at me.

My tremulous smile as I introduce myself.

A beat. My teacher laughs, her teeth glinting scythe-like in the light.

There is something wrong here and I don't yet know how to grasp it. With a smile, she asks me to repeat my name. I do. She laughs again.

I watch as she makes a great show of rolling out a scroll, printing the letters in big blocks, pausing for dramatic effect between each one. As I sit down, she sellotapes the long piece of paper in front of my desk and smiles again. 'Just so we get it right.'

[Pause]

It begins when I'm four. It begins in the cold months. Begins with sweat reeking of spices. With the packed lunch of jollof rice in the stained container. The 3 o'clock pick-up time with Dad. Him asking, 'Weren't you hungry?' The worry in his eyes. The sitting on the curb in the winter watching early sunset and eating orange grains before the long walk home.

This is how I begin to learn hunger is control, is a kindness, is just a feeling that passes. The pavement underneath my crossed legs is freezing, but I'm so warm in the middle. 'I was playing chasing all lunch,' I say. 'Forgot!'

I am a doughnut baby, all sugar with a big hole in the centre. When Dad unfurrows his brow, delights at my popularity and tugs at my beaded braids, I grin. This feeling is so good.

My little girl hands holding his heart, protecting him from pain with half-size palms. *Bun go Barr*. Upside down. A reverse in the order of things. This feeling could keep me fed till next winter. Further even.

[Play]

I am thirteen.

Dad isn't doing good. 'Doing *well*', Mum says. *Doing well*, we repeat. Grammar is a thing to cling to, a thing to steady us on this spinning world.

At afternoon nap, I stare at the great white ceiling and the Bible verse stickers on the wall. I study them carefully. Mum cares about the language we use. Pidgin is banned, but saying *The devil is a bastard* in times of great stress is allowed. So, the things we say are *Daddy isn't good—well. Ms Clarke said my slip wasn't signed. Where's my tie? Please pick your brother up from the ground. Come and let's pray. Adanna, I'm warning you* and BASTARD.

I've not been eating for four weeks. I've been taking my sandwiches and making missiles to fling behind the big bush in the neighbour's garden. Shooting stars of lettuce and mayo and good Irish ham. I've been coming back with the hunger of doing something wrong, and the satiated feeling of emptiness. The pure feeling of control.

Mum catches me the day before the BIG VISIT. We've been hearing about the big visit for weeks. Daddy might be able to come home, might be able to breathe okay, but only if we pray every morning. Only if we believe in it so much, we tremble. Magic is evil, but this is holy. When I don't eat nowadays, I feel like God likes me more.

Mum calls on God when she catches me.

'*Chineke*! Why have you given me this evil child? Adanna? Adanna? Adanna? How many times did I call your name?' She tugs on her earlobe, her knuckles blanched.

'Are you from the devil? Are you a witch? Are you a bastard?' she bellows. Mums voice is so loud it feels like a physical thing, shoving me inside the house alongside her furious hands.

'I *wish*, I'm literally praying to God that I am.' I try for sarcastic, but my voice when I scream back, is more heartbroken.

When she slaps my face, I feel full.

'I wake up every morning—every blessed morning—to clean, to cook, to care for you children. Every morning! With the money we don't have. You don't even know what I do for you, what I—her voice breaks—what I have been trying to do for you.' Mum jabs a finger at the Trócaire box on the counter. Points at the face that looks like mine. She trots out the well-worn saying, in sync with every Irish mammy before her.

'There are children *starving* in Africa—'

'Well then, I wish I was in Africa!' I scream back.

The fight lasts a full hour. Hurricane girl and her tsunami mother. I lock myself in the bathroom and pretend to die. Sit in silence until she's convinced that I've killed myself. I think about doing it out of spite, instead of the normal desperation.

She bangs on the door like she's begging for her knuckles to become pulp.

When I finally unlock the door, she is silent and drawn, her eyes like pinched sweet wrappers. Empty and garishly shiny.

Our faces are mirrors. The hatred bouncing between the two surfaces again, again, doubling as we stand in the light of the hallway.

We enter the car in silence. I press my face into my baby brother's hair. I stopper up my nose and remind myself how to lie.

When I enter the sterile room, Dad and I stare at each other. '*Kedu?*' he asks. I remember to saturate my voice with honey and light, remember my teacher saying: *Adanna likes to tell tales.*

'Ọ dị mma!' I trill. 'Did you know Caoimhe invited me swimming with her and the other girls this weekend? Mum doesn't want me to go though. Even though I told her it'll be fine!'

'I didn't even know you could swim!' 'I'm part *Mami Wata*,' I wink.

Dad laughs and laughs. I twist my rings and eat the salt from the packet on the table.

When Dad asks about school I tell him my new biology fact: jellyfish are actually invertebrates. Just clouds that hurt and sting but have no spine. They lash out when touched, let sea water in and always, always float.

[Rewind]

I have swimming lessons every week. At the first one, I stand at the edge of the pool, in Dealz fabric. My toes curl around the lip like limpets, dark knees locked.

'Jump in, Adanna!' Caoimhe calls. She says it like A-day-nah. 'Don't even think about it!'

'Caoimhe! Do you want to kill the poor girl?' Kate says. 'Sure, they don't have water in Africa!'

'Kate!' Caoimhe says, but her laughter rings right up to the ceiling.

In the pool, I float. I do not sink; I don't even think of sinking. I do not think at all. I wait till the very last blink of a second—the very last shut of a minute— and I open my mouth. Wider than the crack in the pavement. Wider than the toilet bowl. Wider than the tunnels I came through. I scream, waiting for the inevitable bubbles.

In that moment, I swear, I feel like lightning.

[Play]

In the hospital room, every time I tell a joke I rub my nose raw. In this circus life of dissatisfaction, of netless tightrope walking, of unruly timetables and loud sounds—*beep! clang! nurse!*—I get very good at performing. I eat the orange slices Dad offers me, juice dripping down my chin. I nearly swallow the rind whole in eagerness. I gift him a beautiful story, of a beautiful life, and make sure to look only at his wide smile.

Dad aims to pat my cheek with his bear paw but gets my ear instead. I giggle, pretending he was on target. I rub my throat and thank the audience for coming to the show.

[Fast forward]

I am fifteen in the hospital, collapsed after another famine day.

'Don't hyperventilate,' the doctor says, sternly, before pressing a burning hot needle to my wrist. I watch the sharp tip puncture my skin.

'You bear pain well,' he says. He says 'you' in plural. I know this by the way he tilts his head at my braids as they *shhh* across the covers. My blood swells in the syringe, the red a war-crime ruby. I sink into the white pillows and think about my dad and sour fruit.

Later, when the morphine is making me formless, I lie on the ceiling looking down at the bed. I forget what it means to be human and I'm grateful for it.

I am the dripping tap. I am the slant of the carpet. I am the full, dark door with no light creeping underneath it. I am the aromatics burning. I am the nail clippings. I am the glue webby hands and the mess they made in class. I am the monochrome palette of the room, the rim of the bedpan, the fluorescent flatlines.

I am the low-flying plane outside the window. I am the elbows pointed heavenwards, cradling the downy soft head resting on the V of the collarbone. I am the sweat pooling in that valley. I am the sweat dripping to the clean floor. I am the moment before the crash.

(A teenage girl is a countdown clock.)

The moment before sleep, I press a hand to my force-fed stomach and think of my dad's recent health check-up. The way the nurse shrugged helplessly. The way my belly cramped.

I am sad.

I am lonely. I am *hungry*.

[Skip]

Now, I'm sixteen on the bus with my dad. My body is a closed accordion, airless and small.

We are on the way to a special doctor. This special doctor will tell me things that will make Dad cry. He will open up my head like a breadfruit, serve it up special and watch me eat every bite.

The bus is a sauna, so when the two women with the buggy get on cold air brushes my face.

The older woman with the corkscrew curls is round and soft, a well-kneaded loaf of bread. She settles on a seat diagonal to us, and the younger one, her daughter, probably, sits next to her. The daughter is nearly my age, I think. She's holding a baby the size of shoebox in her arms.

When we lock eyes, I smile.

My dad's voice echoes as he tells the bus driver where to drop us off. 'Just before the SuperValu, please!'

He shouts it really, but the bus driver nods because he knows us. This is our route home, our seats, and Dad's balance has now become the business of strangers.

Dad's voice still rings in my ears. I hate the squirm I feel inside, the mulch of shame. I know how to quiet myself. I understand having notions; my dad doesn't. He believes in the kindness of people; I believe in the fear of them. I believe in the holiness of embarrassment and the sickness of sticking out like a sore thumb. I look at him and will him to be quiet. The lady on the intercom says the next stop, repeats it *as Gaeilge*.

When the woman calls us niggers the first time, I blink and check behind me. I then look at my dad. He hasn't reacted so I dismiss myself. Then she says it again, this time tougher. The one-two punch of the double barrel 'g', the low blow of the hard 'r'. I let the meaning trickle in and blink hard.

This isn't real, I decide. People don't do this in real life. I look at the security camera screen. I look for the beetle-like shape of a microphone, then finally look back at her.

'The absolute *cheek* of you,' she starts. 'Thinking you can come here and start screaming down the bus, like there's not a bell in front of ya, and a baby beside ya! Would you cop on to yourselves?'

I look at her, look at her daughter, look at the baby with the milk bubbles gathering at the corner of its cupid bow mouth. Dainty spectators.

My mouth is so dry, the gum inside it rolls like a tumbleweed. Every word I've ever known evaporates.

'Fucking niggers,' she mutters.

Dad doesn't even flinch. He stares forward, his face a stagnant lake. My eyes tennis ball between them and every time I look at him, I feel woozy with fury. My hands itch to slap, to shield. I feel nauseous.

Sixteen years, I think. Sixteen years I've gotten away with it.

'He wasn't trying to be rude,' I shakily begin. 'It's just that he has a cane and—'

She cuts me off with an 'I don't care'. Turns back to her hideous daughter, her idiot grandchild.

I whip around in my seat to look at everyone else, see their eyes study the spider in the corner, the red of the bell, the smiling kids in the advertisements. 'Join us on the journey' is splashed in lurid text above the grinning face of a brown woman.

The unfairness of it burns through me. Like the embarrassment of being picked last. Like the unwanted nicknames in secondary school. Like four, like thirteen, like fifteen.

This anger, this *anger*. So heavy, like a sunken stone. So hot it feels like love. I like the heft of it. I could bludgeon her if I tried. I want the mush of face contact; I want wet thud. I shift in my seat to face her, a snarl on my lips. The pendulum swings, the weight shifts at the fulcrum, my mouth opens—

Ding!

The doors open and the air rushes into the vehicle. Dismount. Battle ended before it began.

I stare at the woman through the window as the bus drives on.

She doesn't even look back.

I turn to my dad, to the softness of his jaw, the soil of his eyes. How many times does it take before you can look through it? I wonder. How many times, until it's all mist? I don't want to know; I fear I'll find out regardless.

I let myself remember I love him ferociously.

Me at sixteen; Dad placing a plate outside my door. Me at thirteen; Dad handing me an orange slice. Me at four; Dad morphing a utensil into an aeroplane, zooming it to my lips. I remember the way my mouth reflexively opened.

Maybe love is closing your mouth around a spoon.

The sky is a swirl of clouds, the sun squeezing its way through.

I feel myself thaw for the first time in years. Feel the full expansion of my heart, feel the soreness in the fillings of my teeth. I feel the fist around my throat loosen. I let my hands return to the natural order of things and allow myself to lean into him.

Allow myself to listen to his heart beating just fine on its own.

'Maybe for dinner, we could get pizza?' Dad muses.

The elasticity of our breaths, the way they bounce in tandem.

'Maybe chipper instead?' I reply.

[Scene change]

Roddy Doyle
The Buggy {short story}

There were people at the far end of the beach. Some adults, a lot of children. An extended family, maybe—he didn't know. He tried to see if one of the adults was carrying a baby or if there was a toddler—a padded lump—plonked on the sand.

He didn't want to walk over, down from the path, across the sand and stones, to the buggy. It was facing the sea. If the people up the beach had been nearer to it, he'd have known that it was theirs. He'd have known that they'd parked the buggy there at the edge of the sea so the baby would drink in the air—the ozone, whatever it was—and sleep, and stay asleep for a while. But it stood out, alone. There wasn't an adult or a sibling, a towel or a bucket, anywhere near it. It made no sense.

It was more than likely empty. That didn't make much sense, either, a buggy abandoned on the beach like that. But he remembered abandoning a buggy himself, years ago—it would have been more than thirty years—when the frame had buckled as he was pushing it up the hill in that place in France they'd gone to on their way to the ferry in Le Havre. Mont-Saint-Michel. A spectacular place, dripping with history and religion, but all he remembered about it was the ache in his arms, and the heat, as he pushed the buggy and the toddler in it up the incline, and the metallic screech as the frame—the sides—surrendered and the toddler seemed to disappear, as if she had been eaten by the buggy. The toddler, Gráinne, was fine—she had a toddler of her own these days—but the buggy wasn't savable. No amount of bending or hammering would have coaxed it back into shape. They'd left it beside a bin and passed three more buggies, buckled and discarded, on their way back down to the car park.

Maybe that was what had happened here. The frame had given up as the buggy was pushed—shoved, forced—across the sand. But he was looking at it and he knew: there was nothing wrong with this one. It was a solid-looking thing; calling it a vehicle wouldn't have been ridiculous. A small adult could have squeezed into it. A hen or a stag party—he could picture the other eejits pushing a little bride or groom from one pub to the next in the buggy he was looking at.

It wasn't buckled, but it might have been abandoned, and he wanted nothing to do with it.

Was the tide coming in or on its way out? He didn't know. He hadn't paid much attention to the tides and their times since he was a kid. He remembered how much he'd loved looking them up in the back of his father's *Independent*, after his father had shown him how to read the charts.

The sea—the wave he was looking at now—stopped a yard, a metre, from the buggy's front wheels, and receded. He waited for the next wave. Exactly the same—from where he stood. It got no closer to the wheels. He looked again, from left to right, to see if anyone was going to claim the buggy before the sea took it.

He should have kept driving. Of course, he should have. He'd been on his way to meet his brother, who'd moved down to Arklow. He'd left the house early—hours early— before he'd wanted to. He'd just been anxious—anxious about finding his brother's place, anxious about the traffic, anxious about leaving the house, anxious about meeting his brother. He'd seen the sign for the beach and he'd turned left, off the motorway. And here he was, about to witness a drowning, an abandonment. Something bad. Something dreadful. An accusation, a misunderstanding, a night in a Garda station, a slot on the news. Or just an empty buggy on a cold Irish beach. A mystery. A story he didn't want to make up, or even think about.

He should have kept driving. He shouldn't have left home in the first place.

He didn't want to do it—he really didn't. He'd go over now to the buggy; he'd look in, he'd bend down. Even here, on the path above the beach, he could feel it. The magic, the curse—the man he'd been thirty years ago. The man who would have known what to do. The man who wouldn't have hesitated. But he was so far away from being that man, he'd have to turn into an entirely different man—a man who wasn't in him.

He could remember being a kid. He remembered being very small. He could remember looking up at the handle of the fridge, in the kitchen. He could remember standing beside his father, resting his arm on his father's knee as his father ate his dinner. He could remember the smell of his father's tobacco. He could remember the paint on his father's trousers. He could remember his father telling his mother that he'd change his trousers after he'd finished his dinner; he was starving and the grub wouldn't taste any better in clean trousers, the trousers weren't the ones eating it. He remembered his mother laughing and calling his father an eejit. He remembered looking up at them—their words and laughter—over his head. That was how far back he could go. But not just that—the little lad was still in him. He was the much, much older version of that child. And the older boys, the other layers of his life—they were in him, too. Not just the memories—it wasn't that they were vivid. They were living things, events—he could live them now. He could scratch at the blue paint on his father's cord trousers. He could hear his mother's laughter—now he could. He could feel his foot hitting a wet leather football. He could hear the chalk on a primary-school blackboard. He could taste the first girl's tongue—he could feel her sweat on his cheek as they kissed, both of them afraid to stop, like they were both cycling bikes for the first time and would fall off if they slowed down or stopped.

But the man—the competent young man he'd been, the father—he couldn't feel him at all.

He could see him. He could see him take Gráinne from the buggy, making a joke of its collapse, making her brothers laugh—*The poor ol' buggy; your bum was too big for it, Gráinne*—and carrying her back down the hill. But he couldn't feel her weight on his arm, or the confidence—the knowledge—that he'd make it all the way without changing arms or putting her down and trying to persuade her to walk.

He could remember another buggy. He was standing

on the platform as the train—the Dart—came slowly into Killester station, with the boys on either side of him. A double buggy this time—before Gráinne was born. He had one boy's hand in his own left hand—the younger lad, Colm—and he held the buggy, folded, in his right hand. The older boy, Seán, held on to the buggy. The train stopped. There was no one getting off, no one there to press the button to open the train door. He forgot that Seán loved pressing the button, that it was his job, the thing that made him more important than his little brother. He let go of Colm's hand for a second, to give the button a jab—and Colm was gone. He had tried to step onto the train; his stride fell short of the gap, and he dropped between the train and the platform, under the train. Someone had seen what had happened and was shouting up the platform to the driver, as he got down on his knees, gently grabbed Colm's outstretched hand—*Good lad, up you come*—and pulled him up to the platform, gave him a hug, Colm smiling, not a bother on him, then got himself, the boys, and the buggy onto the train, and dealt with Seán's tears.

If the train had been moving, if Colm had slid further beneath it, if the guy on the platform hadn't been there to shout the warning to the driver—all of these possibilities rattled away inside him as the train left the station and the boys sat so they could both look out the window and get ready to be surprised by any trains dashing past in the other direction. *Ambush*!

But, really, he'd been fine, even happy. He'd known that he'd just have had to reach down, his arm in the gap between the train's green side and the rain-drenched cement of the station platform, and hold Colm's hand—not even grab it—

just hold it and lift the boy effortlessly to safety. He'd have managed it. He remembered examining the soaked knees of his jeans and brushing the grit off them with his open hand. Mission accomplished.

He looked at the hand now, his right hand. It wasn't the same one—it wasn't the hand that had saved Colm. It wasn't the age, or the liver spots. It wasn't even the hand. The hand, his arm, shook sometimes—just slightly—when he had to reach out to grab something, and sometimes he was happier holding a mug or a glass in both hands till he became used to the weight. But it wasn't his hands or his arms or aging or anything. It was him. Just him. That phrase from the pandemic, 'essential worker'—he'd been an essential father. He could remember rescuing Colm, but he couldn't imagine it—he couldn't feel it. He couldn't believe he'd done it. He *didn't* believe he'd done it. Or any of the other things he'd done when he was a father. Not just observed or witnessed, stored away for later. Done. Picked up, set down, pushed, pulled, fed, tickled, comforted. His physical life beyond children, too. Ran, gasped, laughed, cried, came. The verbs—the action words. He had the words, but the actions? He could walk and drive and eat and sleep. He could go through the motions. He could get through the day.

But he didn't live.

The tide was coming in—the sea was closer to the buggy. Another minute and the waves would be digging under a front wheel.

There was another buggy story. He'd pushed the buggy, empty—he couldn't remember which buggy; they'd gone through five or six—down to the shops, with Seán walking beside him. Seán was grand walking anywhere, it didn't really matter how far. But, coming back, he often went on strike. Setting out, he'd object to the buggy—*Buggy's for babies!*—but on the way home he'd sit on the ground, plonk himself down, in puddles, or right in front of shopping trolleys and pit bulls and pensioners, and refuse to walk. Even then he objected to the buggy. He wouldn't climb into it or let his father pick him up and fasten him in. This particular time, Seán—the adorable little bastard—shoved the buggy out onto the road, right in front of an oncoming car. The driver braked, but the car hit the buggy side-on— he'd never forget the noise, the thump. The buggy went into the air and landed clean, all four wheels at once, facing the car, and the driver, a woman with a carful of her own babies, stared out at the empty buggy and screamed and screamed and fell out of the car and looked under it and on the roof for the missing baby—*Oh, Jesus, oh, Jesus, oh, Jesus, oh, Jesus*— while the missing baby, Seán, pointed at her and laughed. *Funneee*!

He could remember it like a scene from a film. It was a very good film. But he wasn't in it.

What happened?

Where had his life gone? Not the years—the blood. Where was the life?

The buggy was listing—it was going to topple. The next wave or the one after, it was going to be on its side and the baby—if there was one—would be strapped in and helpless.

If there was one.

He'd forgotten how hard moving across soft sand was; his ankles were already aching. He nearly fell—the sole of his shoe slid on a stone. He watched a wave wallop the wheel—

he saw the buggy pushed back. He didn't seem to be getting any closer—he'd left it too late. His shoes were full of sand—there was a stone digging into his heel. But the ground was more solid; there was a layer of stones, a thick band that stretched along the beach. He got over the stones quickly enough, and he was nearly at the buggy—he could feel the handle, *all* the handles, in his grip—when a wave slid up over his shoes and he was lifting his feet, moving like a mad thing, his feet smacking the water, and he caught the buggy, he grabbed one of the handles and pulled it back with him, up to the bank of stones, and he knew before he looked. He had the buggy by both handles now, and he parked it, still facing the sea, and looked—no baby. He was relieved—and disappointed—and angry. His feet were freezing—his legs, up to his knees and past them—fuckin' freezing. And he laughed. He was angry, and delighted to be angry. He was soaking and didn't know what he'd do, and he didn't care.

—Oh, God. Thank you!

It was a woman, a young woman running at him, sliding over the stones.

He checked again—the buggy was empty. He wondered why she was thanking him.

—I forgot all about it, she said.

She looked the part, the young mother, exhausted and lovely. But she didn't have a baby, on her hip or in her arms.

He held on to the buggy.

—You're drenched, she said. I'm so sorry.

He shrugged. He wasn't sure if it was a proper shrug. He was gripping the handles and leaning over the buggy, protecting the baby that wasn't in it.

She was a bit uncertain—he could see that. She'd expected

him to roll the buggy across the stones to her, or to turn it around and offer her the handles. It probably looked like he needed the buggy to hold himself up. He looked down. He was wet past his trousers, halfway up his jumper.

—I left my phone in the car, she said. Are you all right?

Jesus Christ, she wanted to phone for an ambulance—for him.

He stood up straight. He let go of the buggy.

—I'm grand, he said.

—You must be frozen, she said.

His job now was to get her to stop talking to him like he was an old man. An old man who'd fallen into the water, or who'd wet himself.

—I'm grand, he said again.

He patted a buggy handle.

—Where's the owner of the vehicle? he asked.

She smiled.

—He's in the car, she said. In the car park.

—If he hasn't driven away, he said. I'm only joking.

She looked behind her, towards the car park that they couldn't see from where they stood.

—I wouldn't put it past him, she said.

He moved first. He walked off the sand, pulling the buggy with him.

—He wanted to go to the toilet like a big boy, she told him. In the dunes.

—Fair enough, he said. What's his name? I feel like I should know.

He pulled at a wet trouser leg where it was stuck to his thigh.

—Seán, she said.

—I've a Seán as well, he told her.

—Really? she said. That's amazing.

They were on the tarmac, off the sand. He let go of the buggy. She took hold of it and pointed it at the car park.

—Tell Seán I said hello, he said.

She laughed. She smiled.

—I will, she said. Bye. Thanks again.

—Seeyeh.

She hadn't asked him if he was okay or if he knew where he was going, or if there was someone he could phone to come and collect him. She'd seen a man who was fine, and she'd walked away. He was freezing, and stiff. He'd drive to Arklow now and change into one of his brother's tracksuits.

He took his phone from his trousers pocket and rubbed the screen dry on the shoulder of his jumper. He went to Favourites and tapped 'Seán.'

—Dad?

—Howyeh, son. Are you busy—can you talk?

—What's up? Are you all right?

He told his son about how he'd been on his way to Arklow, about how he'd been early so he'd stopped at the beach. About how he'd gone for a walk. How he'd seen the buggy facing the sea. How he'd seen the tide coming in, how he'd dashed down to the sea to rescue the buggy.

He didn't hesitate.

—There was a baby in it, Seán.

—Ah, Jesus—a baby? Are you serious?

—I couldn't believe it, he said. Fast asleep.

—No!

—Yeah.

There—in the car park beside the Irish Sea—he'd never felt happier. He watched the mother drive slowly to the gate, stop, then turn left, out, onto the road. He waved at the back of the car. A Volvo, he thought it was. Black, or very dark blue.

—Was the baby okay?

—Ah, yeah, he said. Not a bother on him. And come here—guess what his name was.

Contributors

Kevin Barry is the author of four novels, most recently *The Heart In Winter* (2024), and three story collections, most recently *That Old Country Music* (2020). He also works as a playwright and screenwriter. He lives in County Sligo.

Estelle Birdy is a writer, book critic and yoga teacher who has lived at the edge of The Liberties in Dublin since her late teens. Born in London, she grew up in the most beautiful county of Louth but is still happy enough to be raising four young Dubs. In her spare time she works for the union.

Niamh Campbell is the author of *This Happy* (2020) and *We Were Young* (2022). She has won the Sunday Times Audible Short Story Award and the Rooney Prize for Irish Literature. Her third novel is forthcoming with Weidenfeld and Nicolson in 2026.

Kevin Curran's third novel, *Youth*, was published to critical acclaim by The Lilliput Press in 2023. It was an *Irish Times*, *Sunday Independent* & *RTE Culture* Best Book of 2023. The paperback edition of *Youth* was published February 2025. He is a secondary school teacher in his hometown of Balbriggan.

Roddy Doyle is the author of thirteen novels, including *The Commitments*, *Paddy Clarke Ha Ha Ha*, for which he won the Booker Prize in 1993, and, most recently, *The Women Behind The Door*. He lives in Dublin.

Anne Enright lives in Dublin, where she was born in 1962. The author of eight novels, two books of short stories and many essays, she is a winner of the Man Booker Prize (2007) and the Irish novel of the year (2007 and 2015). A former Laureate for Irish Fiction, she is Professor of Fiction at UCD. Her book of essays *Attention* will be out in November 2025.

FELISPEAKS is a Nigerian-Irish visionary artist celebrated for their profound exploration of identity, social justice, and personal growth through poetry, performance and theatre. As well as being featured in the Irish Leaving Certificate Curriculum, their compelling work transcends borders, leaving an indelible mark on international literature.

Sarah Gilmartin is an Irish writer and arts journalist. Her short fiction has been published in *The Dublin Review*, *New Irish Writing* and *The Tangerine*. She won the Máirtín Crawford Short Story Award in 2020. Her novels *Dinner Party: A Tragedy* (2021) and *Service* (2023) are published by One. She is the 2025 writer-in-residence at Dublin City University.

Róisín Kiberd has written for *The Stinging Fly*, *The Dublin Review*, *The Guardian* and *The New York Times*, among others. She teaches at the University of Galway, and is nonfiction editor of *The Stinging Fly*. Her book, *The Disconnect: A Personal Journey Through the Internet* was published by Serpent's Tail in 2021.

CONTRIBUTORS

Caitriona Lally has published two novels, *Eggshells* (2015) and *Wunderland* (2021). She won the Rooney Prize for Irish Literature in 2018 and a Lannan Literary Fellowship for Fiction in 2019. She was the inaugural Rooney Writer Fellow at the Trinity Long Room Hub in 2022, and was one of the 2024 New Voices 20 Best New Irish Writers.

Belinda McKeon is the author of the novels *Solace* (2011) and *Tender* (2015). She is also a playwright. She lives in County Louth, and is director of the MA in Creative Writing at Maynooth University.

Deirdre Madden is a novelist whose works include *Molly Fox's Birthday* and *Time Present and Time Past*. She is the recipient of a 2024 Windham Campbell Award for Fiction and is a member of Aosdána. She is also a Fellow of Trinity College, Dublin, where she taught Creative Writing for over twenty years. A study of her work, *Deirdre Madden: New Critical Perspectives* (eds. Anne Fogarty and Marisol Morales-Ladrón), was published in 2022 by Manchester University Press.

Paula Meehan was born and raised in Dublin's north inner city. Her poetry has garnered widespread popular and critical acclaim. *The Solace of Artemis* (2023), winner of the Pigott Prize and *As If By Magic: Selected Poems* (2020) are published by Dedalus Press, Dublin. She is a member of Aosdána.

Thomas Morris is the author of *We Don't Know What We're Doing* (2015) and *Open Up* (2023). He was born and raised in Caerphilly, South Wales, and lives in Dublin.

Niamh Mulvey is a novelist and short story writer. Her novel *The Amendments* was published in 2024 by Picador and was nominated for an An Post Irish Book Award. Her short-story collection, *Hearts and Bones: Love Songs for Late Youth* was published in 2022 and nominated for the John McGahern Prize.

Nuala O'Connor lives in Co. Galway. Her sixth novel *Seaborne*, about Irish-born pirate Anne Bonny, is nominated for the Dublin Literary Award and was shortlisted for Eason Novel of the Year at the 2024 An Post Irish Book Awards. Her fifth poetry collection, *Menagerie*, is published by Arlen House, spring 2025.

Sean O'Reilly has published a number of books, including *The Swing of Things*, *Watermark* and the short-story collection, *Levitation*. Originally from Derry, Northern Ireland, he teaches on The Stinging Fly Fiction Workshop and is a member of Aosdána.

Keith Ridgway's first novel, *The Long Falling*, was published in 1998. Since then his books have included *Animals*, *Hawthorn & Child*, and *A Shock*. His short fiction has appeared in *The New Yorker, Granta, Zoetrope, Inque, The Atlantic, The Stinging Fly*, and others.

Peter Sirr lives in Dublin. The Gallery Press has published his eleven poetry collections, most recently *The Swerve*, (2023) and *The Gravity Wave* (2019), a Poetry Society Recommendation and winner of the 2020 Farmgate Café National Poetry Award. *Intimate City: Dublin Essays* was published in 2021. He teaches literary translation in Trinity College and is a member of Aosdána.

CONTRIBUTORS

Stephen James Smith is a Dublin-born poet, writer, performer, playwright, and educator. Their short poetry films have captivated millions, earning them the opportunity to perform around the world alongside notable names like Eddie Vedder, Patti Smith, Bono, Imelda May, and Glen Hansard. As a recording artist, Stephen's work has been lauded both nationally and internationally, leading to Stephen being dubbed 'Dublin's unofficial poet laureate.'

Réré Ukponu is a 25-year-old writer from Dublin. She has been published in *The Irish Times*, *Metro Éireann*, *The Stinging Fly* and *Internazionale Magazine*. She is currently studying Medicine at University College Cork, where she is a Quercus Creative and Performing Arts Scholar. She got her love of words from her grandfather, who is the best storyteller she knows.

Karl Whitney is the author of *Hidden City: Adventures and Explorations in Dublin* and *Hit Factories: A Journey Through the Industrial Cities of British Pop*. His journalism has appeared in the *Guardian*, *Irish Times* and *London Review of Books* and his essays about writing are published regularly in the *Irish Examiner*.

Editor

Declan Meade is founding editor and publisher of *The Stinging Fly* literary magazine, which he established in Dublin in 1997. He has edited several other anthologies, including *These Are Our Lives* (2006), *Let's Be Alone Together* (2008), *Beyond The Centre* (2016), *Stinging Fly Stories* (with Sarah Gilmartin, 2018), and *The Writer's Torch* (with Phyllis Boumans and Elke D'hoker, 2023).

Permissions

We are grateful to the following for permission to reproduce copyright material:

Short story 'There Are Little Kingdoms' by Kevin Barry, first published in *There are Little Kingdoms*, The Stinging Fly Press, 2007, copyright © Kevin Barry, 2007. Reproduced by permission of the author and C&W;

Extract from *Ravelling* by Estelle Birdy, Lilliput Press, 2024, copyright © Estelle Birdy, 2024. Reproduced by permission of the author and Lilliput Press;

Extract from *We Were Young* by Niamh Campbell, Orion Publishing Group, 2022. Reproduced by permission of the author, and Orion through PLSClear;

Short story 'Adventure Stories for Boys' by Kevin Curran, published in *The Stinging Fly*, Vol 2(37), 2017. Reproduced by kind permission of Kevin Curran;

Short story 'The Buggy' by Roddy Doyle, first published in *The New Yorker* 16/06/2024, copyright © Roddy Doyle 2024. Reproduced by permission of the author and C&W;

Essay 'Dublin Made Me' by Anne Enright. Commissioned by the Museum of Literature Ireland as part of ULYSSES European Odyssey, funded by Creative Europe, ulysseseurope.eu. Reproduced by permission of the author and the Museum of Literature Ireland;

'Dublin: A Poet's View' by FELISPEAKS was commissioned for *Dublin Exchange, Reflections from a City in Flux*, edited by Ruth O'Herlihy, René Boer and Gary Hamilton and published by Story, Building, www.storybuilding.ie. The piece was subsequently broadcast on *Sunday Miscellany*, RTÉ Radio 1, 13/10/24, copyright © FELISPEAKS. Reproduced by kind permission of FELISPEAKS and Story, Building;

Extract from *Service* by Sarah Gilmartin, copyright © Sarah Gilmartin, 2023. Reproduced by permission of the author and Pushkin Press;

Extract from 'The Night Gym' by Roisin Kiberd, first published in *The Disconnect*, Serpent's Tail, 2021, copyright © Roisin Kiberd, 2021. Reproduced by permission of the author and C&W;

Extract from *Eggshells* by Caitriona Lally, The Borough Press, copyright © Caitriona Lally, 2015. Reproduced by permission of the author and HarperCollins Publishers Ltd;

Short story 'For Keeps' by Belinda McKeon from *All Over Ireland, New Irish Short Stories*, Faber and Faber, 2015, copyright © Belinda McKeon. Reproduced by permission of the author c/o Rogers, Coleridge & White Ltd., 20 Powis Mews, London W11 1JN;

Extract from *Authenticity* by Deirdre Madden, copyright © Deirdre Madden, 2002. Reproduced by permission of the author and A M Heath & Co. Ltd. Authors' Agents;

The poem 'In Solidarity' by Paula Meehan, *The Solace of Artemis*, Dedalus Press, 2023. Reproduced by permission of the author and Dedalus Press;

The story 'all the boys' by Thomas Morris, from *We Don't Know What We're Doing*, Faber and Faber, 2015, copyright © Thomas Morris, 2015. Reproduced by permission of the author, Faber & Faber Ltd and The Wylie Agency (UK) Limited;

The story 'Stringing Up The Brides' by Niamh Mulvey, *The Stinging Fly*, 2011. Reproduced by kind permission of the Niamh Mulvey;

Short story 'Jesus of Dublin' by Nuala O'Connor, *Joyride to Jupiter*, New Island, 2017. Reproduced with kind permission of Nuala O'Connor;

Extract from *Levitation* by Sean O'Reilly, The Stinging Fly Press, 2017. Reproduced by kind permission of Sean O'Reilly;

The essay 'Undublining' by Keith Ridgway, 2025. Reproduced by kind permission of the author;

Extract from 'Noises Off: Dublin's Contested Monuments' by Peter Sirr, *Intimate City: Dublin Essays*, The Gallery Press, 2021. Reproduced by permission of the author and The Gallery Press;

The poem 'Dublin You Are' by Stephen James Smith was commissioned by Dublin 2020, European Capital of Culture, in 2015. First published in *Fear Not*, Arlen House, 2018, copyright © Stephen James Smith. Reproduced with the kind permission of the Stephen James Smith;

Short story 'Famine Days' by Réré Ukponu, published in *The Stinging Fly*, Vol 2(50), 2024. Reproduced by kind permission of Réré Ukponu;

Extract from *Hidden City* by Karl Whitney, Penguin Ireland, copyright © Karl Whitney, 2014. Reproduced by permission of the author and Penguin Books Limited.